SPIRAL STAIRCASE

SPIRAL STAIRCASE

John Wainwright

St. Martin's Press
New York

Library of Congress Cataloging in Publication Data

Wainwright, John William, 1921-
    Spiral staircase.

    I. Title.
PR6073.A354S6   1984   823'.914   83-21120
ISBN 0-312-75243-1

First published in Great Britain in 1983 by Macmillan London
Limited.

First U.S. Edition

10 9 8 7 6 5 4 3 2 1

Tallboy didn't like the guy in the white coat. Maybe it was the coat; too clean, too starched, slightly too large for the man wearing it. Maybe it was the stethoscope dangling from one pocket, the scarlet rubber looking like spilled guts gorged with blood. Somebody else's blood. Or maybe it was what the man was saying, and the way he was saying it. Something. Whatever it was, Tallboy didn't like him.

'The ecclesiastics might call him a lost soul, but it's not as easy as that. Professionally, I can't subscribe to the "soul" theory, of course, but he's certainly lost. Again . . . wrong. Wrong tense. He *was* lost. I think he's found himself again. At the very least, he *thinks* he's found himself. He won't talk. Except under sedation he refuses to say a thing.'

'Dope,' growled Tallboy.

'Mild sedation, superintendent. I'm not talking about "truth drugs". He's under my care. I'm allowed — even required — to prescribe medicines as I see fit. He doesn't object. He takes them without a murmur. Dalmane, if you must know. Quietener-downers. Check it out, if you like. Capsules. They're prescribed by the thousand. They relax people. That's all.'

'And make them talk.'

'No! Dammit man, we're on the wrong side of the Iron Curtain for what you're suggesting. He needs them. They help. He thinks he has no friends. He truly believes that. That he's forfeited all right to friendship. That's one reason why he won't talk. Dalmane helps . . . just a little. He opens up a little. Doesn't hate himself as much.'

There was a pause before the guy in the white coat continued. 'You know the history of his trouble?'

'Better than you do,' said Tallboy coldly.

'Generalities.' The guy in the white coat unlinked his fingers long enough to make a movement meant to erase all previous talk and explanations. 'The human being is an animal. That's not a premise, that's a fact. He eats, he sleeps, he defecates, he procreates. His basic urges are warmth, hunger, fear, sex and self-

5

protection. All the rest is up here.' He tapped the dome of his skull. 'The pleasures of music, of literature, of art. The complex code of conduct we call civilization. Concrete things, like motor cars, aeroplanes, television sets, typewriters. Even conversation and the ability to read and write. To communicate. Abstract things, like justice, compassion, self-respect, a conscience. All up here.' He tapped his skull again. 'And much of that lot — *most* of that lot — opposes the natural, basic, animal urges.

'Take any other animal — a horse, a dog, a cat — and give that animal what you and I take for granted. Not the luxuries. What we like to call "the bare necessities" of life. That animal would have the instinctive sense to know it lacked nothing. Nothing! Were it capable of so thinking, it would count itself in clover. Happy to just take that and live a damn good life. No worries. No problems. No anything. But lock that animal up — remove its freedom and what have you got?'

Tallboy didn't answer.

The guy in the white coat continued, 'That, with an animal. A form of madness. Now . . . *add to that the limitless complexities of the human brain.*' He paused and sighed. 'One day we'll come up with a better answer, but until we do, people like me will never be out of a job. We'll have knots to untie. Knots we'll *never* untie because — and because of this brain we're so proud of — the human animal moves in its own peculiar and unique way.

'The non-human animal — figuratively speaking — moves in a straight line. Birth to death. A few minor adventures on the way, but in effect a simple journey from A to B. Not so the human animal. That brain of his has to be paid for, and the first thing that goes is the straight line. Too easy. Too uncomplicated. Too simple to understand.

'Instead a spiral staircase. Dark and without windows. Round and round. The way we all go . . even the best of us. Some rush. Some go slowly. It makes no difference. We're all the same in that respect. Our natural instincts are shackled by the mores and customs dictated to us by our superior minds. Therefore, instead of a straight line, a spiral staircase. Up to the battlements where the crows wait to peck out our eyes, or down to the dungeons

6

where the rats wait to tear the flesh from our bones.

'And the reason, superintendent? Oh yes, there's a reason. Unlike our happier, Stone Age ancestors, we're too wise — too learned — to merely *accept*. Our minds have out-paced our feelings. That a thing *is* is not enough. We demand to know why it is. My profession — the profession scorned by so many, including you — exists because the human animal has become *too* civilised . . .'

The newspapers called it *the Time of the Vigilantes*, and the name stuck. In the localised history of Bordfield Police it was given the same name; these crackpot names are handy pegs on which to hang periods of terror, periods of excitement, periods of mass hysteria peculiar to the twentieth century. The Dunkirk Period. The Swinging Sixties. The Age of the Mods and Rockers.

So with crime. The name Donald Neilson means little to those not professionally interested in murder and its kindred subject-matter, but mention the Black Panther and most people remember. John George Haigh — who's he? But they recall the Acid Bath Murderer. Another George — George Joseph Smith — another man with an eye for baths. Who remembers anybody called Smith? But the Brides in the Bath . . . that rings bells, even though World War I was making the headlines at the time. Jack the Ripper. The Boston Strangler. The Park-Avenue Bandit. The Black Dahlia. Dozens of them. Scores of them. Each reduced to a form of journalistic shorthand and fed to a newspaper-reading public ready to be titillated by hinted-at horrors as a means of breaking down the cold-blooded boredom of an everlasting, and very real, international horror called living.

But rest assured, the Time of the Vigilantes was real enough. It was a little too real, a little too hairy, to the men and women of Bordfield Police. To them, it was an affront. Even an insult. To the media it meant good copy, but to the over-worked coppers it meant mob-rule in the streets and the implied accusation that official law-enforcement had broken down and wasn't worth a damn.

It lasted less than a month. Temporarily, it scared the pants off the riff-raff. It shot the crime statistics through the roof. But in the long run it did far more harm than good . . . to everybody.

I know. I organised it.

The name? *My* name? Lennox. The first name is not important. For some few years I have not enjoyed the luxury of a first name; become an inmate of one of H.M. Prisons and the first name is spoken once, at the reception desk — a formal verification that the right man is being locked away — thereafter, a number replaces the first name and only the surname remains. A small thing. Unimportant, perhaps. But when I came out and Chris Tallboy called me "Lenny" I almost broke.

Tallboy was once my colleague. He is, thank God, still my friend. He is a chief superintendent of police. I, too, was once a chief superintendent; a detective chief superintendent, and Head of Bordfield Regional C.I.D. Bordfield being one of the regions which make up Lessford Metropolitan Police District. I killed a man.★ The reasons are unimportant other than that, at the time, it seemed the right thing to do. Chris Tallboy did his duty, as I knew he would. He arrested me, charged me with murder and, in so doing, broke his own heart a little. The charge was reduced to manslaughter — perhaps the circumstances *did* send me a little crazy — and a humane judge sentenced me to what was, in effect, a mere nominal term of imprisonment. Four years remitted to three.

And yet . . .

Three years can be an eternity. Little more than a hundred and fifty weeks. Slightly more than a thousand days. An eternity of counting. In the prison system — any prison system — that is the hidden secret torture. Counting! You count the days, even the hours. You count the weeks and the months. You count the bricks. You count the steps from your cell, along the gallery and to the iron stairs. You count everything because, despite the games-rooms and the gymnasiums, the books and the exercise periods, only two things really matter. How many? And how long? How many more slop-outs? How many more times will the door be slammed and the key turned? How many more queues for food? How many more nights? How many more dawns?

★*Dominoes* by John Wainwright, Macmillan, 1980

The lags insist that the only way to digest a prison sentence of any length is to accept it day at a time. No past, no future or you'll go mad. Only "now" matters. But they, too, know. 'Now' lasts forever, therefore they, too, count. They know exactly how many shuffling steps it needs to circumnavigate the exercise yard. How many cell windows can be seen from any point in that yard. They can identify a warder before they see his face by the fall of his foot and the number of paces he takes to reach their own cell. More than a thousand men, all locked away and all counting; all silently counting different things at different times. Was Bedlam one wit better?

That and the hatred.

I expected, and could understand, the hatred. Of course they hated me. If not for what I was, for what I'd been. Every one of them was there because a policeman had put him there. Guilty or innocent — and with some I learned to doubt their possible guilt — the pigs were their enemy, and I'd been a pig and would remain a pig to the end of my days.

The chief warder tried to warn me. A stern man, a just man, but a man as much a part of the system as any of the prisoners. 'Tread carefully, Lennox. In this place, it isn't the screws you'll have to watch.' It was meant to be kindly advice; as far as his pride would allow him to go without an open admission that the warders merely locked doors. Three days later I was in the prison hospital with a badly bruised back and a cracked rib; my cell-mate vaulted down from his top bunk and "accidentally" landed on me with both feet as I was bending to tie my shoe-laces. Five times in all — five times in three years — I ended up in the prison hospital. My fingers were smashed in a suddenly-slammed door. My forehead was opened up enough to need seven stitches; a skilfully executed ankle-tap as I started to descend the iron stairs . . . and every man on those stairs stood aside to allow me free passage to the concrete floor. The two other times were "shiv jobs". Shivs, knives — shaped and sharpened in secret in the workshop — were made, hidden and discovered with almost monotonous regularity. Whenever necessary, a shiv was always available. Both my "cut-ups" took place in the crowded slop-room. The first was meant to kill, but it was badly executed and all it did was scar me for life along the lower abdomen. The second I saw coming — I had become "stir-wise" by this time — gripped the blade and almost broke the lunatic's wrist as I twisted it from his hand. Recollection suggests I went a little berserk. I had him bent backwards over the slop-sink, with my fingers on his throat and the point of the shiv plucking the skin at his groin. 'Anything else — *anything!* — and I'll geld you.'

More stitches in the palm of my hand, another spell in the prison hospital, but I had sense enough to keep the shiv and to keep it hidden. Thereafter, I was left alone. I had learned a lesson the hard way; that to give terrorists a monopoly of terror is no answer; that only when *they* are terrorised can there be peace. The so-called "Balance of Terror". It works. Internationally, nationally and even on a one-to-one basis.

I think the governor was glad to see the back of me. I'd learned the rules. Not the official rules — they were simple enough to learn — but the *real* rules. The rules laid down by the inmates. I could have named the man who ankle-tapped me, and the two men who came at me with shivs. I didn't. Not because I was afraid, but because the harsh pride of caged men had become part of my personality. Little things pleased me. The cool sheets of a hospital bed and the temporary privacy of the ward. The reluctant respect in the eyes of some of my fellow-prisoners when I refused to name names, even more, after that second shiv attempt. Nevertheless, the governor was glad to see the back of me. An ex-detective chief superintendent was a little like having dynamite locked away inside his prison.

Freedom, even after only three years of imprisonment, can be a little overpowering. Even frightening. The flat, high, featureless walls; the angular, enclosed spaces; the doors — doors everywhere and all with locks — produce a form of temporary agoraphobia. When the last door — the wicket-door let into the main gates — closes behind you, you suffer a moment of sheer insanity; you want to turn, hammer on that wicket-door and beg to be re-admitted. It doesn't last, but it's *there*. The wide drive leading up to the gates, the highway at the mouth of the drive and, beyond the highway, the whole world. It seems too much to take at one gulp.

Then I saw the car. A Ford Cortina. I didn't recognise it — it wasn't the car he'd had three years ago — but I recognised the man as he opened the door and climbed from behind the wheel. Chris Tallboy.

I hadn't expected it. Not even half-expected it. We'd exchanged letters. A mere half-dozen letters. Stilted and awkward, but the only letters I'd received and the only letters I'd written. No apologies; Tallboy was too good a copper ever to apologise for doing his job. Nor had my letters hinted at mock-forgiveness. He didn't *need* forgiving and would have thought less of me had I suggested it. And yet he'd driven more than a hundred miles to greet me on that grey morning in late February. He must have come down the day before and spent the night somewhere. The knowledge, the realisation, cancelled everything out. It gave me what I hadn't had for three years. A friend.

And yet there was embarrassment. We walked towards each other slowly. Very slowly. I suspect his thoughts paralleled my own. What greeting? What sort of words to use? How to *say* the right thing in such circumstances?

Thank God for good women!

The passenger door of the Cortina opened and Susan Tallboy climbed from the car. *She* didn't hesitate. *She* didn't have to think. *She* did the right thing — the magnificent thing — instinctively. She half-ran, overtook Chris then, without a word, flung her arms around my neck and buried her face in my shoulder. I remember the hint of carefully used perfume; without doubt, the most beautiful scent ever to touch my nostrils. The touch of her hair against my cheek. The tiny muscle-spasm as she gulped back the tears of welcome. Then Chris had my right hand in a double-grip and was pumping it up and down and gabbling, 'Lenny. Lenny. It's good to see you. God, it's good to see you, Lenny.'

And that's when I almost broke.

*

13

I sat in the front seat alongside Chris. Susan sat in the rear, and beside her there was my tiny suitcase containing all the personal bits and pieces I'd taken with me into prison. We talked little; odd spurts of conversation about men — usually police officers — we both knew, and what had happened to them. But conversation wasn't necessary. It was almost an intrusion. There is a form of silent companionship which needs no talk. Indeed, talk can sometimes ruin its warm intimacy. Sufficient it was that I'd been one — no wife, no family and, I thought, no friends — and now I was part of a trio. I had everything. More than I'd dreamed of. How could mere talk improve upon perfection?

He chose the A1 north. A typical choice. The A1 is a homely road; better by far than the M1, despite the traffic roundabouts. Motorways are a means of moving from Point A to Point B in the shortest possible time. You drive along a motorway, but with a road like the A1 you journey. The farmland is there on both sides. Each filling station has its own character, and the cafés vie with each other for custom, knowing that they are *not* the only place serving food in fifty miles or so of cramped monotony and that, having suffered that monotony, what awaits is neither better nor worse. There are even pubs scattered along the A1.

We stopped at one of the pubs for an early lunch.

It was a nice pub, with a good restaurant, and gradually we relaxed and talk became easier and less intrusive. I remember the food. Fine food and fine wine. More wisdom from Chris; he'd allowed the taste of prison breakfast — what little I'd eaten — to leave my mouth before feeding me with dishes it was a pleasure to eat.

Chilled melon smothered in granulated ginger.

'There's a job waiting for you, Lenny.'

'A job?'

'If you want it. I think you should take it. There's a flat attached.'

Susan added, 'It's a nice flat, Lenny. Comfortable. Plenty big enough for one.'

'Unless you've a job lined up.'

'No.' I shook my head. 'I haven't a job lined up.'

14

Nor had I. It came as something of a shock to realise that I hadn't given the matter of eventual employment a moment's thought. Some mad imp of mischief had insisted that I was still a copper; that the job I liked, the job I'd been trained for, was still waiting for me. One more aspect of prison-life lunacy. The Day. That as all that mattered. The horizon ended there. Well, the Day had arrived, I'd reached the horizon . . . and, left to myself, there'd have been nothing.

Chris said, 'You'll have talked to the welfare people.'

'No.'

'The prison visitors. You'll have . . .'

'No.'

The last three years had coarsened me. That second "No" wasn't too far from a snarl, *and* I'd interrupted him in mid-sentence. I'd lost touch with simple good manners.

In a low, but apologetic, voice I said, 'The do-gooders, Chris. I want no part. I used to think they were wasting their time. I now know the truth of it. They *are*.'

'Are *we* "do-gooders"?' asked Susan softly.

'God, no!' I was shocked that the thought had crossed her mind. I tried very hard to get the truth across. 'We . . . *You*. You don't know. You can't even guess, Chris. We — you — the police . . . you only see them when they're licked. When they're on the defensive. Inside *there*. They rule. They're their true selves. What have they to lose? They revert back. They become what they are. Animals.' I touched my forehead and held my hand open to show the scar. 'Those — and across the stomach — for no good reason. To maim, to kill. That's their *true* opinion of coppers. Of authority of any kind. Open the gates, offer them freedom . . . they'd kill every warder before they left. And the do-goodery crowd butter them up. Make excuses. They don't *need* excuses. They don't *want* to change. All they want is . . .'

I closed my mouth and there was a silence. They thought I was overstating things. A reaction to the last three years, perhaps. Neither of them voiced the opinion, but it was there in their expressions. I sipped at the wine and let the moment pass. The waitress cleared the dishes and brought on the main course. Fillet

15

steak, with every vegetable in season; fresh vegetables, cooked to perfection. The sort of meal I'd occasionally remembered. Even promised myself.

'Fifty pounds a week,' said Chris suddenly.

'What?'

'The job. Not much of a wage,, but the flat's free. So is lighting and heating.'

'Oh, I see.'

'Furnished,' he added.

'Sounds reasonable.'

'A place of your own. Your own front door.'

'And *I* have the key to the lock.'

Immediately I'd said it I realised it was not a kind remark. It smacked of ingratitude and self-pity. These two people deserved more. Much more. What they'd done — what they *must* have done — and I was repaying them by making smart remarks.

'I'm sorry,' I said awkwardly.

'Steak okay?' Chris nodded his head.

'Fine. Perfect.'

'Wine?'

'I'm sorry, Chris,' I muttered. 'I — I haven't yet grown used to being polite.'

'Forget it.' He grinned true friendship. '*We're* new at this game, too.'

I ate in silence. Chris made gentle, husbandly conversation with his wife. 'More sprouts, darling?' 'No, I've quite sufficient.' 'More wine?' 'Just a snidge please, pet.' That sort of thing They tried very hard not to make it sound like a cover-up, but it was. Maybe, just *maybe*, they'd made a mistake . . . that was what they were both thinking. It was there. As obvious as if they'd voiced their misgivings. And I felt ashamed.

In a gentle, as steady a voice as possible, I said, 'Tell me about the job, Chris.'

'It's at a bank. One of the high street banks.'

He said it in something of a rush; as if to get the pill down before it choked both of us.

Equally hurriedly, Susan added, 'A sort of caretaker-cum-supervisor. Letting the cleaners in and out.'

'Double-checking, each evening. Making sure everything's locked and secure.'

'With this tiny, self-contained flat above the bank premises.'

'I'm an ex-con,' I said gently. 'Just out.'

'You're an ex-chief superintendent,' said Chris.

'An ex-*con*,' I insisted.

'Dammit Lenny, you're not a thief. You've not been inside for stealing.'

It was an argument. A tissue-thin argument, and neither Chris nor Susan were foolish enough not to recognise it for what it was. Somebody had done some very hard asking. Even pleading. Equally, somebody had gone out on a particularly slender limb.

The stench of prison was still on me. For three years my daily companions had been men to whom banks were merely a means of reaching the high life the easy way. I might have become friends with them. I might even have absorbed some of their basic philosophy. A risk, therefore, but on the other hand a peculiar defiance. A dare. That I — a man who throughout his life had not merely upheld but enforced the law, yet for once only had seen fit to break that law — could be ever other than trustworthy.

I murmured, ' Somebody's neck is very handy for the axe.'

'Yours,' said Chris bluntly.

'Ah!'

'Lenny,' he growled. 'Straight talk. Right?'

'The only talk worth a damn.'

'Unofficial watchman. That too. And if there *is* a break-in . . .' He left the end of the sentence unspoken.

I said, 'Ah!' again.

'What you'd expect. What you'd once have accepted as normal.'

'Number One Suspect.' I sighed. 'As you say . . . what I'd expect.'

'It should . . .' he hesitated, then said, 'It should make you keener than ever. Put that extra edge on things.'

'Is that the argument you used?'

'One of them,' he admitted.

'Lenny.' Susan looked sad. Almost disappointed. 'Suspects are eliminated. You know *that*, too.'

I smiled. The waitress arrived to clear away the main course dishes, and serve the sweet. Crêpes Suzette. We ate, first in silence, then with small talk. I felt something of a louse; by all the rules of the game, I should have been down on my knees thanking these two for something I hadn't expected and didn't deserve. Instead . . .

I was grateful. Of course I was grateful; more grateful than I could say. But my freedom could still be measured in hours, and not too many hours at that. The bars and the walls have an effect. It is there and it cannot be sloughed off like so much dead tissue. It goes deeper than that. The pinheads of suspicion mix with the corpuscles of the blood and, if they are removed at all, it is a long and sad process. It takes patience. It takes understanding. Above all, it takes self-examination and the acceptance of an untarnished truth. Meanwhile, one miserable part of me insisted that there was a "catch". There *had* to be. The prison code . . . nothing for nothing. I was wrong — I knew I was wrong — but one part of me refused to be *convinced* I was wrong.

The cottage. It had once been Blayde's cottage. Blayde, a one-time fellow-copper, who'd built it stone by stone and timber by timber with his own two hands. Built on the outskirts of Beechwood Brook Division. Built with love and skill, then willed to the Tallboys.*

It was where our journey ended and as always I was amazed that a man who was more than a mere "loner" — a man who was basically *lonely* — had been capable of designing, then creating, a house that was, from the start, a home. Complete with a cat. That was its name: Cat. I knew its history; I'd known Blayde and Blayde had told me. A stray, half-wild creature. Some tom from a farmyard litter, and in the beginning Blayde had fed it milk at the rear door of the cottage. Cat had made the first move. Cats always do; they have a wisdom combined with an independence lacking

Blayde R.I.P. by John Wainwright, Macmillan, 1982

18

in the canine make-up. *They* choose. Cat, it seemed, recognised its human counterpart. A solitary fighter, who refused to run with any pack. Cat moved in with Blayde and, for the first time in his life, poor old Blayde had a friend he could completely trust. (It's anybody's guess what Cat thought when, as repayment for that trust, Blayde had his masculinity painlessly removed!) And when the Tallboys took over, Cat went with the cottage. It is also a measure of the Tallboys' understanding that, when they took over, they tacitly accepted the feline proposition that *they* were the guests.

Cat stayed and, gradually, condescended to become part of another family.

Cats. I have this thing about cats. Forgive me, but they bring back memories of what, at the time, I didn't recognise as the happiest years of my whole life. A good woman was my wife. Good, but by no stretch of the imagination beautiful. Not even moderately handsome. Like me, in fact. Mildly eccentric, and not giving a damn about the rest of the world. Halcyon days, when we masked our love for each other behind gentle insults. I lived for policing. She lived for her cats. Russian Blues, bred and cared for like the peers of their breed that they were. I made believe they were a nuisance; that she thought more of her cats than she did of me. But we both knew. They were beautiful animals, and in their own way they were substitutes for the children we couldn't have.

She died, I sold the cats, the house and the furniture. Not to have rid myself of everything other than memories would have sent me into the nearest mental home within months. I continued policing, but even that had lost its previous fascination. And when I killed a man . . .

But enough of this. Suffice to say that Cat made me as welcome as Chris and Susan. As we entered the cottage he uncurled himself from his corner of the hearthrug, stretched luxuriously then, with tail as rigid as a flagpole, sauntered across and tentatively allowed the fur along one of his sides to touch the cloth of my trouser leg. I bent and scratched him gently between the ears and, after that split-second of doubt which was part of his personality and a throw-back to the long-gone days of his half-

19

wild state, the purring started. Deep-throated and soft, with a regular rise and fall, which to cat-lovers is a sure sign of complete acceptance.

'You're favoured.' Susan slipped out of her coat and kicked off her shoes. Chris was garaging the car. 'We almost had to bribe him to acknowledge our existence.'

'An old friend.' I continued to scratch the top of Cat's head. 'We've met before.'

As I straightened, she said, 'Throw the chip away, Lenny.'

She didn't look at me as she spoke. She was draping the coat over her arm and collecting the shoes.

'Before Chris comes in.' She turned and stood looking at me. Not a tall women — in her stocking feet looking even smaller — but a woman of great stature. Almost young enough to be my daughter and, indeed, our relationship bordered upon that of father and child. But a determined woman. A one-man woman, and that man was Chris . . . and, for him, *anything*. She said, 'Close the door, Lenny. Please! It's in the past. Close the door, otherwise you'll let both of us down. We want to help. We're not "do-gooders". We just want to help because we both know you. Love you. For what you *were*. For what we both know you can *become*. But — and please understand me — we won't fight you. We'll help you, but we won't fight you. We won't try to *make* you do anything. It's your choice, Lenny. Make it. Make the right one.'

We both heard Chris enter the house. She smiled quickly, then turned and made for the stairs leading to the bedrooms.

Later I was shown to the spare bedroom. The clothes I'd left at my lodgings, prior to my trial, had been collected, laundered and dry-cleaned and were neatly tucked away in the wardrobe and drawers. New pyjamas, socks and a pair of carpet slippers were there for my use. Then a long soak in the hot, oil-scented water of a bath removed the last of the jail-stench.

That night we sat and talked into the small hours. Susan stayed with us until almost midnight, and the three of us sipped drinking chocolate and did what I once thought I'd never do again. We indulged in a veritable orgy of "bobby talk". Of Susan's father,

Ripley, who'd once held the position of Beechwood Brook divisional officer, now held by Chris.

'He'd have found a way.'

'Chris, darling, he was never better than you . . . and *you* can't get round them.'

'Get round who?' I asked.

'The professional police-baiters,' sighed Chris.

'As bad as that?'

'Lenny.' He moved a hand in a gesture of helpless disgust. 'Since the riots. Since some damn fool came up with the scheme for making coppers glorified parsons. You get a search warrant, swear it out, do everything strictly by the book. Who the hell cares? As *you* go in the front door some clown is already nipping out of the back on his way to the nick to lay a complaint. You aren't even *in* the bloody house and already you've been accused of harassment. It's a game and the rules say *we* must never win.'

It was an exaggeration, of course. But not too much of an exaggeration. Three short years . . . but things had changed very dramatically.

We talked of Rucker. The never-to-be-forgotten and universally hated Rucker. The day Gilliant, the chief, made him my opposite number and promoted him to Head of C.I.D. Lessford Region a lot of beer had been watered down by tears.

'Nobody quite like him,' I chuckled, and was quietly surprised to realise that it was the nearest I'd come to laughter for a very long time.

'Today they'd crucify him.' And there was not a hint of laughter in Chris's remark.

'The — what d'you call 'em? — police-baiters?'

'The men. His fellow-coppers.'

'For God's sake! He had his faults, but he was a magnificent thief-taker.'

'It isn't the same, Lenny. It isn't the same job. The joy's all been squeezed out of it.' He blew out his cheeks in disgust. 'We damn near have to say "please" and "thank you" to the men — *and* the women — we supposedly have authority over. Discipline's up the spout. Nobody guards anybody's back.

21

Rucker? One of *his* little outbursts — just one — and some pasty-faced young copper would have him on the carpet for using "insulting language". That's the way things are these days. They wear the uniform and damn-all else.'

'Not all of them,' murmured Susan.

'Enough,' growled Chris. 'You only need a handful of death watch beetles. Eventually the whole beam turns to powder.'

It came as a shock. Not just the picture of the old force, as painted by Chris, but also his own bitterness. As I remembered him, Chris Tallboy wasn't a man to complain too readily. He'd had his ups and downs; every copper worthy of the name rides an everlasting switchback. But he'd always come back swinging. The good ones always do. He'd hammered his way to the top, without stamping on anybody's neck and, to my knowledge, nobody had ever denied his right to climb the ladder to his present position. And every inch of the way he'd had Susan, which meant he'd always enjoyed a good home life upon which to build a sense of proportion. Now, he seemed to be going overboard a little, and that wasn't the Chris Tallboy I remembered.

I sipped drinking chocolate and enjoyed the taste of a good cheroot. That was another thing. The cheroots. Time was, I smoked like a mill chimney, and always cheroots. Cheap cheroots. The cheapest on the market. Trash, I suppose. But I'd acquired the taste and, when I'd been up there in the driving seat, I'd allowed myself the luxury of that personal gimmick. Cheap cheroots and a snazzy dress sense. The Tallboys had remembered the cheroots and, rightly, had figured they hadn't been available inside. A whole box had been waiting there for me in the spare bedroom. Not cheap ones. Good ones, with which to start a new chapter of my life.

Small things. Important things. The meeting, the meal at the pub, the clothes, the cheroots. The job waiting for me was the main thing, but the small periphery kindnesses were the things that mattered. *They* had the effect of admitting me once more to the human race. Of cancelling out much of the mental sourness brought about by three years in prison.

I therefore wanted to know things. Why? Why this basic

change in Chris's outlook on life in general and law-enforcement in particular? Why the bitterness? Why the tone of near-defeat from a man I'd once known as being almost fanatical in his professional pride?

I asked. I forget the exact words I used. I know I chose the words very carefully. Wasn't blunt. Wasn't rude. Nevertheless, I asked.

'Mob rule,' he said bluntly.

'Nasty, but not the end of the world,' I teased.

'How the hell do you know?'

'Darling!' Susan jumped in and reminded Chris that I wasn't seeking an argument.

'Sorry.' He combed his fingers through his hair then, in a low voice, said, 'I've tasted it, Lenny. Just a taste . . . no more than that.'*

'And?'

'We're not equipped to handle it. We're not para-military. Never will be. And that's what it needs. Beyond a certain point, that's the only answer. Otherwise it's anarchy and we needn't be there.'

'Guns?' I suggested.

'Whatever's needed,' he grunted. 'Flame-throwers if necessary. Certainly water-cannon.' He paused then, in a passionate voice, continued, 'Lenny, it's got well beyond the stage of the old-fashioned truncheon charge. It can flare up like *that*.' He snapped his fingers. 'And when it does — when the mobs rule the streets — what the hell have *we* got? Plastic shields. Crash helmets. Shin pads. Boxes to protect our balls. For Christ's sake! They're pelting us with home-made fire-bombs. They're out to kill. To maim at least. We're the enemy. Dammit to hell, *we* are. Not the crooks, not the tearaways, not the arsonists. How it's been done — God only know how it's been done — but the public's been brainwashed into thinking *we're* the enemy. Smart-arsed sods who sit in a television studio and churn out never-ending guff about "police brutality". Not a blind word about the extremists. Not a

Anatomy of a Riot by John Wainwright, Macmillan, 1982

hint about what the mad bastard was up to before some hard-working copper stopped his gallop the only way possible. *We're* the bully-boys. Not the louts who sling bricks through shop windows. Not the rent-a-crowd set who chase decent people off the street. Us! I tell you . . .' Again, he combed his fingers through his greying hair. 'The hooligans run things these days, Lenny. The hooligans, backed and encouraged by people who want us out of the way as a first step towards a take-over.'

'You think it's political?' I asked sombrely.

'Damned if I know.' He took a deep breath, then lighted a cigarette before repeating, 'Damned if I know, Lenny. Some of the top men in the service hold that opinion . . . and voice it occasionally. Take your pick. There's a new excuse — another explanation — every day of the week. The one thing I *do* know. Compared to what it was, this damn job isn't worth a candle.'

It was past midnight. Susan had gone to bed and the drinking chocolate had been replaced by whisky and water. I was enjoying my last cheroot of the day, Chris was smoking a cigarette and the talk had moved from outraged generalities to more intimate and parochial subjects. The cases we'd shared; not the headline-hitters, but the less flamboyant and, at times, more interesting cornering of miserable culprits.

'The old lady,' chuckled Chris. 'The one Preston interviewed and didn't known she was a little off balance. She carried a whole dinner service to the police station. All white. Swore blind Preston had pinched the Willow Pattern from them.'

'Where's Preston these days?' I asked.

'Up north, somewhere.'

'Another force?'

'A step up. He applied, and the chief gave him a glowing testimonial.'

'Probably glad to see the back of him.' I grinned.

Odd. I was a copper again. Of course, I *wasn't* a copper, could never again *be* a copper, but the feeling was still there. One of them. Party to the unique "in" jokes of the service. Dropping, quite naturally, into the colloquialisms which to an outsider would have meant nothing. "Taking the dew off his rose". "Playing the hard and soft game on him". God, I was happy, and for the moment the last three years hadn't even happened.

Very casually, I asked, 'Who's in my old chair, these days?'

'Badger.'

It was a one-word answer and, I suppose, that should have hinted at *something*. The combination of whisky and conviviality didn't go with one-word answers.

'Who's Badger?' I asked.

'From one of the mobs down south.'

'Oh! Any good?'

'Unusual.' The impression was that he contemplated expanding upon the answer, but instead said, 'Very unusual.'

There was a silence. For my part it was not an awkward silence. Indeed, it was a very comfortable silence; I was relaxed and happy and free to go to a warm bed at any o'clock I chose. I was in the company of a friend who had proved himself to be a *real* friend, and I was enjoying the solace of good tobacco and nice booze. Less than twenty-four hours previously . . .

Believe me, it was a *very* comfortable silence.

Chris broke the silence as he said, 'He — er — he had a lot to do with getting you the job.'

'Eh?'

'Badger. He pulled the job for you. I suggested it, but I wouldn't have got far alone.'

'Good of him,' I murmured.

'Bordfield. His region, not mine. And he knew the manager. Said the right things at the right time.'

'I must thank him.'

'Yeah.'

Thereafter, the talk dwindled into tiny spurts of small-hours chat while we finished our drinks. Then I squashed what was left of my cheroot into the ash-tray, left Chris to open the curtains and check the doors and went to bed.

The next three days gave me back much of what I'd lost in jail. Not least, self-respect. It was February and the gardening year was on the move. I'd once had a belly, now I was merely "thick" and those years inside had, at least, hardened the muscles and made me fit. I spiked the lawn for them, then gave the vegetable patch its spring dig. It was no hardship. It toned me up and did a little to repay them for their kindness.

On the second day (the Friday) I caught a bus to Bordfield. I called at my old bank, checked that they'd kept their eye on my savings, then withdrew the lot, closed the account and transferred everything to the bank at which I was going to work. A sense of humour had returned. The expression "sitting on your money" took on a new meaning and amused me a little. I told the teller who I was and asked to see the manager.

He was a tall man; thin, sad-eyed and with a slight stoop. He gave the impression of a man who'd suffered a great loss yet, when he smiled, it wasn't the practised grimace of the guy who supposedly lives in your wardrobe. His name was Stowe. Reginald Stowe.

He closed the door of his office, waved me to a chair and said, 'It was thoughtful of you to call, Mr Lennox.'

'It was far more than thoughtful of you to offer me the job.'

'Mr Badger assured me you were just the man we needed.' He opened a cigarette box on his desk, and I helped myself. As he flicked a lighter he asked, 'Do you know Mr Badger?'

'I've heard of him,' I said carefully.

'A fine man. A fine officer. I'm prepared to accept his judgement in just about everything.'

'And Chief Superintendent Tallboy,' I added quietly.

'Ah, yes. Him, too. But I don't know Mr Tallboy as intimately as I know Mr Badger.'

I left it at that, and we talked of the salary and the duties the job entailed. We left his office and he led me out of the bank and to a tiny, oak-panelled door alongside the main entrance.

'There's another door, a sort of rear entrance, which leads directly into the premises of the bank. But this is your front door, as it were. The door you'll normally use when entering and leaving the flat.'

It was a solidly built door, with a damn good lock. A Chubb

26

Castle mortice deadlock. Some security-minded person had realised that if there was a way from the flat to the bank, the flat door had better be as safe as the bank door.

'Three keys,' he said. 'You have one, I have one and one remains in the bank strongroom.'

'And the other door?'

'The same. A similar lock. Both doors locked at all times, if you please.'

'Naturally.'

There was a small landing at the top of the stairs. To the right, a second flight of stairs led down to a closed door.

'The door leading to the bank premises.'

'I see.'

A door opposite the head of the main stairs led into the flat. It was a nice flat; compact, but with a neatness of layout worthy of admiration. A main room with windows looking out onto the street in front of the bank. A well-planned kitchenette leading from the main room. At the rear, a moderately-sized bedroom, with a tiny bathroom and toilet en suite. Finally a smaller room which might, at a pinch, be used as a second bedroom, but more likely would be used as a fairly spacious boxroom. The whole place was fully equipped; fitted wardrobes, central heating, an electric fire, a bed, tables and chairs. Even bed linen and pans, a kettle and crockery.

'You'll find cutlery — things like that — in the kitchen drawers. Glassware — those sort of things — in the wall cabinet. Hopefully, the only thing you will have to provide is food and clothing.'

'That's fine.'

'Laundry once a week. Mondays. Collection and delivery. If you'll have it ready the cleaning lady — one of the cleaners employed by the bank — will collect it when she comes to straighten up the apartment. Part of her job is to give this flat a quick clean each morning before she finishes work.'

I nodded. There wasn't a lot I could say. The truth is, I was more than a little flabbergasted. This wasn't just a job . . . it was a *gift*. Chris had performed a near-miracle and the unknown

27

Detective Chief Superintendent Badger had more "pull" in Bordfield than I'd ever had. I was an ex-con, well into the middle-age bracket and the unemployment figures were swanning around numbers usually reserved for astronomers. And this little beauty had been handed to me on a plate.

He said, 'You start Monday.'

'Yes.'

'I'll leave you a key to the flat in case you want to bring anything over — books, clothes, things like that — before you move in.'

'Fine.'

'I'm afraid there's an inventory. Everything itemised. Banks tend to be rather tiresome in such matters.'

'Understandable.'

'I'll have the chief clerk here on Monday morning. Half-nine be convenient?'

'I'll be here.'

'He'll check the inventory with you and at the same time give you a key for the door between the flat and the bank.'

I thanked him, we shook hands and I left.

How to explain what it was like to carry a key in my pocket for the first time in years? Silly. Childish. But at the same time monumentally important. I kept slipping my hand into my hip pocket and fingering it. I called at a leather-goods shop and bought a key-wallet; an expensive housing for this key, with hooks which would never loosen their grip and a zip which would last a lifetime. The key deserved nothing less. A key to an expensive lock, and the expensive lock was part of my own front door. I had a *home* again. I was trusted. Which meant I was respected. Which, in turn, meant I was once more a complete man.

All because of one tiny piece of metal in the shape of a key.

I called at a neat little café and ordered an early afternoon snack. Hot muffins, running with melted butter, and tea served in a teapot, with milk jug, hot-water jug and sugar bowl. I'd slotted back into civilisation as if I'd never been away.

And as I sat there, I pondered upon the man I'd just left. Stowe, the bank manager. A sad man and yet — and of this I was

28

sure — not a naturally morose man. Not one of those born misery-guts who blight everything by their never-ending wretchedness. By the very nature of their profession, bank managers must be careful optimists. Their job is to encourage, to give hope and, very often, to take a calculated risk. Indeed, what was *I* but a calculated risk? More than that, they have to look the part . . . *and* act the part.

Stowe, therefore, was unhappy, and because of what he was he had *reason* to be unhappy. A personal reason. An unhappiness he could not hide. Something big enough, hurtful enough, to swamp a professional personality which had taken him to the top office in a large and important city. Not some tin-pot branch in a market town. But Bordfield. Population past the half-million mark. A metropolitan district; what had once been known as a county borough.

A recent death, perhaps? I thought not. His suit had been of mid-brown and without a black armband. His tie, too, had been brown — of a shade matching that of his suit — with a motif of tiny yellow shields. Mourning — even unofficial mourning — would have called for a dark blue suit and a plain, dark tie.

Already, I liked the man enough to find that his unknown tragedy saddened *me* a little.

At the same time, I was pleasantly surprised to discover that the tricks of *my* profession — of my once-upon-a-time profession — hadn't deserted me. I could still see things, note things, then follow a line of logical reasoning. The manner, the profession, the clothes. With Stowe, the three things didn't quite jell. To the-man-in-the-street . . . nothing. He wouldn't have noticed, and *had* he noticed, it would have meant nothing. He would have dismissed it as none of his business. But to a trained and experienced jack, *everything* was his business and *everything* had to have a reason. "Once a copper, always a copper". How true. And I almost grinned with secret delight as the realisation hit me.

I left the café and walked to the garage.

One more good turn from Chris. He'd taken my old VW Beetle and arranged for it to be stored and periodically checked at one of the Bordfield garages. Not quite as outrageous as it might seem to those not privy to normal but unofficial police practice. In each police area there is a chosen garage; a night-and-day job, complete with breakdown truck. Accidents happen all the time. Cars have to be towed from the scene and, if the towing vehicle belongs to a garage, the smashed car will be taken to that garage. Whether or not possession is nine-tenths of the law, the fact remains that the chances of that garage collecting the job of repairing the smashed car are very good. Garages therefore vie with each other to be the one the cops always call out. Favours are offered, and favours are accepted. Free servicing of the private cars of policemen. Cost-price tyres. That sort of thing. The cost of storing the VW, therefore, wasn't going to knock me sideways. In the event, it cost me nothing and a complete oil-change, a tank full of petrol and a tyre check were thrown in for good measure.

The proprietor, Alf Black, knew me and greeted me like an old friend.

'Almost a museum piece, these days.' He jerked his head at the VW. 'Good nick, too. You could get more for it today than you had to pay when you bought it.'

'It's not for sale.'

'Don't blame you.' He led the way into the tiny, plaster-board-walled office. When we were seated, he said, 'Good to have you back, Mr Lennox.'

'I'm not "back".' I stripped the cellophane from a cheroot. 'Not the way you mean.'

'Pity. We could do with some of the old-time bobbying round here.'

'As bad as that?' I picked an oil-stained box of matches from the crowded desk and lighted the cheroot. 'Three years isn't a lifetime.'

'It is, these days.' He frowned his annoyance. 'A place like this. It's a full-time job keeping the buggers out.'

'Breakers? Thieves?' I sounded surprised. I *was* surprised. If places like Alf Black's garage tempted the lifters things really *had* deteriorated.

'Naw.' The annoyance turned to open disgust. 'Destructive bastards. They don't pinch much. A few cans of aerosol paint to

30

write mucky words on walls with. That's about all. But the bloody damage! You wouldn't believe. Just for the sake of smashing things. Windscreens, headlamps, slashing tyres to hell. It's getting so insurance companies just don't want to know.'

'Garages?'

'Any bloody thing. Yobs. Bloody punks. What the hell they call themselves these days. If it's breakable, they'll break the bloody thing. Just to show they've been around. Shop windows. I dunno how many but at least a dozen a week. The buses. The crews won't take 'em out after eight Fridays, Saturdays and Sundays. Too many drivers and conductors been knocked about. It's like living in a bloody jungle.'

'And the police?' I asked gently.

I thought he was going to spit, but instead he snarled 'They're shit-scared. They don't want to know. Mate . . .' He leaned forward in his chair, and his eyes shone with furious outrage. 'I've *seen* 'em. Young kids — still with the nappy marks on their arse — turn and walk the other way. No bottle. Not like the old days. Christ, I can remember the time . . .' He stopped, settled back in the chair, gave a twisted grin and shook his head. 'I don't have to tell *you*, Mr Lennox. You knew *how* to bobby.'

A mechanic ran a final check on the VW prior to the stamping and signing of the required MOT Certificate, and meanwhile Alf expanded on the same theme. "Bloody kids". That's what it boiled down to. By "kids" he meant everybody from teens to twenty, regardless of sex or upbringing. He was a prodigious swearer — to his credit, he rarely used obscenities — and his indignation was bespattered by basic Anglo-Saxon cuss-words. 'Another bloody war. That's what we need. Get the young buggers off the streets, and give 'em summat to do.' Nor was he in any way prejudiced as far as colour was concerned. Like most of his kind, he was more impressed by what a man *did* than by what a man *was*. 'They blame the bloody nigs, but they're no worse than the home-grown sods. I've seen some of the bloody skinheads. What they want is six laceholes up their arse.'

It was quite impressive and, having collected the VW, I decided to drive around the town, and perhaps judge the extent of

31

his exaggeration.

There was no exaggeration. In retrospect, I think the immediate trauma of freedom had blinded me until Alf Black had opened my eyes. For whatever reason, I was suddenly aware that Bordfield had lost its pride. Never a spa town, nevertheless it had once had an air of lived-in untidiness. Not dirty, but "regularly used". It was a place of industry — some of it heavy industry — and commerce; not a place to go to for a holiday, but for all that a fine shopping centre and a place whose natives were proud to have been born there. Its monuments, civic buildings, office blocks, cinemas and the like had been kept moderately clean. Always some main building had just had, or was just having, a new coat of paint and a general face-lift. The pokey squares and gardens — the tiny, scattered lungs of the city — had enjoyed trim lawns and unimaginative but weed-free flower beds; rowan trees, plane trees, even an occasional willow; benches on which tired housewives could rest and ease the weight of their shopping-bags, where elderly men sat and, like elderly men the world over, put the world to rights, where red-legged pigeons fluttered from the ridges of nearby roofs and pecked and strutted among crumbs thrown by city-dwellers brought up to believe that the pigeon was a pet rather than a pest.

All this had changed. Vandalism and the product of sick minds had worked ugliness into its very fabric. Many of the benches had had timber torn away and their cast-iron scroll-work smashed. Trees carried knife and hatchet scars and lower branches had been ripped almost clear of the trunks. Idiot slogans had been painted on dozens of flat surfaces by aerosol spray-cans. I counted seven boarded windows in the area where the main shopping centre was situated. Groups of youths at street corners; some of them skinheads, some of them with hair beyond shoulder-length; one with a Mohican haircut, one with spiky hair dyed a brilliant purple, one with hair dyed an unnatural yellow; all wearing clothes which amounted to a uniform of whichever clan they claimed as their own. Their female counterparts, their sex burlesqued and destroyed behind equally outlandish clothes and hair-styles. A mad world, peopled by destructive lunatics. And *these* were free to roam the streets while other lunatics, who were at least *men*, rotted in cells.

Completely illogical, but all the way back to Beechwood Brook I muttered to myself about the injustice of wrong people being in prison. Thieves, tearaways, even murderers. At least they'd had *reason*. They'd had *cause*. With each of them, there'd been a breaking point — a temptation they'd been too weak to resist — but, however reprehensible, it could be understood. Understand me, I wasn't manufacturing excuses. I'd lived with them for three years. I'd witnessed their perversions, been victim of their petty hatreds, learned to know the level of their intelligence. In the main they were scum and a disgrace to the human race, but even with scum there are degrees. A handful were beyond hope of redemption, but the rest . . .

Dear God, they were monuments of respectability when placed alongside this small army of strutting hooligans who, merely for the sake of wanton destruction, were burying a city — *my* city — beneath the offal of their own madness.

My expression must have reflected my thoughts when I arrived at the cottage. Chris was on duty and Susan had a scratch meal ready pending the main meal of the day when he returned home.

We sat in the kitchen, nibbled scrambled eggs on toast, sipped hot, sweet tea and chatted. It was homely. Nice. And I found myself wondering why — indeed *how* — people like Chris and Susan and the louts I'd seen on the streets of Bordfield could inhabit the same world.

'Disappointed?' Susan asked the question gently, and with the hint of a frown.

'Eh?' The question puzzled me.

'About the job? The flat, perhaps?'

'Oh, *that*? No, that's fine. Couldn't be better.'

'You *look* disappointed,' she accused.

'Er . . . disgusted.' I chose the word with some care.

'The flat? The . . .'

'No. Some of the yobs hanging about the streets.'

'Oh?'

'Alf Black — the garage man — he tells me they run riot. I drove around. Saw some of the vandalism. Then the yobs. I hadn't realised.'

'I think it all started on the football terraces,' she opined solemnly.

'Aye. Maybe.'

'Then some of the modern pop music. Some of the groups. They set out to shock . . . the kids follow *their* lead.'

'My pet, they aren't "kids",' I said gently. 'That's what shocked me. Old enough to have the vote. Some of 'em old enough to be married and *have* kids.'

'The cinema, perhaps. The television. Sex and violence. It's a very marketable commodity these days, Lenny. The hard-sell people push it for all they're worth.'

She was making excuses. Stock excuses. She, too, had been subjected to a "hard sell" campaign. With her it was parlour psychology, hawked in the pages of the popular press. I'd gumption enough to realise that, too. But I wasn't there to argue. I was there to ask.

I said, 'What about the police?'

'Beechwood Brook doesn't get much . . .'

'Bordfield has a police force, too. What about them?'

'I wouldn't know.'

She was wrong of course. Well, not *wrong* exactly. She was treating my questions like tennis balls being aimed at her. Dodging them in case they hit and hurt. Of course she "knew". She was Chris's wife, and Chris was the sort of copper who shared secrets with his missus, knowing that the secrets would be safe. She was also Charlie Ripley's daughter . . . and he'd been one of the best coppers ever. She "knew". She just wouldn't open up.

It irritated me a little, but I hadn't the heart to fault her. Apart from her loyalty to Chris, who the hell was *I* these days? Not a copper any more. The other thing, in fact. A man just released from jail. How did *she* know how I felt? How could she be *sure*?

'A big mistake,' I mused.

'What?'

34

'Making it one bumper-bundle. Lessford. Bordfield. The county. It can't be handled. Too many coppers in the wrong place at the wrong time. Different tactics, too. Your dad. A hell of a copper, but a *county* copper. Collins, on the other hand . . .'

'Collins is dead,' she said gently.

I breathed, 'Christ! I didn't know.'

I suddenly felt very mortal. Very vulnerable. Henry Collins had been something very special; one of a select band and probably best of them all. He'd worked Lessford. Chief superintendent in charge of Hallsworth Hill Division. Chief superintendent, uniformed, but in his own quiet way a regular "king-maker". I could name chief constables and assistant chief constables — damn good men — who'd freely admit they learned their job while working alongside Henry Collins.

'When?' I asked.

'About a year ago.' She hesitated, then added, 'He was mugged.'

'Mugged? Henry Collins?'

'He was an old man,' she reminded me quietly.

'How?' I asked hoarsely.

'On his way home one night. After a concert, I think. Walking. For his age, he was a fit man. He took a short cut. Two street lamps were smashed. Somebody jumped him. Stole his wallet and wrist-watch.'

'Somebody?'

'It's . . .' She glanced down at her plate as if embarrassed. As if it was her fault. 'It's undetected.'

'They killed him?'

'No.' Her voice was as hoarse as mine. And as low. 'He died in hospital. About three months later. He wasn't — y'know — young any more. They hurt him badly. About the head. About the body. I . . .' Again the embarrassed hesitation. 'I don't think he really wanted to live. He was disgusted. So *disgusted*.'

I used my fork to push scrambled eggs around on my plate. Slowly. Carefully. Making silly patterns. Something to do with my hands. Something upon which to concentrate my mind.

I muttered, 'He was a good man.'

'I know.'

'No, I mean a *good* man. Too good for that to happen. At times, too good even to be a copper.'

'I know,' she repeated gently. 'He was our friend, Lenny. Like you are. We knew him . . . well.'

'No.' I raised my head and stared at her. Sadly I said, 'Compared with me, he was a bloody saint. Honour the dead, but that's not it. When he was alive, I'd have said the same thing. The only man I've ever met. He never did an evil thing. Never had an evil thought. A genuine one-off. Nothing deliberate. It — it was quite natural to him. There just *wasn't* anything bad about him.'

That night was one of those nights you remember. The gloom of the bedroom occasionally washed by the reflection of passing headlights. The spasmodic sounds of the countryside; the velvet scream of an owl; the distant bark of a dog fox. I heard them because I couldn't sleep. And I couldn't sleep because of memories and mental pictures.

Collins. Slim and slightly hawk-nosed. Clean to the point of fastidiousness. Perfectly mannered in a strange, old-fashioned way. He'd worn his uniform with quiet elegance. With equal elegance — with equal natural ease — he could have worn a plumed hat and cloak. All who knew him agreed. That was his real "age"; the age of the cavalier; the age of impeccable manners; the age of blazing honour.

And this man had been a copper, and one hell of a copper. One *hell* of a copper. He'd handled cases, situations which would have broken ninety-nine men in every hundred; been a friend of Ripley and Sullivan . . . men who themselves had grown to be legends in their own lifetime. A group of officers — county, Lessford, Bordfield — from the Golden Age of policing; Ripley, Sullivan, Raff, Collins. Men who'd set a murderously high standard in law enforcement and of them all — each a giant — Collins had been the greatest. The greatest, yet the gentlest. That had been his magic. Something only he possessed.

And now some lout . . .

God, if one of them had still been alive. Any one of them. Alive and in harness. He'd have taken Lessford apart, brick by brick, but he'd have found the animal — maybe animals — responsible. He'd have nailed him to the floor of a Crown Court dock, forced a conviction from any jury under the sun, then visited Collins's grave and stood there in solemn satisfaction.

If only one of them . . .

I almost sat up in bed. One of them *was* still alive. Or was he? Dammit, I hadn't known about Collins until a few hours before. A lot of people die in three years. Especially people no longer young. But if there was justice in the world, David Raff would still be alive. And of them all, David Raff had been closest of all to Collins. All through his police career, Raff had played counterpoint to Collins's virtuosity; they'd been as close as any two men, any two coppers, could ever be. Same force, same division, same cases. Collins with a slightly younger Raff keeping pace and alongside. Dear God, Raff *had* to be still alive.

I dropped off with that hope — that prayer — dominating my mind and then I dreamed. A bad dream. A nightmare.

I was back in that damn cell; that cubicle of confined stench. And men I'd known — men who'd shared the landing and whose only common cause was their hatred of me — were crowding in. Laughing. Waving shivs. I was being cut to hell. I was being murdered, inch at a time. But I was protecting something. Something huddled in a corner; something I wouldn't let them touch. A huddled figure; dark and almost unrecognisable. I hadn't time to turn my head — to even glance at it — but I knew it was Collins. Collins, there in the corner. His head caved in and dead as a nit. But I had to stop the bastards from killing him. Whatever the cost — even if they carved me to shreds — I had to stop them from killing him . . . even though he was already dead.

Christ!

I woke in a muck-sweat. I must have made some noise; shouting, screaming maybe. I was awakened by the light being switched on, and Chris was there in pyjamas and dressing-gown. Looking worried as he approached the bed.

'You okay, Lenny?'

'Eh?' I blinked the last of the nightmare from my eyes and

wiped my mouth with the back of my hand. My face was sweat-lathered. I moistened my lips and, feeling like some ham-actor in a Hollywood war film, I muttered, 'Sorry, Chris. A bad dream. Did I — y'know — did I disturb you?'

'Not to worry.' He sat on the edge of the bed. 'Feel like a drink? Something to steady you down a little?'

'No.' I hoisted myself into a sitting position. Ran the palms of my hands down my soaked cheeks. I repeated, 'Sorry Chris,' hesitated, then added, 'I was back inside.'

'It's not out of your system yet.'

'No.'

'Maybe you should see a medic.' He took cigarettes from the pocket of his dressing-gown and offered the opened packet. I took one and he flicked a lighter. The cigarette wobbled as he continued, 'Mild sleeping tablets, maybe.'

'It isn't that I can't sleep.'

'No.' He inhaled, then exhaled cigarette smoke. 'But you want *restful* sleep.'

'What the hell's *wrong* with the force these days?' I almost snarled the question.

The change of direction puzzled him, and he scowled non-understanding.

I moved the hand holding the cigarette in a vague, conciliatory gesture and in a quieter tone said, 'Forget it. Collins . . . Susan told me. It's — er — knocked me over a bit.'

'Brought on bad dreams?' He drew on the cigarette. 'I wouldn't blame you.'

'It didn't help matters,' I fenced.

There was a moment or two of cigarette-smoking silence then, in a more reasonable voice, I asked, 'Chris, what *is* wrong? Time was, killing a cop was long-term suicide. They were *always* caught.'

'Not any more,' he grunted.

'Why?'

'We're licked,' he sighed. 'We go through the motions, but we're licked.'

'For Christ's sake! The criminals these days aren't any . . .'

'Not the criminals.' He folded forward and rested his elbows on his knees. 'Not the criminals,' he repeated sadly. '*They* haven't beaten us. It's something else. Something more subtle. Something more dangerous.'

I waited. He seemed to be gathering his thoughts. Seeking some way of telling it. I glanced at my watch on the bedside table. Three o'clock, near enough. A nice time for confessions. A nice time for heart-opening. What was coming, whatever was coming, was going to be the truth as Chris Tallboy saw it.

'Damnation, it's not even the bad guys,' he said at last. The admission seemed hard to make, but having made it, it seemed to free the rest. 'Misguided, maybe. Holding like hell to the mucky end of the stick. Some people — some of the big-wigs of the various forces — say politics. Anarchy through the back door. That sort of thing. I don't go for that. No way. Sure, the agitators have climbed onto the band-wagon, but they're not pulling it. There aren't enough of 'em. All they're doing is cashing in on a good thing.' He paused long enough to draw on the cigarette then, still bent forward and still talking in a low voice, as if explaining his own tentative conclusions, he said, 'Lenny, we have a fine Criminal Law. Short of killing and stealing, it lets people do almost whatever they've a mind to do. Preach revolution on the box. Okay. They *can*. That's what "democracy" means in the UK. Play hell about the coloureds. Any damn thing! But too many people — too many *decent* people — are grabbing the wrong idea. Because they're allowed to say it, it *is* so. A cock-eyed argument, Lenny. A crazy, back-to-front logic. The freedom to say it means it must be the truth. The *freedom's* stopped being important. What that freedom *allows* is all that matters.

'The "Mrs Grundies" have taken over. Everybody's part of some damn "underprivileged minority group" these days. Equality under the law doesn't mean a thing. Christ, I remember the day — *you* remember the day — black, white, brown, yellow, pink or polka-dot — if they were bent, if they stepped too far out of line, they sucked the hammer. Colour didn't come into it. Class didn't come into it. If he was a suspect, who the hell he was, you quizzed him . . . hard. If you thought you'd the right guy, you booked him and no messing. But not any more, Lenny. Not any more.'

There was another pause. A long pause this time. Filled with bitterness and the humiliation of a proud man unable to come to terms with his pride. I stayed silent. The pale reflection of this state of affairs had filtered through into the jail, but imprisoned men don't waste too much time worrying about the niceties of the outside world. I was, in effect, being brought up to date on public opinion. One aspect of public opinion. And (the truth) it scared me a little.

'We can't do our job, Lenny,' he said at last. 'We can't do our job because busybodies won't *let* us do our job. Everything has to be explained and excused. Accounted for. Justified. The stupid bastards won't *trust* us. Lawyers — I swear it's no less than the truth — lawyers, solicitors, even barristers specialise in hampering the police. Not *defending*. Far more than that. It's a damn good job. It pays well. Hot-shot groups of high-sounding lunatics pay good money, and smart-arsed lawyers are eager to grab that money. For what? For what boils down to obstructing the police. That's what. That really is *what*. What the hell the case is. Riot, murder, arson. What the hell it is. Start asking questions. Just start *asking*. They're in there screaming "police harassment!" Petitions. Public meetings. Every damn stop in the organ pulled out, before we even *start*. And the hound responsible — whoever he is — sits there laughing. He knows. The crazy people are building a wall round him. He doesn't even have to worry. We can't get at him. The harder we try, the higher they build the wall. Lenny . . . *we can't do our job*.' He almost sobbed the words. 'Decent people have been conned rotten. The do-goodery crowd have got what they always wanted. There aren't any criminals left in the world. Only "sick people" and "mixed up kids". Nobody's just plain rotten . . . except us, of course. We're the only bastards left around.'

It was the end of his tirade. He straightened, took a deep, deep pull on the cigarette and allowed the smoke to trickle down his nostrils. The smile was twisted and without humour.

'That's the score, Lenny. Collins was mugged. He died . . . period.'

'Period, my arse,' I growled.

'Live with it, Lenny.' As he spoke he stood up from the bed. There was total defeat in his tone. 'Be grateful. You aren't one of *us* any more. It's we who have nightmares. Every night. Every day.'

Saturday, February 27th. A day to remember. The day I saw Gwen Raff for the first time in years. She'd grown old; too old, too fast. God, she'd *really* taken some stick.

The Raffs lived in the end house of a terrace on the outskirts of Lessford. A nice neighbourhood; a neighbourhood peopled by solid citizenry who went about their business and minded their own; not a "blue-rinse" neighbourhood, but a patch of Lessford the Conservatives didn't need to tout. That sort of place. No two-car families, but everybody *had* a car. One car and not too many kids. Neat little front gardens with privet hedges. A vegetable patch, maybe a tiny greenhouse in the back.

A nice house, and the Raffs had lived there since David Raff had left the force. That much I'd remembered. What I'd *not* remembered — what I only remembered when Gwen Raff opened the door to my ring — was that Raff had retired early because of a mental breakdown. The pressures had become too heavy. It happens; it happens often enough to merit the description of "occupational disease". With some men it's ulcers. With others it's a mental thing and, very often, the breakdown of a good marriage.

The Raff marriage had taken the strain, but the haggard eyes of Gwen Raff told their own story. The eyes, the pallor and the snow-white hair.

For a moment she didn't recognise me then, when recognition came, it was accompanied by a look not far removed from panic.

'Lenny!'

'Gwen.' I tried a smile; a movement of the lips meant to reassure her.

'What — what is it?'

'David in?'

'Er — yes.' The hesitation almost made me wish I hadn't come. 'Yes . . . of course.'

That, too. The "of course". As if it had been a particularly stupid question. As if to say, 'He's *always* in.'

'Could I see him?'

'Why? what about?'

The woman was suffering. She was terrified. She'd once been a friend. At a guess, she still wanted to be a friend, but she did nothing to indicate that I was welcome. Not that I was *un*welcome. Just that I'd created a situation in which she was uncertain.

In a gentle voice, I said, 'It's about Collins, Gwen. I've just heard about him. What happened to him.'

'He's dead,' she said in a flat voice.

'That's what I mean.' I was almost coaxing her. 'Dead. Murdered. And it's still undetected. I'd like a chat with David about it. I thought — y'know — he might like to help.'

'Help?'

'David.'

'David? *Help?*'

There was something not too far from hysterical disbelief in her tone. In the way she stared at me, as if I'd suggested something well beyond the grounds of possibility.

In an awkward voice I mumbled, 'Y'know . . . help. Advise, perhaps. He was close to Collins. They worked together. They were friends. I thought he might be able to . . .'

'Come in.' It was a sudden decision and she stood aside. 'Come inside and ask him.' She cleared her throat gently. 'Just don't expect too much.'

When I'd seen her, I'd been shocked. When I saw *him*, I could have wept. The front room, with the half-drawn curtains; a token invitation to death to come as a blessed relief. The armchair, with the blanket tucked around his legs and feet. The dull eyes, staring ahead at some invisible point well beyond the walls of the room.

She said; 'Mr Lennox has come to see you, darling.'

'David,' I greeted hoarsely.

42

He didn't heed. Didn't move his head. Didn't even try to re-focus his eyes.

I'd known this man in his prime. Alive. Vital. Full of fight and afraid of nobody. And now *this*! The word "zombie" flicked across my mind. The "undead". The wispy hair seemed to ruffle in a breeze that wasn't there. If he was breathing — and he must have been breathing — there was no hint of a rise and fall of his chest. White bristles covered his cheeks and chin like hoar-frost.

As if reading my thoughts, she murmured, 'I — I try to shave him, sometimes. It's difficult.'

'A . . .' I couldn't take my eyes from his face, and I found it difficult to speak. 'A doctor.'

'There are limits,' she breathed.

'Nevertheless, he should . . .'

'*He's not going inside.*' She hardly moved her lips. Her teeth were clenched. It was a creed — *her* creed — and no power on earth would make her abandon that creed. 'What he was, Lenny. What he still is. My husband. Who'd love him more than I love him?'

I shook my head slowly. In sorrow. In amazement. There are definitives. Adler, playing the harmonica. Turner, painting a landscape. Olivier, delivering a Shakespearian line. Definitives. You see or hear them once . . . and you know that that's *it*. Never better. Never as heart-stopping. Never even as good. This woman — this Gwen Raff — had touched a definitive; touched it, and would hold it whilever breath remained in her body. Wifely devotion. Something at which younger, lesser people sneer. But this lady had transformed it into her own personal religion.

It was hopeless. I knew it was hopeless. Whoever else, not Raff. I'd arrived with such plans, such schemes, such possibilities. But there was nothing. Nor could there ever *be* anything.

I breathed, 'David, old son . . . you're loved. Gwen. A lot of other people. If you can understand anything, understand *that*. You're not alone. What the hell else, you're not alone.'

I did something which, in any other circumstances, would have been melodramatic. Even hammy. I leaned down and touched the wispy hair on the top of his head with my lips. Then I turned and walked from the room.

In the hall Gwen touched my hand with her fingers. A gentle brush of "Thank you". It was unnecessary — of course — he'd been my friend, and was still my friend.

In a hoarse tone, I started, 'Isn't there anything . . .'

'Nothing.' She was already shaking her head. 'Dope. They can ram him full of dope. Kill his mind completely. They'd do that inside, thinking they were doing him a kindness. They'd be wrong. He knows. He *understands*. Somewhere, deep down, he understands. People *haven't* forsaken him.'

'You're a hell of a woman,' I sighed.

'I have friends.' She managed a smile. 'You, for example. Dick Sullivan. We're not alone.'

I caught my breath and said, 'Sullivan?'

'Dick comes by about once a month. Sometimes more. Dick and Mary Sullivan. Sometimes Dick sits with him, while Mary and I go to the cinema . . . something like that.' She paused, then in a tone which held a challenge, added, 'He knows Dick. Recognises him. Even though he doesn't show it, he recognises him. Now he'll know you. Remember *you*. He understands. I don't care what they say, he *understands*.'

'Of course he understands,' I soothed. 'Why shouldn't he? A blind man hasn't lost his sense of touch. His sense of smell.'

It meant nothing. Cost nothing. It was merely comfort to a fine woman who deserved every gram of comfort available.

I drove slowly back to Beechwood Brook. Slowly and carefully, because I wanted to think. To take stock of things. Of my life, for example, and what had *been* my life.

The force; the unique society which, unless *it* rejects you, you can never leave. And, even as an ex-jail bird, it hadn't rejected me. First, Chris. Now Gwen Raff, on behalf of David. To them I was still "one of". Okay, I'd given my one-time profession a major slice of my life, and now it was repaying me. I was a lucky man. I think the Prodigal Son must have felt a little like I felt. If not, he was a graceless bastard.

Take Raff. Poor, crazy Raff. Ex-cop, therefore a fellow-ex-cop took time off to sit with him; to share with him the silent, crazy world into which he'd been dropped. Comradeship, my friend. The comradeship of the force, and a comradeship which knew no limitations. It choked me a little to know that these people still counted me as one of their number. Despite the three years. Despite everything and anything I was still within the pale. Chris and Susan. Gwen and, through her, David. Had Collins still be alive . . .

And Sullivan.

I hadn't know Richard Sullivan too well. Not as well as I'd know Henry Collins or Charles Ripley or David Raff. I'd met him a few times, and we'd hit it off fine, but I hadn't really *known* him.

Nevertheless, I'd heard of him. Come to that, who hadn't? The big man in North End, when Lessford had been a city with its own force. Who *hadn't* heard of Sullivan? Who hadn't heard of North End? In the old days — back to the Golden Age — when North End Division had been a force within a force; a perpetual "war zone", with gangs battling it out for supremacy when they weren't joining forces to give the hard-pressed cops an even harder time. And, time and again, Sullivan and his "cowboys" had taken them on, man-for-man, blood-for-blood and hammered them into some sort of submission. Sullivan had *been* North End, and North End Division was next door to Hallsworth Hill Division, and Sullivan and Collins had been buddies.

Therefore, Sullivan.

Who else *but* Sullivan?

In retrospect, and with that immaculate wisdom which is a by-product of hindsight, I can see now that I was almost as crazy as poor old Raff. Put it down to shock. To trauma. To a natural over-reaction. Hide a man behind bars for three years, cut him off from even half-decent society, call him a criminal — one of the worst types of criminal — and treat him as such. Take away all hope of future, all hope of respect, all hope of *anything*.

Then, not even overnight, but *instantaneously*, slot him back into a niche not too far removed from the one he'd enjoyed before.

45

Without warning. Without giving him a hint of expectation. Respect and honour returned to him on a golden platter.

What the hell else but daydreams? What the hell else but the conviction that the word "impossible" merely fills a slot in a dictionary?

Then drop it to him — almost off-handedly — that a fine man he's always held as being something very special has been mugged and killed by scum . . . and that the scum still walk the streets.

What the hell else?

It explains my state of mind as I drove back to Beechwood Brook.

A sombre euphoria. An illogical, mental gratification in which I was some sort of resurrected embodiment of the old days — *our* old days — complete with shining armour, white charger and even a loyal squire, in the person of Richard Sullivan. I tell you at that moment, on that drive back to Beechwood Brook, Don Quixote would have been proud to ride alongside me.

What stupidity! What *Boy's Own* mush! But understandable. Very understandable.

Take an enclosed community. Any enclosed community. A religious order, a public school, a prison. Anything. Force a normal mind into the matrix of that order and watch the warp. For good or bad, it will come. A different slant. An out-of-true perspective. An imbalance of priorities. And with the warp will come an immaturity; a return to innocence, perhaps. If so, a return to an innocence for good, or for evil, or for stupidity, or for a mix of all three. See it in clerics, see it in professional soldiers, see it — see its darkest side — in truly evil men. No greys. No in-betweens. Nothing else but absolutes.

It was happening to me. Indeed, it had *happened* to me although, at the time, I was unaware of it. Which in turn meant that Chris and Susan couldn't be told. They were well beyond the boundaries of my world of immaculate vengeance. They represented "officialdom", whereas I was Superman, the Lone Ranger and Robin Hood all rolled into one.

That in retrospect and with the wisdom of hindsight. But as I drove back to Beechwood Brook . . .

I moved into my new home on Monday, March 1st. I'd spent the Sunday moving what private bits and pieces I owned into the flat, and on Sunday evening I'd insisted upon repaying some of their kindnes by taking Chris and Susan out to dinner at a good restaurant. By mid-morning on the Monday the inventory had been checked and signed for, I'd taken over the key to the inner door and the chief clerk and I had time to sit back, sip newly-brewed tea and smoke; he a pipe, I a cheroot.

He turned his head, surveyed my tiny room, and observed, 'Not a bad little place.'

'I'm lucky,' I agreed.

'So I'm told.'

It was said without malice. It was even accompanied by a faint smile.

His name was Curtiss and, at a guess, he was in his early forties. He had the smooth politeness of a good bank-man, but without smarm. A few more pegs and he, too, would be manager of an important branch . . . and I didn't doubt that he'd get there.

'A week ago, I was in prison,' I said gently.

It seemed stupid not to make the admission. Soon, if not already rumour would be spreading among the bank employees.

'I know.' He drew on his pipe. 'Stowe told me. In strict confidence, of course.'

'Ex-cop,' I added. 'Ex-detective superintendent.'

'You had Badger's job.'

I nodded.

'Know him?'

'Not personally.' This time, I paused to draw on the cheroot. 'I've heard of him, in the last few days. I'm told he helped with this job.'

'He's a string-puller.' It was a statement of fact, but without apparent criticism.

'I'm told that, too,' I murmured.

'No half-way with Badger.' He moved the mouthpiece of the pipe a few inches from his lipe and grinned. 'You approve or you disapprove.'

47

'And you?'

'I rather like him. He gets things done.' He journeyed the pipe to his mouth for a moment, to keep the tobacco smouldering. 'There's a clique. This town, every town. The so-called "professional" men. Solicitors, accountants, bank managers, house agents, building society managers, that sort of thing. Various all-male get-togethers. The Rotary Club. The Round Table. A general you-scratch-my-back-I'll-scratch-yours set-up. Back-door pull. They virtually run the town. Badger's in there with 'em.'

'But not you?' I ventured.

'Sure.' He smiled. 'I'm in there too. I'm ambitious. But I'm also *aware*.'

'About Badger?'

'There's a reason.' He chuckled quietly. 'There's always a reason. Badger's reason.'

Beyond that, he refused to be drawn. Nothing specific. No details. He indulged himself in some very nifty verbal footwork, but with a smile hovering near his lips. He left me with the distinct impression that Badger was the undoubted power behind any throne Bordfield might possess. That for good or evil, Bordfield was *his* midden.

A good omen. Like the old days. Specifically, like *Sullivan's* days of North End power.

When Curtiss had left I passed another minor milestone in my life. I cooked my first meal. Nothing too ambitious — egg, sausage and chips, to be precise — but it was edible. Even enjoyable. And after clearing away and washing the crockery, I telephoned Bordfield Regional Headquarters and asked to make an appointment to see Detective Chief Superintendent Badger. Courtesy demanded that I thank him for what he'd done for me, but there was more to it than that. I wanted to see this man. Size him up for myself. He was occupying my old chair, in my old office. I was curious. Taking Tallboy's assessment, and placing it alongside Curtiss's assessment, what remained was something of an enigma . . . and enigmas hadn't been too thick on the ground in my day.

At 6 p.m., on the button, the young cadet tapped on the door, then led me into the last room I'd worked in prior to jail. It hadn't altered, I swear! Common gumption insisted that it must have been re-decorated, but if so no imagination had been wasted. The colour scheme was still the same; cream cheese and plain chocolate. The same chairs in the same places. The same shelves, holding the same leather-bound law books. The same old desk; even the same old scar at one corner where (before *my* time) some damn fool had thumped it with something very hard and very heavy. Even the carpet — yes, even the worn parts.

It was like stepping into the past. A sudden and unexpected time-warp and, for the moment, it staggered me a little.

Then I saw the man and I knew that *something* had changed.

His age — strictly speaking, his lack of it — widened my eyes slightly. He was some few years from the half-century mark — hardly past forty, at a guess — and the slightly brash panache of youth rose easily on a frame which, even at first glance, was in prime condition. Then the eyes. Few men have blue eyes; not that pale, almost translucent blue which, supposedly, is only found in murderers. Badger had them, and they fairly shone from a face whose only wrinkles were at the outer corners of his eyes. A strong face; fine-boned, but not thin; bronzed with health and with a mouth wide but slightly thin-lipped. A very imposing character. For his age, and for the rank he carried, a *very* imposing character. The impression was that few people argued with him and that those who did rapidly wished they hadn't.

He stood up, walked round the desk and held out his hand.

'Mr Lennox.'

'Chief Superintendent Badger.'

We shook hands as the cadet left the office and closed the door. Badger waved me to a chair; the chair once reserved — *still* reserved — for special guests. He returned to his own chair behind the desk, gave a smile which was as near a laugh as not to matter, then spoke.

'The legend. I've been waiting to meet you.'

Nice going, from a top cop to an ex-con, but it pleased me. He seemed to mean it. His voice had a slight, mid-Atlantic drawl, as if at some time he'd mixed with either Americans or Canadians and some of the speech mannerisms had rubbed off.

'I owe you a debt,' I said solemnly.

'No way.'

'I could have been cap-in-hand outside the Prisoners' Aid office.'

'You? Cap-in-hand?' This time he gave the laughter right of exit, and it came from the back of his throat. Deep. Almost bawdy in its fullness and freedom. 'Mr Lennox, I've . . .'

'Lenny,' I murmured. 'I answer to "Lenny".'

'Great. Lenny, I've been checking your record, when your ass was where mine is. Some of those cases! You could knit fog.'

'The old days,' I sighed.

'Yeah, the old days,' he echoed.

There was a silence as we both paid momentary tribute to "the old days".

'Like the place?'

As he asked the question he tossed a packet of cigarettes across the surface of the desk. It seemed in character that the cigarettes were Pall Mall. Equally, that the matches which followed the cigarettes were book matches.

As I took a cigarette, I said, 'The flat?'

'I told Stowe it might be a little small.'

'It's fine.' I lighted the cigarette. 'I'm a tidy man. Prison does that for you.'

The blue eyes seemed to drill holes in me as he said, 'Don't wear it, Lenny. It's no hair shirt. What you did? Who knows? Maybe me? Maybe anybody? I've talked with Chris Tallboy. He was *there*. It takes a big man to do what you did . . . then take the rap.'

He helped himself to a cigarette. He did it the "un-English" way. He didn't fumble around at the open end; he flicked the bottom of the soft pack with his finger, then chose one of the cigarettes that popped up. He tore a match from the book, and joined me in cigarette smoking.

In a softer tone he said, 'The Specials?'

I stared at him.

'I could get you in. No sweat. You'd be holding rank within months.'

'Bloody blacklegs,' I growled.

'Yeah.' The smile came and went. 'Just a suggestion. It had to be made.'

'No professional copper likes part-time bobbies. If you don't know that . . .'

'I know it. I know it,' he said, soothingly. 'Just a try-on. No more. I had to be sure.'

'Why?' I drew on the cigarette. 'Sure about what?'

He left his chair and walked to a corner cabinet. I knew from the old days what that cabinet was used for. Booze. With his back to me, he opened the door of the cabinet and I heard the chink of glasses and bottles. He didn't ask. Didn't give me a choice. Maize whisky; bourbon. I spotted the label, and again it was completely in character. He spoke as if he was talking to somebody inside the booze cabinet.

'I need somebody on the outside, Lenny. Somebody I can trust. *Really* trust. No pay. No cherries. Just some guy who can get where I can't get. Do things even *I* can't do.' He turned and handed me a glass. 'What say, old-timer?'

'An informant,' I said, and even to me the word sounded sour.

'Oh, no.' He shook his head, then closed the door of the cabinet, leaving his own glass inside. 'I have enough snitches to fill a snake pit. I can tell you which dog pissed up against which lamp-post. That I can do. But I need more.'

'From me?'

Slowly, pointedly, he said, 'From an ex-con who *isn't* an ex-con.' Then, before I could answer, he sat down at the desk, reached for the telephone and continued, 'Sit tight, Lenny. Put the booze out of sight. Then listen and watch. We'll talk about it later.' He lifted the receiver to his mouth and said, 'Okay. Jennings and Swan. Bring 'em in.'

Jennings and Swan. Detective Constable Jennings and Detective Constable Swan. As they walked into the office I recognised them for what they were. Immediately. The slight swagger. The hint of newly-acquired arrogance. The clothes which, while not a uniform, nevertheless were a uniform; culled from cheap fiction and cheap films, the right and proper gear worn by all "jacks".

'Detective Jennings. Detective Swan.' Badger stared at them across the desk. 'Okay. Who gives the explanations?'

Jennings said, 'Sir, I don't know what . . .'

'First, I'll see your scars,' snapped Badger.

'Sir?' Jennings looked puzzled.

'Your war wounds. Those honourable stripes that aren't yet healed.'

'Sir, I don't know what . .'

'Last night you were out drinking. You listening to this, Swan?'

'Yes, sir.'

'Listen good. It's important. Last night you were out drinking.'

'Alone, sir,' cut in Jennings. 'We were off duty. We pal around together and . . .'

'The hell you were alone! You each had a slag dancing attendance. You picked 'em up at the town centre. You used your car, Jennings. Before you dropped 'em off — before you each went home to your waiting wife — you screwed the ass off 'em. You in the back, Jennings. You in the front, Swan. The exact location? In the Post Office car park behind Central Station. A spot already fixed. A spot already well-used. It should be locked. It *isn't* locked. You have a working arrangement with the fink whose job it is to *keep* it locked.' Badger paused, then before either of the men could say anything, continued, 'Understand me — both of you — I don't give a damn about your morals. You can saw yourselves in two the hard way for all I care. Just that I know these things and have statements to back 'em up. Is that clear?'

Jennings breathed, 'Yes, sir.'

'Swan?'

'Y-yes, sir.'

'Okay. Now let's get back to the boozer, where you were showing these ladies of the street your muscles. There was a fight. Tell me about the fight, Jennings.'

52

'It was — it was a fight, sir. That's all.'

'Not by a country mile that's not "all", Jennings. There's the little matter of Police Constable Grimble. Remember Grimble?'

'Yes, sir.' Jennings almost groaned the admission.

'Out for a quiet drink. Off duty, like you two. Unlike you two, alone. Tell me what happened to Grimble, Jennings.'

'He was — he was . . . jumped. Sir.'

'Jumped?'

'Yes, sir. He was . . .'

'He was minding his own damn business.' Badger's voice was ugly with contempt. 'He was out for a quiet jar, then he was "jumped". Right?'

'Yes, sir.'

'Who did the jumping?'

'Kendal, sir.'

'Kendal?'

'Kendal . . . and five of his soldiers.'

'His *what*?'

'His gang, sir. Five of his . . .'

'Don't call the bastards "soldiers", Jennings. They're not *soldiers*. They're scum, Turds. Crow-shit. You get the message, Jennings? Do I make myself clear?'

'Y-yes, sir.'

'Swan?'

'Yes, sir.'

'So,' Badger ground on, 'Constable Grimble gets jumped by six bastards who should have been drowned at birth. And two of *my* men — two creeps who glory in the name of "detectives" — sit back and watch it happen. Six turds drag Grimble outside and give him a very neat going over. And where is Grimble, right now? For your sweet information — in the unlikely event that either of you is remotely interested — he's in a hospital bed hurting like hell. A broken jaw, a broken arm, busted ribs and close on fifty stitches. Six-to-one. Those were the odds. You miserable goons. They were the odds he faced. You could have cut those odds down to two-to-one. And why didn't you? I'll *tell* you why you didn't. You were too damn interested in the jumping *you* had planned. What the hell happened — who the hell got hurt — you were gonna shove it between the legs of two poxed-up cows you'd already propositioned.'

Badger jerked open a draw of the desk. He pulled out a folder ands slapped it on the surface of the desk. He tapped the closed folder with a forefinger as he continued his tirade. He used a cooler tone. A tone which refused to admit even the possibility of bluff.

'In case you think I'm guessing. It's all here. Statements and signatures. Times, places and names. I could take Kendal and his rats to court, but these people wouldn't give evidence, and *you'd* fold. So, instead . . .

'Starting tonight. Starting at ten o'clock tonight. Into uniform. Both of you. You, Jennings. You, Swan. You pound pavements. Night patrol duty. Foot patrol. And night duty till I say "when". It's arranged. It's fixed. The beats, too. Hand-picked. The dirtiest, toughest beats in the whole city. Real "punishment beats". They're all yours. And you're gonna work 'em. Till *I* say. Any squealing — any resignations — and a photo-copy of this file is sent, registered post, to both your wives. You want that? Start jibbing. Start even complaining. That's what's waiting for you. And don't think these people won't give evidence against *you*. You're not Kendal. They'd enjoy it.' The smile was tiger-cruel. It sat easily on the thin lips. 'Book a bed. Both of you. Warn the emergency ward to be on stand-by. You'll need it. What Grimble has is a "slight inconvenience" to what's waiting for you two. Now . . . *out*! And start sweating.'

'Impressive.'

Jennings and Swan had left. Badger had brought his drink from the booze cabinet then, having settled back in his chair, had lighted another cigarette.

I therefore murmured, 'Impressive,' because that seemed the word he was waiting for.

'You did things in your time,' he reminded me.

'True.'

'More subtle, maybe?' He seemed to be spoiling for an

54

argument.

I said, 'You don't need *my* approval.'

'I get vibes,' he growled. 'Those two yoyos. You're sorry for them, maybe?'

'It's possible.'

'Me? I'm sorry for Grimble. It makes more sense.'

'Me, too.'

'Look, Lenny . . .' He seemed to make a conscious effort to cool down. 'Those two clown-dogs. Forget 'em. They had it coming. Creeps like that the C.I.D. can do without. They're back on the beat. Okay they're back on the beat. Nice guys work beats. Even the beats those two are going to. The truth? In this chair — when you were in the driving seat — would you have done less?'

'That much,' I agreed. 'But not the other thing.'

'Oh, *that*?' He sipped the drink, then his face relaxed into a grin. 'Snitches, Lenny. We were talking about snitches. Remember?'

I nodded.

'I have a barrelful. That's how I know the exact where, the exact when and the exact what. But, tell me Lenny, you ever know a snitch put his name on a piece of paper?'

'No.'

He lifted the file and tossed it onto my lap. I opened it. It held perhaps a dozen sheets of quarto-size pages. All blank.

'Bluff, Lenny.' He drew on the cigarette. 'To keep their bowels loose. That's all. They feel like screwing around? That's *their* business. But they did dirt on Grimble and, for that, they sweat.'

I handed him back the file. He replaced it in the desk drawer, then eyed me quizzically.

'Questions?' he asked.

As I hesitated, he pushed the packet of cigarettes a few inches nearer. I leaned forward, helped myself, then lighted one with a match from the book.

I waved out the match, then said, 'Kendal? He's new to me. He wasn't around three years ago.'

'Walter "King" Kendal,' he mused. 'One of the new breed. A pain in the ass, but a power to be reckoned with. I'm told he can pull in close to a hundred soldiers if need be.'

'Soldiers?'

'It's a word.' He moved his shoulders. 'The mobsters of the 'thirties used it. Hoods, hooligans, tearaways, soldiers . . . what the hell? Kendal flashes the word around. Who cares? We all know what it means.'

'A hundred?' And, if I sounded dubious, who could blame me? 'That's a small army.'

'I have good snitches, Lenny. They don't feed me crap.'

I allowed the remark to go unchallenged and waited.

'Y'see, friend . . .' He leaned forward and rested his elbows on the desk surface. 'Kendal is a little like a weed, and the creeps up top won't give us the right to use the only weed-killer capable of clearing the ground. Sure, I could take him to court. Him. Every snot-nosed bastard he orders around. But what then? Up come the funny-farmers. Up come the creeps who figure a cop should be a glorified scout master. "Deprived childhood". "The Economic Climate". "Environmental Disadvantages". They write books on the goddam excuses these days. They give out university degrees to young finks who wouldn't know how to take a kid's pants down and tan his ass . . . or want to know. And the magistrates listen. And the judges listen. And the whole stinking world comes up with a thousand-and-one different answers. And *we* ain't included in those answers.

'So, like weeds — Kendal and his kind — they grow, they take over, they establish themselves. And good people can't walk out nights, because the cops don't rule the streets these days.' He paused, sighed, then enjoyed two deep draws on his cigarette before he continued. 'A crazy state of affairs, Lenny. A very screwed-up state of affairs. I need help — unofficial help, as much help as I can muster — to straighten things out a little.'

'From me?' I asked carefully.

'I was hoping.'

'*My* neck on the chopping-block?'

'It fits. It's been there before, and *I* hold the axe.'

I was being propositioned. In the privacy of a detective chief superintendent's office we were waltzing around "unlawful means", and we both knew it. It has been done in the past, it will be done in the future, but it always was and always will be a very dangerous pastime. Absolute and unqualified trust is a first necessity. The knowledge that the man guarding your back will still be there when the blood and snot start flying — put very crudely. And, although Badger had already impressed me, I still didn't *know* him.

'Nothing for nothing,' I murmured.

He raised an eyebrow.

'The flat,' I amplified. 'The job.'

'You have 'em. You keep 'em. No strings.'

'No strings.' I smiled a little sourly. 'Other than my own conscience.'

'Lenny,' he said bluntly, 'I don't give a monkey's toss about your conscience. Maybe you have one, maybe not. Who cares? What you hold, you keep . . just that I could use you.'

I pondered it for a moment, then said, 'This Kendal character. How far does his influence reach?'

'Way out.' The hand holding the cigarette moved in a vague gesture. 'Like I say, he's been allowed to grow, to spread. Bordfield. Lessford. Some few . . .'

'Lessford?'

'Yeah, Lessford.' He nodded. 'Twin towns — twin cities — the scum move between the two. They don't need passports. They don't need visas.'

'He knows what goes on?' I pressed.

'Crime-wise?'

It was a damn-fool word. Part of the mid-Atlantic phraseology he favoured. But I knew what he meant and I nodded.

'You name it, he could put a name to it,' he said bitterly. 'The old gang routine from the Big City. Break the law, but only with his say-so . . . and with his percentage.'

'Everything?'

'I'd say everything.' He nodded slowly. 'He has this area by the balls, Lenny, and he ain't afraid to squeeze.'

'Henry Collins,' I said gently.

He looked a question.

'Ex-Chief Superintendent Collins,' I amplified. 'He was divisional officer of Hallsworth Hill when Lessford had its own force.

'Oh — er — yeah.' His slow nod of recollection was accompanied by a frown. 'Yeah. Some months back. He was mugged, right?'

'Murdered,' I corrected him.

'I don't recall he was . . .' He stopped, snapped his fingers once, gently, then said, 'Sure. You're right. He died in hospital.'

'Making it murder.'

'Making it murder,' he agreed.

'Could Kendal name his killer?'

'That I wouldn't know.'

'Not *would* he. *Could* he? I'll take an educated guess.'

'Well . . .' He rubbed the side of his jaw. 'Yeah. I'd say he could. He has his listening posts and — although I hate to admit it — they're good. Yeah, *he'll* know. But don't get ideas, Lenny. He won't say.'

'We're not talking about interview rooms,' I said coldly. 'We're talking about Kendal and what Kendal knows. I've just ended a three-year education course in the infliction of pain. I now know all the finer points of making a man scream. I'm no longer a copper, therefore I don't have to consult any rule-book. I don't *have* rules.' I paused, stared hard at this man who a few moments before had been keen enough to propostion me. I ended, 'Henry Collins was a fine man, Badger. A fine policeman and a very good friend. Rest assured, this Kendal bastard will talk . . . eventually. He'll be eager to talk. He'll be eager to tell. That's *my* side of the bargain.'

'You have a deal, friend.' He stood up from the chair and held out his hand. 'We both have a deal. Shift the garbage from the streets and Kendal's yours till hell freezes. Till you force the name you want from him.

We shook hands on it. He had a good, firm, dry grip. The grip of a man I was prepared to trust.

That evening, having carefully re-checked every door and every drawer in the bank, became one of the evenings of my life. Solitude, without loneliness. A place of my own. A home, where I could come and go as I pleased. Warmth. Comfort. To loosen my tie, to shrug off my jacket, to kick off my shoes . . . and know that I *could* without spoiling my manners, without some loudmouth pipsqueak bawling me out.

I fixed myself salami sandwiches and hot, sweet tea. I pulled an easy chair to the window, turned off the light then pulled back the curtains. I sat munching and sipping; watching and remembering.

The double-deckers trundling along the main street; the centre of the city which once more was *my* city. At regular intervals; like great illuminated pendulums keeping the city ticking over. Diesel-engined monsters on rubber tyres.

So different from the tram-cars . . .

Those old trams. Rattling and swaying from Station Square and up Halifax Road. Noisy, jangling creations. All the way to Elland, past Birchencliffe. Comfortless things, with their slatted seats, and despite their noise travelling at little more than a slow run. "Move along inside there. Only five standing. Sorry, son. Full up." Not that it mattered. Start jogging and you were half-way to the next stop before the old tram caught up with you. Then a quick sprint and you were clear of the town centre at the next stop and, as a passenger alighted, you climbed aboard. Early teens, mid-teens . . . you could do it without even being breathless.

Almost opposite the bank one of the two remaining cinemas. The Odeon: Odeon One, Odeon Two, Odeon Three. The new-style, three-in-one picture house. Just a trickle of people turning into the lighted entrance. Soft porn, a promise of gory violence and an old Disney classic. Who the hell was making *good* films these days?

Not like The Ritz: standing for more than an hour in the rain — there was always a queue, with the uniformed doorman separating the queues into customers waiting for various-priced seats — then sitting, soaked but enthralled while Ringo, in the person of John Wayne, sniped at the racing Apaches from the roof of the swaying stagecoach. *The Petrified Forest* and Bogart taking his first firm step towards immortality as Duke Mantee. Charlie Chan and Warner Oland admonishing "Number One Son" in a bland, sing-song voice. Cops-and-robbers, Hollywood style, with every gangster hiding a heart of gold and G-men cutting the opposition to shreds with Tommy-guns, but not a drop of blood in sight. The great "dream factory". Today? Close-up fornication and an everlasting gush of Kensington Gore.

And yet some things remained the same.

The window was higher than the orange/yellow street lighting. A thin, misty rain floated down and turned the road and pavements into dull mirrors. It was like watching a world through a transparent curtain of fine gold and, beyond, a mirror-image of that world. And kids were still in love. Despite the dress; the jeans and the shapeless jerseys, the untrimmed beards on faces too young to carry beards, the couldn't-care-less, floor-mop hair-styles. Dammit, they were still in love and showed it. They held hands as they walked. They laughed and chattered. Their step had that spring unique to an age of basic innocence. God, the world was *theirs* . . . if it could be kept from the hands of rogues and scoundrels.

I finished the tea, I finished the sandwiches, I smoked a cheroot, but I continued to sit at the window. Past mingled with present, dovetailed in, sometimes fitted and sometimes didn't. A great mix of nostalgia and envy. What had been and what *might* be were I still of an age at which good things could be encouraged and *made* happen. Too much evil around. Too much evil, and too much innocence. And the innocence would go under, and the few good people left would weep . . . but it would be too late. Far too late.

It was almost eleven o'clock when I pushed myself from the chair, closed the curtains, snapped on the light, tidied up, bathed and went to bed. But the mood — an echo of the mood — continued in the darkness of the bedroom.

A new bed; a new bedroom; *my* bedroom. For the first time in years I wasn't a "guest". The night noises were different. Not the grunts and creaks — the snores and farts — of prison small-hours.

60

Not the punctuated silence of night in the country I'd listened to at Chris's place. Instead, the city's pulse; a slower, gentler pulse than that of daylight, but the pulse of a giant which dozed but never slept. The lifeless 'toot" of a diesel train pulling into or out of the main-line station. The town hall clock chiming the quarters and striking the hours. The traffic quietened, but never stopped. In the distance, closing then leaving, the sound of a siren; police or ambulance; audible proof that life — perhaps death — was also part of this cat-napping monster. And, not too far away, the steady slap of rope against some flag-pole. And voices. Shouts. Dogs barking. Cats courting. So much noise, but such muffled noise; not brash and *fortissimo*, as in daytime, but muted and *piano* as if night and day were parts of the same great symphony with contrasting movements.

Just before sleep a thought touched my mind. That I was alone. Probably more alone than I'd ever been before in my life. In the centre of Bordfield; surrounded by stores, offices, banks, a cinema, the whole paraphernalia of a major city . . . but in the *centre* of that city. Not where people actually live and sleep. Somewhere, at the back of my hazy mind, I remembered reading an article. A Sunday supplement, perhaps. Something, somewhere. That in Piccadilly — Piccadilly Circus, the nub of one of the greatest cities on earth — looking down on the circus itself . . . one flat. The single living quarters to boast "Piccadilly Circus" as its address. One of those silly, off-beat facts you read and can't forget. I'd been fascinated. What was it like, alone and living on top of a great milling ocean of life?

Well, now I knew.

Sullivan was in his greenhouse, poking and touching tiny lettuce plants in a propagation tray.

'Cos,' he murmured. 'Crisper than cabbage. And tastier.'

'You like living here at Upper Drayson?'

'Mary likes it. It's nice in summer. Rough in mid-winter, but very nice in summer.'

He replaced the top of the propagation tray, half-turned his head and squinted at the clouds through the glass.

'It's positioned a bit out,' he observed. 'This greenhouse. In the right place it could have caught at least another two hours of sun. I should have consulted Steve.' He touched the damp surface of potting compost in a seed-tray. 'Steve designed the bungalow.'

'I know.'

'The whole lay-out. Just as Mary wanted it.'

'Uhu. I know.'

'He's down south now. Bath. A good firm of architects. He gets on well with them.

'I'm glad.'

He dusted his hands together, then reached up and slightly re-arranged flower pots on one of the shelves. He did it slowly. Deliberately. With great care.

'Fresh vegetables, Lenny. Nothing like 'em. With the deep-freeze, all the year round. You're staying to lunch?'

'Mary suggested I might . . .'

'Of course you are. Steak and kidney pie. Fresh vegetables. Real *taste*.' There was a slight pause, then in exactly the same tone, 'It's good to see you out, Lenny.'

'Thanks.'

'I mean it. Any time . . . call in any time.'

'Thanks.'

He continued moving the pots then, again in the same tone, but much softer, 'Christ, I'm bored.'

'You have a hobby.'

'This?' Again he dusted is hands. He leaned across the strip of brick-bordered soil at his feet and re-stacked a bundle of canes in a corner of the greenhouse. He seemed unable to keep still. Unable to just stand and hold a real conversation. 'They write about this, Lenny. Lots of books. Even poems. "Nearer to God in a garden . . ." That sort of crap.'

'You don't like gardening?'

'It gets me from under Mary's feet. It helps keep me fit.'

'But that's all?'

From the canes, he moved to empty flower pots. Re-stacking them. Dusting their already clean sides with the palm of a hand.

'I play bowls in summer.'

62

'Bowls?' I said politely.

'An old man's game.'

'I wouldn't call it an . . .'

'No. Nor would I. You walk miles. Bloody *miles*! Back and forth across the same blasted green. Bloody *miles* . . . going nowhere.' In a voice tinged with sadness. 'For Christ's sake, don't retire, Lenny. Drop dead on the job, just don't retire.'

It was a Richard Sullivan I hadn't met before. He'd said "bored" and that, perhaps, was part of it. But not all of it. I think the unspoken — not-to-be-spoken — fear of growing old was in there somewhere. The warrior deprived of all causes. And, of course, the husband; a husband whose wife had stood aside and allowed her mate complete freedom to carve a name for himself; who'd watched him battle with the hooligans of North End and neither complained nor dulled his enthusiasm by revealing her own anxiety. That, at a guess, was also a major factor. He'd owed her eventual peace. He still owed her peace, but peace and a man like Sullivan were not easy companions.

Therefore, he fiddled with things. He kept his fingers, his hands and his eyes occupied. As if guilty of treachery to the woman he loved. As if struggling to suppress something of which he was ashamed. His voice, too. Muted. A little bitter. Carrying more than a touch of self-pity, and with it even more guilt.

'Gwen Raff telephoned.'

'I called.'

'Poor old Raff.'

'I hadn't realised. It came as a shock.'

'What a sodding job!' He tossed a piece of broken crock into a plastic pail. 'Raff out of his mind. You doing a stretch inside. What the hell *for*, Lenny?'

'Reasons,' I murmured. 'Difficult reasons to explain.'

'Reasons!' He almost spat the word. He thrust his hands into the pockets of his trousers and, almost defiantly, growled, 'Lenny, they should shoot us when we've finished. Put us out of our bloody misery. *This* is no life. I don't grumble. Not to Mary. I've no right to grumble — good pension, nice home, fine wife — everything! But bugger-all really. Farting about with lettuce seeds. Watching the path — all the time, watching the path — bloody nigh praying I'll see one of the old gang strolling down ready to talk about old times.'

'The old gang?' I said gently.

'Bear — Winnie Bear — remember him? He drops by about once a week. And Sykes. Remember Sergeant Sykes? I sometimes play bowls with Sykes.' He grinned ruefully. 'I've seen him take one of the woods and throw it as far as he could across the green. Sheer bloodly frustration.' The grin grew into a quiet chuckle. 'They damn near drummed him out of the Brownies. "Ungentlemanly Behaviour". Christ Almighty! You should have heard his language when the club president tried to choke him off.'

'How many?' I asked, and there was the hint of breathlessness in my tone.

'What?'

'The old gang? How many still in touch?'

'Oh . . .' He squinted at the glass of the greenhouse. 'About half a dozen. Maybe more. Bear and Sykes. Greenapple, remember Greenapple?'

I nodded.

'Harris.'

'Harris?'

'Aye, even Harris. He has difficulty in walking far. His joints have stiffened. Needs sticks. Two sticks. But — just occasionally — he drives out here. He can still drive if he's careful. And we talk. Natter. Y'know . . . remember things.'

Hope and disappointment. Names; some I knew, some I didn't know, some I'd heard of via reputation. Some were still fit; moderately fit, like Sullivan and myself. Some were crippled, either in mind or body. The expression "Old Crocks" flashed through my mind. And they were, too. Men at the wrong end of middle-age . . . but *men*. And they'd all been coppers, and damn good coppers at that. Get them into a team, give them one last fling — one final victory to remember . . .

The trouble was, I didn't know how the hell to approach it.

Despite his outburst of self-disgust, I wasn't sure. Dick and Mary Sullivan lived a happy, peaceful life; something they deserved; something they'd worked for. Me? I had nobody. I had nothing to lose. I could afford the gamble and, if the gamble didn't come off, so what? At worst a name in an obituary column and "no flowers by request". Not much of a price to pay for the love of a good woman and the friendship of fine men. But other people? I hadn't the right to involve, or even suggest.

It was a nice meal. A very nice meal. Steak and kidney pie and quick-frozen, garden-fresh vegetables. 'Dick grew them. He's getting better each year.' That touch of wifely pride cut like the blade of a knife. We had wine, too. Good wine. 'Another of Dick's hobbies. It takes patience . . . and time.'

'The one thing I've more than enough of,' grunted Sullivan.

We sat over cheese, biscuits and coffee. Sullivan smoked a pipe, Mary Sullivan smoked a cigarette and, after asking permission, I lighted up a cheroot.

'Not as bad as they used to be.' smiled Mary. She nodded at the cheroot.

'No.' I returned the smile. 'I've — er — I've acquired some degree of taste.' Then I screwed things up by adding, 'It's a thing you learn in prison.'

'Knock it off, Lenny,' growled Sullivan.

'Sorry.' And I genuinely *was*.

As if to fill an awkward space, Mary said, 'Gwen Raff telephoned. She said you'd called.'

'Uhu.' I nodded.

'That you were very upset about Henry Collins.'

I made a noise denoting agreement. I daren't trust myself to speak. Not at that moment. The angels were on my shoulder; Mary Sullivan, of all people, was guiding the conversation along lines I hadn't had the courage to approach.

'Who the hell *wasn't* upset?' Harsh disgust was there in Sullivan's tone. 'Who the hell still *isn't*?'

'Undetected,' I allowed myself to say gently.

'And *there's* a bloody fine thing.'

'It should have been cleared.' I eased the boat a little farther

65

from the shallows.

'It *would* have been detected.'

'You two!' Mary Sullivan suddenly seemed to become aware of certain possibilities. 'How do you *know*? *Everything* wasn't detected. You weren't . . .'

'We bloody well *were*.' Sullivan's jaw jutted a little. His eyes glinted. 'A fellow-copper. A man like Collins. Don't anybody ever tell me it wouldn't have been detected.'

'I'm told, I said softly, 'that Kendal could name the killer. That the chances are he could.'

'Kendal,' said Sullivan slowly.

'Know him?'

'One more king of the castle. That's what he calls himself. "King". "King" Kendal. They come and go. They never last.'

'You toppled a few,' I ventured.

'Lenny!' Something not far from panic was in Mary's voice.

'Mary, my love.' I forced myself to say it. I didn't want to hurt her, but more than that — far more than that — I wanted the other thing. 'Henry Collins was one of us. Like Dick is. Like David Raff is. Something's happened. Something very wrong has happened. Somebody has to right it . . . *somebody*.'

'There's — there's still a police force.'

'Would you call 'em that?' The contempt in Sullivan's question was without bounds.

I looked at her, saw her lower her head and close her eyes, as if in defeat. Slowly — oh, so slowly and oh, so sadly — the tears crept from behind the closed lids. What I felt? The truth is, I felt nothing. I'd come to Sullivan hoping for help and, without much prompting, he'd offered it. I hadn't pushed. I hadn't pleaded. I hadn't had to do either. Collins had been that sort of man. Had inspired that sort of loyalty.

In honesty, I don't think Mary understood. As she saw things, she'd failed as a wife . . . that at a guess is what she thought. The simple, uncomplicated logic of a good woman who's given her whole life, and all her love, to one man. All that, but not enough to hold him. But men can love men, too. Not carnally, but honourably. A totally different love, but a love women rarely understand. Collins would have done the same. Raff, too, had *he* been able to understand. With luck a handful of us . . . and we'd *all* understand.

But Mary Sullivan?

Never.

'She'll get over it.' Sullivan's voice was tight and brittle. 'Give her time. She'll accept it.'

There wasn't much I could contribute along those lines, therefore I said, 'Badger reckons he controls about a hundred men.'

We were out in the garden again. Strolling side-by-side, up and down the path between the beds of turned earth. A soft, springy path of pine needles. Even *I* knew that old gardener's trick. One of the best ways of all; two inches — three inches — of pine needles, and forget the weeds; no weeds and easy on the feet. Sullivan must have spent a lot of hours and lot of energy in that garden. For a non-gardening enthusiast it must have been prolonged hell. He still smoked his pipe. I puffed away at a cheroot. We talked quietly, but with great seriousness.

'Badger?' he said.

'I've met him. So far, no complaints.'

'Yankee father, I understand.'

'Oh?'

'Sort of reverse GI bride. Bridegroom, in his case.'

'It explains something,' I grunted.

We reached the end of the path, turned and began the return stroll. Beyond the trimmed hedge a field rose in a gentle slope to a tiny wood at its brow. Above the trees the sky was a uniform gun-metal grey. A dreary, featureless day, but as far as two far-from-young ex-coppers were concerned, a very important day.

'How many?' I asked.

'Count on half a dozen.' Sullivan moved his pipe in a tiny wave. 'Maybe more. No promise of numbers, but an assurance of reliability.'

'All one-time-coppers?'

'Of course.' He seemed surprised at the question.

'I think . . .' I began slowly. 'I think Badger expects something of this sort.'

'An unorthodox type. So I've heard.'

'I can put a name to another unorthodox type,' I grinned.

He chuckled and said, 'More than one.'

'We're out-numbered,' I reminded him.

'We always were. But — as usual — we have the *quality*.'

'And, of course, bags of modesty.'

Like naughty schoolboys we walked alongside each other. Smiling at our memories. Eager, I think, to prove that we hadn't lost all the cunning of the once-upon-a-time. What nervousness — what doubts — we might have had we masked behind quick bursts of soft laughter. Silly non-jokes. Reminders of other times when we'd risked reputations and got away with it. Strangely, the years seemed to fall away. The mind became young again; sharpened by what lay ahead; calculating, planning, calling upon a whole range of experience with which to counter impossible odds. I caught sight of Mary, watching us from the kitchen window. I saw her expression and looked away hurriedly.

'Bit at a time,' mused Sullivan. 'Never a frontal attack.'

'Against those odds!'

'Nibbling. Destroying the morale.'

'The only way,' I agreed.

'You're the boss, of course.'

'Look, I'm not sure I'm the . . .'

'Somebody has to give the orders. Make the decisions. The rest of us have to obey. That's part of our strength. You're the boss, Lenny. Anybody not prepared to accept that isn't in.'

I hadn't particularly wanted it. I certainly hadn't touted myself. Nevertheless . . .

Nobody felt more strongly about Collins's murder than I did. I think I made-believe I wanted justice whereas, in fact, I wanted vengeance. Inside those prison walls the two words had been interchangeable. There the eye-for-an-eye concept had *been* justice; no accusation, no hearing, no awaited verdict. Like for like . . . and if the wrong man got it, hard lines. The *right* man would know what was on its way, and sweat a little.

Maybe I *was* the one to run things. The guy giving orders. Maybe the others were still too much "ex-cops". Tough, but a mite too "gentlemanly". For me? This wasn't a game — this wasn't a skylark — this was a war, complete with casualties.

I visited Upper Drayson on Tuesday, March 2nd, and before I left we'd agreed that Sullivan should have three days (until Friday, March 5th) to sound out and gather together a tiny army of like-minded men. Ex-coppers, all of whom had known Collins. All of whom had proved themselves in past tight corners. All of whom were fit and active for their age. All of whom were prepared to accept orders and obey those orders without question.

Those, we agreed, were the minimum requirements. Anything less and we were storing up trouble for ourselves. Anything more . . . that would be a welcome bonus.

Meanwhile, I carried out my duties at the bank conscientiously and carefully. I got to know the cleaners; was friendly enough with them, but kept them at arm's length and wasn't *too* friendly. I passed a quick time-of-day with Stowe and Curtiss. The rest I nodded a silent greeting to if and when they noticed me.

The flat became a home, as opposed to somewhere to sleep and eat my meals. This, with astonishing speed. The shops were on my doorstep. On an impluse I bought a vase and flowers . . . the difference they made was almost beyond belief. I bought a small, stereo radio, and when I felt like it was able to enjoy the soothing influence of good music. I arranged for a daily delivery of *The Lessford And Bordfield Tribune*, and was thus able to keep abreast of local as well as national news. In effect, I became a "citizen" and something more than a piece of flotsam floating around on the tide of a large city.

I could have relaxed. I could, very easily, have settled into a comfortable rut of quiet respectability . . . had it not been for the fact of Henry Collins's death, and the cause of his death.

It was about six o'clock — a few minutes after six, perhaps — when the doorbell rang. I went down the stairs and peeped through the thick glass of the spy-hole before unlocking the door. Basic precautions. I lived in a bank — at least *over* a bank — and already I'd trained myself never to forget the fact. It was Thursday the 4th — and I knew of nobody likely to call at that hour on that day. It was also dark outside and this, along with the distortion brought on by the curvature of the convex surface of the glass, momentarily prevented me from seeing other than a completely out-of-proportion face. Not at all recognisable. I peered through the spy-hole and, after a few moments, the visitor stepped back to look up at the lighted window of the flat. Then, as he backed off, I recognised him. Sergeant Sykes. An older Sergeant Sykes; greyer and with lines of living etched deep down the sides of his mouth. Nevertheless, Sergeant Sykes.

I opened the door and another re-union took place.

Up in the flat I settled him into one of the armchairs, brought two cans of beer from the fridge, and we settled down to talk. I allowed the how-are-you and the good-to-see-you-again small talk to evaporate as we drank beer straight from the cans.

Then I said, 'Dick Sullivan tells me you're a bowls enthusiast.'

'Bugger bowls!' He wiped his mouth with the back of a hand. 'That's not why I'm here, Mr Lennox.'

'Lenny,' I insisted.

'Mr Sullivan says we're in business again.' He stared into my face as he spoke. 'That we're out to show 'em how it should be done . . . unofficial, like.'

'Back — er — "in business"?' It seemed safer, for the moment, to pretend ignorance.

'That you're the boss, sir. That with a bit o' luck we'll nail the bastard who mugged Mr Collins.'

'I answer to the name of "Lenny",' I murmured.

'No, sir. Not if you're the boss. Not if what Mr Sullivan says is right.'

'Okay.' It wasn't much of a risk, therefore I took it. 'Let's work on the assumption that he *is* right. Why visit me?'

'We both know each other, sir.'

I nodded.

He sipped his beer, then continued, 'We both like — both respect — Mr Sullivan.'

'We're in agreement so far.'

'Now, sir . . .' He leaned forward a little in his chair. 'You and me . . . we've nobody. We're alike. Your missus is dead, my missus is dead. We've damn-all to lose if things get sticky. Mr Sullivan *has*. He has a wife and son. Both of 'em grand people.'

'Open your heart up, sergeant,' I said. 'You've come a long way to say something. Go ahead and say it.'

'Don't call for volunteers, sir. That's what I mean. If there's a chance of shit flying — a chance of being caught — detail somebody. Detail *me*. I'll not let you down. You have my word.

Whatever else, I hadn't expected that. And yet, I should have done. Sullivan, Collins and that rare brand of everlasting loyalty such men create. With the possible exception of the armed forces, no other profession on God's earth could have engendered that depth of respect. Nor was it meant to be flashy. If the "yeoman type" still exists, Sykes personified that type. I knew him of old. I'd known him and worked with him when the odds had seemed impossible. Almost as impossible as they seemed at that moment. And never once had I known him to budge. Never once had I known him to play to the gallery. And yet I couldn't grant him his request. Not without qualifications.

'The right man in the right place, sergeant,' I said quietly.

'Sir, all I'm asking . . .'

'I know, I understand and I admire you for it. But the odds are stacked too heavily against us. We can't afford the luxury of shielding even *one* man.' I paused and watched the quick scowl of worry cross his face. 'This I promise you, between these walls: if it's level-pegging — if it doesn't matter whether it's you *or* Mr Sullivan — I'll turn to you, every time.'

'That's all I ask.' He nodded slow and solemn thanks. 'You're a good man, sir. I don't give a damn what the odds are. With you up front, we'll knock the living crap out of 'em.'

'I hope so.' I tried to sound as certain as he did. I sipped beer from the can, then continued, 'When I checked you through the spy-hole, I couldn't recognise you. It's what we need. Distortion of faces . . . just in case. Hallowe'en masks. Face *and* head. Thin rubber. You know the sort of thing I mean.'

'Yes, sir.'

71

'We need some. A dozen, to be on the safe side.' I pushed myself from the armchair and walked to the tiny bureau where I kept my cheque book. 'All different, if possible.'

'Novelty shops,' he suggested. 'Joke shops.'

'A job for you, sergeant.' I wrote out a cheque as I talked. 'Never more than two at one shop. Tomorrow have a ride round. You have a car?'

'A Mini.'

'Fine. Leeds, Bradford. Maybe as far afield as Manchester. No more than two at one shop. All different . . . then *we'll* know. Change clothes. You know the tricks. Spectacles. No spectacles. Mac. No mac. Walking-stick. A different description at each shop. A different speech pattern.' I tore out the cheque and handed it to him. 'It's made out to cash. Pay it in, then draw some out. Enough, but not enough to raise eyebrows. Park your car carefully. No traffic wardens. Multi-storey car parks, if possible. And, for Christ's sake, no accidents. Drive carefully.'

'Leave it to me, sir.' He finished his beer, placed the empty can on the carpet alongside the chair and stood up. He held out his hand. 'Thanks for the chance, sir. I'll not let you down.'

We shook hands and he left.

The first step; the first positive, practical step. I turned out the light, opened the curtains and watched the street below. Slowly, I finished the beer in my can. Now it was more than talk. More than wishful thinking. This evening, the cheque. Tomorrow, the masks and a get-together with Sullivan. Out there — maybe down there in the street — yobboes under the control of this man Kendal still thought they were safe. The coppers were wary of them. The general public were terrified.

Well, we'd see. We'd bloody well *see*.

And after we'd twisted a few tails — after we'd dropped a few balls into the meat-grinder — we'd have a quiet, man-to-man talk. Just Kendal and me. We'd talk about Henry Collins and who killed him.

The next day (Friday the 5th) I had my second meeting with Badger. I was undecided. Indeed, I was more than undecided; I'd more or less reached the conclusion that a meeting with "officialdom" wasn't called for — wasn't even wise — until I knew the strength and possible weaknesses of my own tiny force. The actual odds didn't worry me too much. A pitched battle wasn't on the agenda. Guerilla warfare was our only hope of success. To hit Kendall's crowd at their weakest point, and when they least expected it. Therefore, security was of the essence. The secret then which, if broken, would rob us of everything. Not only where we were, but *who* we were. Not to be seen with Badger too many times; not to be seen with *any* police officer in fact.

You will note that by this time I had assumed generalship. I was even thinking of the men willing to follow my lead as an "army". Nobody can accuse me of not working very hard at self-delusion!

In the event, I almost collided with Badger.

I'd gone for a walk; to stretch my legs a little away from the slightly cramped confines of the flat. No particular route. Certainly no destination. Merely a brisk stroll along the pavements while the rain held off. It was pure coincidence that I passed the main entrance to the Town Hall and Crown Courts as Badger was hurrying down the shallow steps. As he reached the bottom step — less than a second after I'd spotted him — he gripped my elbow and fell in step alongside.

'I know a nice eating-house, Lenny.'

'Eh? Oh! Hello.'

'Join me, old-timer.'

'I — er — I don't think I've . . .'

'Sure, you've time.'

'I'm — y'know — not really hungry.'

'Okay. Smoke one of those cigar things and watch.'

I agreed. I forget what words I used, I was busy working out how the hell *he* knew about "those cigar things". The only other time I'd been in his company I'd smoked his cigarettes.

It was a cafe. Back-street, pseudo-Italian and moderately clean. It called itself a "pizzeria", and that's what it sold: pizzas, and if the way he trenched into the multi-coloured disc was anything of a hint Badger had a real weakness for pizzas. I sat opposite him, smoking a cheroot and sipping frothy coffee. The tables were fine for two people; with four the elbows would have needed to be strapped to the sides. Each table was in what I suspect went under the name of "alcove". It was, in fact, little more than an open-ended horse-box; clean enough, dimly lit but (and this was the important thing) providing absolute privacy.

As far as I was concerned, it had to be pure top-of-the-head stuff. Taking it as it came. Allowing the conversation to trundle along at his speed. *He'd* extended the invitation. *He* knew why. My job was to sit tight and make appropriate noises.

'Things moving?' he asked breezily.

'One spin of the earth, another day gone,' I fenced.

'The flat, I mean. The job.'

'What else would you mean?'

'Who knows? Things happen all the time. Goddam juries.' He waved his fork. Like most Americans — in his case, half-American — the knife provided by the management was superfluous; he ate one-handed; using the edge of the fork as a blunt knife, then spearing the piece of pizza and transferring it to his mouth. He also used the fork as a sort of makeshift baton with which to conduct his side of the conversation. 'The creep was Judas-guilty. But that don't mean a damn thing.'

'Wrong verdict,' I sympathised.

'Like always.'

'A Crown Jewel job?'

'Some stupid dame leaves her car unlocked. This jerk lifts a fur coat from the back seat.'

'Not according to the jury.'

'Lenny, old buddy, I don't have to tell *you*.'

'We were taught,' I said airily, 'that all police interest should cease when the accused stood for trial.'

'Like hell!'

'We should not concern ourselves with the outcome. Guilty. Innocent. It should make no difference.'

He growled, 'Like a square world and dropping over the edge.'

'He'll come again,' I soothed. 'He'll see another fur coat. They always do.'

'Yeah. Meanwhile Kendal thumbs his nose at us.'

'Kendal?' I tried to make it a complete non-question.

'Who else?'

'The accused?'

'Jesus H Christ, no!' He tapped the air with the fork. 'That boy takes his cut. He don't *do* anything.'

I refused to be drawn. Badger was clever; he'd edged Kendal's name into the conversation very smoothly. Fine. That was the character I wanted to talk about. At a guess, the character we *both* wanted to talk about. But with me it had to be egg-shell gentle. However off-beat Badger's policing might be, it remained *policing*. What I was planning amounted to simple brigandry. No holds barred, and to hell with the law. It would have been stupid — disastrous — to have shown even mild interest in Kendal.

For a few minutes he concentrated on chewing pizza. I concentrated on smoking a cheroot and sipping jazzed-up coffee. I pulled a paper napkin from its holder on the table and dabbed the moustache of foam which had gathered on my upper lip.

Then, through a mouthful of pizza, he said 'Y'know, Lenny, you're a strange guy.'

'I wasn't aware.'

'For an ex-cop . . .'

'How about an ex-con?'

'Ex-con my left ballock . . .'

'I wouldn't know too much about your left ballock, chief superintendent.'

'I told you before. I've read the old reports. I know what you did.'

I drew on the cheroot, held the smoke in my lungs, then allowed it to trickle free past pursed lips.

'What you did,' he repeated gently.

'Go back far enough. You'll find I once wet my nappies.'

'Yeah.' He tried to chuckle, and almost choked. When he'd regained control of his breathing, he said, 'This Kendal goon . . .'

'Am I interested?' I asked.

'He has this place by the nuts . . .'

'For three years, I slept and ate with his kind.'

75

'Even on authorised strength, we couldn't cover every corner . . .'

'I even grew to like a few of them.'

'Take the Star Bingo Hall . . .'

'Some coppers, I didn't like.'

'Saturday nights, they pay big prize money . . .'

'Some coppers I positively hated.'

'People come away with fat wads. Elderly people . . .'

'But that's way back in the past, chief superintendent.'

'Lots of dark streets around the Star Bingo Hall . . .'

'Maybe I was happy — maybe I wasn't — it's hard to remember.'

'We try to provide a parked squad car . . .'

'So I don't remember.'

'Sometimes we can't . . .'

'It's a trick I learned.'

'And when there isn't one, there's always a mugging . . .'

'You learn these tricks, inside.'

'The germs are always around, checking whether or not the squad car's in position . . .'

'Lot's of tricks, chief superintendent.'

'And if it isn't, some poor fink gets clobbered . . .'

'Three years, and nothing to do but learn tricks.'

'That's how well organised the bastard is . . .'

'So you learn a lot of tricks.'

'And tomorrow we can't spare a car . . .'

'Like not remembering, not getting involved, not caring a damn.'

'We can almost pencil in "Robbery" and "GBH" before the evening starts . . .'

'Like taking a nice flat over a bank, taking an easy little job, not figuring you owe anybody or anything any favours.'

'Now in your day that wouldn't have happened, Lenny. Would it?'

'What's that?' I pretended to notice the question.

'An observation, old-timer. That's all.'

'Sorry. I didn't hear what you . . .'

76

'Forget it. Finish your coffee.'

'No thanks.' I pushed myself up from the table. 'The only liquid I like with a head on it is beer. Thanks, nevertheless.'

'Any time, Lenny. Any time.' He waved his fork. 'Be seeing you around.'

'It's possible. It's a small world.

I walked back to the flat. The rain had started; not much, but enough to make most people hurry. I didn't hurry. I needed time to think. Who'd been pulling who? We'd talked over each other. Two conversations with, on the face of it, no point of contact. But *he* knew what *I'd* said, and *I* knew what *he'd* said. And *he'd* been the one to suggest a visit to the café.

People said he was cunning, foxy, devious. Sometimes with smiling approval, sometimes with worried disapproval. But *how* cunning, *how* foxy, *how* devious? With what end in view?

I knew what *I* wanted. I wanted Kendal and, through Kendal, whoever had killed Collins, and to get there I was prepared to wade through as many "soldiers" as Kendal cared to throw in my direction. But that was a very personal thing, whereas Badger . . .

Badger was still the "x" in the equation and, as a calculated risk, that's what he had to remain. At least for the time being. One thing for certain. He'd given me my first target. Tomorrow night outside the Star Bingo Hall. Not much. Nothing big. Possibly a try-out. A try-out for him. A try-out for me.

It would be foolish not to take what had been offered.

The list read:
Sullivan
Bear
Sykes
Cockburn
Butterfield
Evans

It was a typewritten list. It gave no first names, it gave no ranks; but I knew, because I'd known and worked with these men in the old days, that the rank spanned police constable all the way

77

up to assistant chief constable. Equally, they represented the old county constabulary and the old Lessford and Bordfield forces.

. I said, 'You've been busy.'

'Give me another week, and I'll double the number.'

I stared at the list for a moment, then said, 'Butterfield. he didn't retire.'

'No.'

'So?'

'He resigned,' said Sullivan sombrely. 'He — er — grew tired of "modern police methods".'

I held the list in my hand, stared at it without actually seeing it and tried to reach a cold-blooded decision.

We were once more in Sullivan's greenhouse. I'd parked the car at the gate, and as I'd walked down the drive I'd seen the light in the greenhouse and Sullivan obviously killing time while awaiting my arrival. It had seemed kinder to by-pass the house; not to subject Mary to any unnecessary embarrassment. As I'd approached the greenhouse, the illuminated glass had looked ridiculously vulnerable. What we were doing — what we were planning — was *very* illegal, and Dick Sullivan couldn't have made himself more obvious had he hired a hall and walked onto a floodlit stage. And yet inside the greenhouse there was a false feeling of absolute security. The single bulb turned every pane into a mirror; reflections of reflections with a ghostly hint of nearby vegetation merely emphasising the black emptiness beyond.

I looked up from the list and, very sadly, asked, 'Are we crazy, Dick?'

'Crazy? I thought you . . .'

'Crazy old men, trying to re-fight old battles?'

'Lenny, the other day you . . .'

'Talk about today, Dick. Talk about this evening.' There was an old, dusty and cobwebbed wash-tub; obviously used to store water, pending its reaching the temperature of the greenhouse. There was a short piece of planking across the rim, a makeshift seat. I lowered my backside onto the plank and waved the typed paper in a gesture of doubt and indecision. 'Old war-horses — all

78

except Butterfield and looked at from one angle *he* couldn't stand the pace. Maybe we should have been sent to the knacker-yard. Instead, we've been put out to grass, and we don't like it there. Is *that* the truth?'

'*I* don't think so.' His voice was almost harsh.

'Or just don't *want* to think so?'

'Lenny, when you came to me and . . .'

'I know. I know.' I waved the paper again. 'Like kids with new toys. But we aren't kids and they aren't toys. I lived with 'em for three years. The recidivists. The regulars. They aren't toys, they're animals. They won't change, because they don't *want* to change.' I sighed. I had a black mood on me, and it swamped the enthusiasm I'd had even as recently as my journey to Upper Drayson. 'Dick, we're innocents. Every copper, no matter how good the copper, is an innocent. We think we can lick 'em. We think we can lick 'em, otherwise the whole thing's a waste of time. The Police Service. Everything. If we accept the proposition that they're unbeatable, it's all for nothing. But they *are* unbeatable. Short of caging 'em for the rest of their natural lives — short of exterminating 'em — they'll return. Like lice. Like locusts. They'll come back. They'll take over. They'll — they'll . . .'

I lowered my head, moved my hands a little and fell silent. Those three years had marked me. I had enough simple gumption left to realise that. The feeling of dark depression, hard on the heels of confidence which had almost touched a pitch of elation. The truth was, I was ashamed of it, but could neither understand nor explain it.

'Finished?' growled Sullivan.

I nodded, without raising my head.

'Come back into the house.' He picked up a shoe-box as he spoke. 'You need a stiff drink.'

'Mary wouldn't like . . .'

'Mary's sitting with Gwen for a couple of hours.'

'Oh!'

I followed him back to the house, slowly and with my head still bowed. What the hell was wrong with me? What the hell had got *into* me? One moment it had seemed not merely possible, but even easy; something to look forward to, a re-establishment of manhood. The next moment, an utter madness; something not to be even contemplated; an acceptance of complete defeat. What the hell was the *matter* with me?

I flopped into an armchair. My arms hung slackly by the sides of the chair. I rested the nape of my neck against the softness of the upholstery and closed my aching eyes. Aching eyes, and a pricking behind my eyes. A gentle throbbing of the brain; something that was not quite pain, but rather like the steady heave of a sea without white-tops. And complete exhaustion. Bone weariness beyond anything I'd ever felt before. A passing thought suggested that I might even be dying, but even that wasn't important.

Sullivan's voice was gruff but kindly as he said, 'Here, drink this.'

It was a tumbler holding what must have been a triple whisky. Neat. I tasted it, and the warmth slipped down my throat and seemed to inject a modicum of life into me. I continued to sip the whisky as Sullivan settled himself in the opposite armchair and talked. He talked as a wise friend. As a man who understands.

'Ripley,' he began. 'You weren't in at the end. Collins and I, nobody else.* I don't want to see another man go down the same path. The death of his wife. That damn wheelchair he was chained to. Even his daughter — Susan Tallboy — didn't know the whole truth.' He paused then, very deliberately, said, 'You're going down the same path, Lenny. I'm no medic. I don't have to be. See it once, from then on you recognise it.'

'I'm — I'm sorry. I don't . . .'

'Manic Depression. That's what the quacks call it. Not just unhappiness. Not just misery. Depression, plunging down to a suicidal level for no real reason. I know. I've asked doctor friends. Ripley worried me. Interested me. So I asked around. No real reason, because they don't *know* the reason. Not the reason triggering the whole thing off. But there's a reason all right. One reason or a series of inter-related reasons.

Death of a Big Man by John Wainwright, Macmillan, 1975

'With Ripley it was the death of his wife, plus his own crippled condition. With you . . .' Again he paused. 'The death of *your* wife, followed by your killing of that man, followed by the spell in jail. Dammit, Lenny, one-two-three. One more than Ripley. *Plus* the news of Collins's death when you came out.'

I was suddenly aware that tears were running down my cheeks. The hell I knew why. The hell I could do anything to stop them. Just that I was so damn *miserable*.

'Manic Depression,' he repeated sombrely. 'That's what's talking, Lenny. Not you. Hell's teeth, of course they can be licked. Of course they can be driven back into their little knot-holes. What the hell they are, they're no worse than the North End crowd. They *can't* be worse. And we wore uniforms. The bastards could recognise us. They knew we were *there*. This time we have surprise and experience. They *won't* know. They won't know a damn thing. Who we are. Where we're going to hit 'em next. God! They'll be dizzy before we've even flexed our muscles.'

There was more of it; much more of it. Pure pep-talk, thrown at me with something not far removed from desperation, mixed with controlled anger. But anger at what? Anger at the crooks? At law-breakers generally and at this character Kendal specifically? Anger at the soft belly of law-enforcement? At the reality, as opposed to the might-have-been, had the bulk of the ordinary people been less apathetic and genuinely backed the coppers in their fight against a two-pronged attack by hooligans and the do-goodery crowd? At age, perhaps? At age and the infirmity — the deep down feeling of helplessness — brought on by age? At *his* age and *my* age and the age of all men — all ex-coppers — of our generation? Or at me? At this weakness which had suddenly shown itself? At this damn maggot which had crawled into my brain and which (or so it would seem) must periodically touch a nerve of indescribable misery and defeat?

Poor old Sullivan. Dear old Sullivan. how he worked! He used words as a life-line and slowly, gradually, dragged me from the morass of self-pity. No more whisky after that one hefty shot — I had to drive a car home — but black coffee and enthusiasm piled upon enthusiasm.

We even planned the tomorrow; the Saturday evening; the opportunity Badger had handed us on a plate.

'A beginning,' said Sullivan. 'A mugger getting his come-uppance.'

'*If* we can pull it.' Some of the doubt still remained.

'Why the hell not?'

'There could be more than one. Two. Maybe even three.'

'Okay. Three of us, plus the decoy.'

'What decoy?' I screwed my face in an effort of concentration.

'One of us has to be decoy,' he explained patiently. 'Not some innocent Bingo player. One of *us*, dressed in drag.'

'I don't see . . .'

'Butterfield. He has the figure.' His enthusiasm wasn't make-believe any more. 'Leave this first one to me, Lenny. I'll fix the details. You have a good night's sleep. Get yourself normal. Final briefing where? Your place?'

I nodded.

'Good. We'll start arriving at five. Twenty-minute intervals. We'll park what vehicles we need along the streets, away from the bank.' He handed me the shoe-box. 'Take this with you. Drive carefully. And don't *worry*. We're back in business, Lenny. Collins was a cop and *nobody* kills a cop and gets away with it.'

Back at the flat I drank more whisky and fought to bring my rocking mind onto an even keel. "Nobody kills a cop and gets away with it". Big deal! But it just wasn't true any more. Once upon a time, maybe. But not today. Cops were vulnerable. They died. Collins had died . . . and somebody had got away with *that*.

Christ, we were playing knights-and-dragons. We were old men in second childhood.

I tipped raw whisky down my throat and, almost savagely, elbowed the doubts aside.

Okay, knights-and-dragons. And with *real* dragons. Sure we could do it. At a canter. Sullivan was one-hundred-per-cent certain. Badger thought so, otherwise he wouldn't have given us this first run. *Sure* we could do it. We'd done it too many times before. We were experts at it. We'd doused more bloody dragons than that in the old days. Slower, maybe. Okay, accept slower. But what we'd lost in speed we more than made up for in cunning. In experience. In not being cramped inside law-books written in safe studies by idiots who wouldn't know street crime from Blackpool rock. But *we* knew. We'd always known. The hard way. The only way.

I fell asleep in the armchair, with the half-consumed bottle of whisky on the carpet alongside my feet.

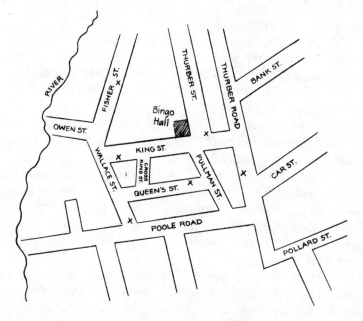

'This.' I tapped the sketch plan as I spoke, and Sullivan, Sykes and Butterfield crowded in a little around the opened flap of the bureau. It was no architectural masterpiece — just a rough, pencil sketch, similar to a few thousand similar sketches made by police officers at scenes of accidents — but it was (to use the jargon of police colleges) a visual aid. It reminded them. It reminded me. It lessened the possibility of a stumer when things started happening.

83

'There it is. The Star Bingo Hall. Main entrance and only exit onto King Street. Starts at eight, goes on till ten. The main prize — so-called *Top Of The Evening* — goes with the last game played. It varies, usually around the hundred pound mark. Sometimes as high as a hundred-and-fifty. Never lower than eighty. If His Nibs is waiting, that's the fish he's waiting for . . .'

Last night need never have happened. I was in top gear again. I'd awakened before dawn, bathed and been up and about before the cleaning woman from downstairs had entered the flat. By mid-morning I was out in the King Street area, making notes and asking indirect questions and, having returned to the flat, I'd drawn the sketch plan.

'Most of the buildings are warehouses and stores. Hell only knows how anybody managed to get a licence — planning permission, whatever it needs — for a Bingo hall in that dog's dinner of riverside streets. There are lamps.' I stabbed the plan with my finger as I continued. 'They're marked with a cross. One in Fisher Street, one in King Street near the junction with Wallace Street, one in Queen's Street, one in Wallace Street near the junction with Poole Road, one in Thurber Street at the junction with King Street, one in Thurber Road. All smashed except the one in King Street itself and the one in Thurber Road. The squad car — when it's around — parks in Queen's Street. An obvious spot. King Street, Thurber Road . . . some sort of illumination. The rest . . . nothing. There isn't even a lamp in Cross King Street.'

I'd telephoned Dick Sullivan. The least I could do was put his mind at rest and, while on the phone, we'd aired a few ideas and made a few suggestions. That afternoon, I'd visited chemist shops and an ironmongers for the bits and pieces we'd decided we needed. What I didn't buy, Sullivan had promised to provide. And on the face of it, it seemed a good scheme. Simple, swift and in no way impossible.

'Sergeant Sykes' van. That's parked in Owen Street. Sergeant Sykes, myself and Mr Sullivan stay with the van until ten o'clock. Any would-be-mugger who uses Owen Street as *his* hide-out won't even be allowed a bite of the cherry.

'At ten o'clock we move out of Owen Street, down Wallace Street to the junction with Queen's Street. You, Butterfield, you're already inside the hall. In the foyer. You come out, holding the wad of notes, looking pleased with yourself, pop them in the handbag — *very* carefully — then turn right and left into Cross King Street. That, hopefully, is where it's going to happen . . .'

For the third time in less than five minutes I checked my wrist watch. Having gone through the rigmarole of synchronising watches before we left the flat the business of split-second timing had assumed a somewhat ridiculous importance. The game of Bingo does not include a time element; anything up to fifteen minutes either way is good guessing in a full evening's session.

Sullivan muttered, 'For Christ's sake, let's move out. If Butterfield gets jumped without us in position . . .'

'He'll yell,' I said irritably. 'We don't want to attract attention. Scare people off.'

By people, of course, I meant potential muggers. Like a kid walking a pavement and deliberately not stepping on cracks, the success or failure of this enterprise had built up to portentous proportions. If we couldn't do this we couldn't do *anything*. Fate was against us, and we might as well forget the whole scheme. But if this first escapade *was* a success . . . anything!

A mist drifted in from the river. It stretched little more than a hundred yards, but it gave good cover. The van was parked in Owen Street, less than ten yards from the weed-choked bank and in the thicker darkness of an archway leading to one of the old warehouses. We'd draped coats and covers over the windscreens and headlamps, in order to kill any likelihood of even a slight reflection, and sacking was already tied to front and rear number plates. We'd been there almost two hours and, despite flasks of hot soup and coffee, the cold dampness was starting to be felt. Other than an occasional car — not more than half a dozen — being driven along Fisher Street, we'd seen nothing and nobody. At times we'd heard shouting (once singing) in the distance, but the warren of streets prevented any real pin-pointing of direction.

Sullivan said, 'I think we should move. I think we should get in place.'

'All right.' I glanced at my watch again. 'One at a time, and keep hidden.'

'I'll go first.'

'Fair enough.' I warned, 'Mask down only when we move in, Dick. And keep the hold-all hidden as much as possible, we don't want *that* snatched.'

'For Christ's sake!' He seemed annoyed that I considered it necessary to have had to remind him.

Nevertheless — and *he* knew it — sillier things had triggered off balls-ups in the past. The reason we'd discarded the original Hallowe'en mask idea was the time element; too long to put on, too long to rip off. Great on television screens, but we'd tried it and the damn things had to be pulled down slowly and carefully, otherwise the eye-holes and the mouth-holes weren't in position and, when you tried to drag them off, the soft rubber sucked at the skin of the face and wouldn't budge easily enough. So stocking-masks. Already over the head and rolled up below the brim of the hat (or in Sykes' case under the neb of the cap), then — like drawing down a blind — down over the face and in position in less than a second.

Sullivan picked up the hold-all and hurried towards the mouth of Owen Street. Through the mist, I saw him turn right and into Wallace Street. The truth was, I hadn't any real doubts. Dick Sullivan was too old a hand at the game to make mistakes. He'd turn left, along Queen's Street, past the junction with Cross King Street, then find shadow enough in which to hide and wait and listen.

I gave Sullivan time to get into position, then I said, 'You too, sergeant.'

'Right.'

'Good luck.'

'And you, sir.'

Sykes checked his rolled-up stocking-mask then, at a normal walking pace left for his agreed position. Right at the end of Owen Street then, like Sullivan, left into Queen's Street, there to find a quiet place before the junction with Cross King Street.

It had been agreed that the ideal location for any mugging attack would be Cross King Street. Open at both ends without a street lamp and masked from any wash of light given by the two unbroken lamps, it was like a black cavern. Away from the Bingo hall it gave a perfect escape route into the unlighted Queen's Street, and from there into the equally unlighted Wallace Street or Pullman Street, then left or right and away into the maze of streets and alleys which made up the rest of the area. *Ergo*, anybody using Cross King Street, when leaving the Star Bingo Hall was asking for trouble, and Butterfield's job was to ask for trouble.

I counted up to one hundred, very slowly, then I too walked to the end of Owen Street. My job was to spring the trap; to cross Wallace Street, walk slowly along King Street — which was lighted by an unbroken street lamp, plus the illumination from the entrance to the Bingo Hall — and, if possible, spot the attacker (or attackers) wait around until Butterfield made an appearance, then close the lid after the attacker (or, again, attackers) had followed Butterfield into Cross King Street. It was a simple pincer movement; simple, that is, as long as *I* wasn't identified as a possible fly in the ointment which, in practical terms, meant as long as Butterfield didn't delay his exit from the Bingo hall long enough to make *me* arouse suspicion.

In the event, the timing was perfect.

As I turned into King Street a trickle of players began leaving the hall. One of them was Butterfield. He was, of course, dressed as a woman; he wore slacks (he'd refused, point blank, to wear a skirt), a woman's overcoat, belted and with the collar turned up against the weather and a head-scarf over the wig which covered his own hair. The cosmetics we'd so carefully applied did the rest. He *was* a middle-aged woman. As he walked down the shallow steps in his low-heeled pumps he carefully folded what looked like a nice wad of bank-notes (the old trick of one at the top and one at the bottom and the rest paper carefully cut to the correct size) and dropped the wad into the shoulder-slung handbag. His fumbling with the catch, and the apparent inadvertency of leaving the flap open, was a minor masterpiece of off-the-cuff acting.

As he left the hall and made for Cross King Street I looked wildly around for any would-be attacker. I heard them, before I saw them. The Norton had been standing, ticking over, at the junction with Pullman Street; the rider and pillion-passenger with their feet planted on the ground. As Butterfield reached the mouth of Cross King Street, the engine roared, the machine swung into King Street, and for a moment I thought we'd bitten off more than we could chew.

We'd expected attackers (hopefully only *one* attacker) on foot. Naturally. In God's name, why naturally? With these people, the getaway was important. As important as the theft. Our cardinal error. We'd been stupid enough to underestimate the opposition.

But not to panic. *Not to panic.* I forced myself to continue my slow walk until the Norton turned into Cross King Street — until it was inside the trap — then I dragged the three-battery torch from my mac pocket and raced for the short, unlighted street.

Two other torches beamed up the street from the other direction. Sullivan and Sykes had guessed what was happening. What we saw was far more than I'd expected. The Norton slowed as it drew alongside Butterfield. The pillion-passenger drove his left hand deep into the shoulder-bag. The fish-hooks (a full dozen, sewn firmly into place with nylon line) bit into the flesh of his hand, and Butterfield hung onto the leather thong of the bag with both hands. We could hear the high scream of the pillion-passenger above the roar of the motor-cycle. The rider tried to accelerate out of trouble. The pillion-passenger screamed even louder, pitched from his seat and, in doing so, caught the rider's side with his right leg and brought machine and rider to the ground.

From then on, it was easy. Sullivan and Sykes arrived at the same time as myself. Quite calmly Sullivan bent, removed the rider's crash-helmet, then swung the length of lead-shot-loaded hose. One wallop, and we had only the pillion passenger to deal with. The screams stopped as Sykes rammed *his* length of hose, sideways on, between the passenger's teeth, and I was already unbuckling the belt of my mac in order to fasten the makeshift gag into place. Sullivan turned to the still-roaring motor-cycle and switched off the engine.

Then we did what we'd agreed to do, but with two instead of one. We carried them into Queen's Street. We handcuffed them around the lamp-standard — both Sullivan and Sykes had brought their darbies from the force as souvenirs when they'd retired — then, while Sykes, Butterfield and I held them upright, Sullivan pulled on heavy gardening gloves, took lengths of barbed wire from the holdall and wired them to the standard. The rider showed signs of returning life, and Butterfield rammed a cloth gag in his mouth and tied it into position with the head-scarf.

And all the time we were aware of eyes watching us. From darkened corners and shadowed doorways. Curious eyes, frightened eyes but — or so the impression was — not hostile eyes. And never less than twenty yards distant. As we'd moved from Cross King Street and into Queen's Street, so the eyes had shifted their position. Watching, but wanting no part. I listened for the sound of approaching police sirens, but none came. In these parts, the police were "the enemy" or, at best, something not worth calling.

From the holdall Sullivan took the notice we'd already carefully spelled out in capital letters with a felt-tipped pen.

WITH THE COMPLIMENTS OF THE CITIZEN VIGILANTE COMMITTEE

We collected the things, threw them into the holdall and hurried away. Sullivan passed the holdall to Sykes, turned into Cross King Street and, as we made our way to the parked van, we heard the Norton approach, then pass us. In Owen Street Sullivan was waiting. he'd removed his stocking-mask and was holding the door of the van open and ready. He was the first one to speak since the start of the operation.

'Pity about the Norton. Time was they ruled the TT track. Still, it's safer in the river.'

Sykes drove. I sat in the passenger seat and Sullivan and Butterfield squatted in the rear of the van. We were well clear of the area — had actually stopped in a deserted street to rip the sacking from the number plates, before continuing — before anything else was said.

Sykes growled, 'First blood to us, I'd say.'

'I'd say,' I agreed, and my voice was pitched a little high.

From behind me, Sullivan's voice was mildly critical.

'Lenny, you forgot to pull your mask down.'

We split before we reached the bank. Butterfield changed out of drag in the rear of the van then he and Sullivan collected their cars. I left the van about two hundred yards from the bank and walked to the flat, leaving Sykes to drive the van home.

I thought about whisky, decided I didn't fancy the taste and instead made strong instant coffee, with plenty of sugar but no milk. It was what I needed. That and a cheroot and a deep armchair in which to relax and think.

"First blood to us."

Well, maybe, but we hadn't caught *all* the eggs. On the credit side, we'd done all we'd set out to do. We'd hoped for one, handled two and, as a bonus, scuttled a perfectly good Norton motor-cycle. To that extent, we were in business. But what if there'd been three? Or even four? We'd taken too much for granted. A hell of a lot. More than that, having shown our hand, there'd *be* more than two next time.

The sign we'd left hanging round the rider's neck, that also hadn't been *too* wise. It had seemed a good idea; to let the opposition know they weren't dealing with a rival gang. To let the police know. Good citizens, who'd had a gutful and were prepared to take the law into their own hands. Fine. But secret organisations — *really* secret organisations — don't even exist. That they're even *there* is denied. Whereas we *were* there, we'd left a visiting card. To that extent, therefore, we weren't secret and (again) to that extent we were that much more vulnerable and had forfeited a weapon which might at some time be useful. Without that "Citizen Vigilante Committee" card it might have been taken for good old-fashioned gang-warfare. It would have sown the seeds of suspicion; villains wouldn't have trusted fellow-villains; played carefully, we could have stirred things up on the divided-they-fall basis, then sat back and watched hooligans destroy hooligans. And that might have been a fine thing. Maybe even better than the "Citizen Vigilante Committee" thing.

On top of which was the little matter of the head-scarf and the belt from my mac. Personal things. The head-scarf had (I understood) been contributed by Butterfield's wife. The belt was *mine*. Four of us, and two of us had left personal belongings at the scene. And forensic scientists could do *very* clever things; build a mountain of evidence from a dust mote; bind a man tightly enough to deny any hope of movement with a single hair. I'd seen it done too many times to have any doubts. What the hell could they do with a head-scarf and a belt?

Yet, oddly enough, I didn't worry too much about the other things. Barbed wire could be bought at any street corner; could be picked up in any field. Handcuffs? Without even checking I knew two places in Birmingham alone where standard police handcuffs could be bought over the counter and no questions asked, no laws broken. As for the fact that I hadn't masked my face. So what? Two pairs of eyes meant two differing descriptions. Coppers are trained to *look*, everybody else merely "sees". And when you're having systematic hell kicked out of you, you have other things to worry about.

Nevertheless . . .

All in all, the planning had been very sloppy. Thanks to Badger the opportunity had been gift-wrapped. The timing had worked out beautifully, but that had been blind good fortune rather than a careful scrutiny of what *might* happen. And the sheer unexpectedness of the attack had given us edge enough to get away with it.

Next time — and there had to *be* a next time — things had to be different. Very different. Not all enthusiasm and little cold-blooded estimation. Next time the planning stage had better be the *important* stage. A careful, inch-by-inch, minute-by-minute examination of what could go wrong, followed by detailed back-up plans and by-pass plans to handle things when they *did* go wrong. We'd counted on luck and this time luck had been with us. But that's not the professional way. With the professional, the only luck worthy of contemplation is bad luck, and bad luck is a very important factor. Bad luck, and what it might lead to, followed by a think-out of countering the possible result of that bad luck . . . that's what *really* takes the time in a good briefing. Smack a man in the mouth. It doesn't end there. What if you miss? What if the angle's wrong? What if he swings at you first? What if he's a bigger man than you thought he was? Those sort of questions — scores of them — they're asked and examined at any briefing worthy of the name and we hadn't asked *one*.

Christ, had we been lucky!

The coffee was cold and the cheroot had burned itself into ash before I got round to thinking about Badger. Detective Chief Superintendent Badger.

Now *there* was a man. There was a perambulating question mark. Good cop? Bad cop? Cunning cop — that without question — but that wasn't the same thing. He knew things. Knew things about me, but that was understandable. A man newly out of prison — ex-high-ranking police officer, or what the hell he was — the local Head of CID *should* know things about him. Things but not *everything*. Even an ex-con was entitled to some degree of privacy. Was allowed to make decisions, without being led up a strange garden path by the nose. Even an ex-con.

I smiled a slightly sardonic smile and, on the off chance that his wraith might be within listening distance, murmured, 'Henry Collins, why did you get yourself mugged? If you had to die, why didn't you die in bed like any decent, God-fearing man? Why in hell did you drop me on this particular griddle?'

I was in bed before midnight and up before seven. It was Sunday, March 7th and, on an impulse, I decided to go to church. No, I wasn't getting religious twinges, but for three years I'd attended Sunday morning hymn-singing (which is what it boiled down to) as a means of off-setting the grinding monotony of prison life. It hadn't, of course, it had merely become one more tiny part of that monotony. Nevertheless, I dressed with moderate care and walked to the nearest church, because . . .

Well, *because*.

I think my private prayers included a quiet chat with a woman who was no longer around; a woman who, alive or dead, was still my wife. Who always would be. I think I asked her to stay close, and do all she could to prevent this silly old duffer who happened to be her husband from making too big a fool of himself. I didn't take the wine and wafers; maybe I didn't feel "pure" enough, but on the other hand maybe *my* brand of religion wasn't able to accept mumbo-jumbo as the high-point of an act of worship. I knew a couple of the hymns, and sang loud and a little off-key. I know I enjoyed myself in a quiet, innocent way and, when the cleric shook hands as we left, I thanked him . . . and meant it.

Back at the flat, I tried egg and bacon for size. It wasn't too difficult; I was rapidly becoming something of an expert with a frying pan. I washed up, cleared away and was pondering possible options with which to while away the Sabbath when the door bell rang. It was a uniformed copper; a young lad, fresh-faced, bright-eyed and not yet with soup splashing down the front of his tunic. He touched his helmet in a half-salute, handed me a neatly done-up parcel and said, 'I was told to give you this, sir.'

I thanked him, closed and locked the door, returned up the stairs and unwrapped the parcel.

The note was typed and unsigned. It read:

Returned with thanks.

Two pairs of handcuffs. *The* handcuffs. They had to be, otherwise what was the point?

I had the impression that somebody was up ahead of me. Watching me. Grinning at me. Knowing exactly which way I was going to twist and turn. Mocking me. Taking me for a complete sucker. I had that very vivid impression, and that that somebody carried the rank of detective chief superintendent.

For a few moments there was a great surge of outraged fury. A fury on a par with that experienced in a slop-room when I'd been within a whisker of castrating a knife-happy lunatic who'd come at me with a home-made blade. For a few moments. No more. Then, like boiling milk dropping down the side of the pan when the flame is lowered, the fury relaxed and stopped bubbling. The return of the handcuffs . . . and with a thank you note. Not merely left at the door. Not even sent back by post. Delivered, personally, by a uniformed constable. A tacit guarantee of immunity, if ever there was one.

Like a see-saw. Like a pendulum. Like a bloody yo-yo. The truth is, the Badger character had me going. From fury to gratitude . . . half the time I didn't know what I felt. In the past, when I'd squatted in the chair now occupied by him, I'd bent the law a little. Every practical copper *has* to occasionally. Bent it — bowed it in order to get ahead of the opposition — but I'd never trampled it into the dirt. But this Badger hound! In effect he'd encouraged — even arranged — deliberate lawlessness. The baddies versus the baddies, and it just happened that Badger was rooting for one set of baddies; rooting for them, because he'd damn near *created* them. Not openly, of course. Oh, no, not openly. Come the enquiry — and as sure as God made green apples there'd be an enquiry if things went as planned — Detective Chief Superintendent Badger could sit there with a shocked expression on his face and say, 'What?' *Me?*' And there wouldn't be one flying, spit-in-the-wind atom of evidence upon which to answer, 'Yes, *you*.'

Come to think of it, maybe that was why he'd returned the handcuffs. The one tenuous link between Queen's Street and the police.

This man was good. Evil, but good.

Sunday crawled its way towards a conclusion. I use the word crawled quite deliberately. All my life I have disliked Sundays. The day which isn't a day; the unwanted orphan reluctantly allowed into the six-day family of the rest of the week. Victoria has much to answer for and, not least, is the still-present sense of mild sinfulness at the thought of treating Sunday as a day no different to any other day.

I recall, quite clearly, that on that Sunday forenoon (when I wasn't worrying about handcuffs, Badger and the previous evening's shindig) I amused myself by elaborating upon "The

Lennox Plan for Economic Prosperity". A conclusion I'd long reached; a scheme I'd toyed with for years, and a scheme which, while in prison, I'd mulled over and — or so I thought — perfected.

Forget the days of the week, other than marker points. Let Sunday be no different than, say, Thursday, Saturday no different than Tuesday. Then put the whole workforce of the nation on a three-on-one-off basis. Work for three days, then have the fourth day off. Let shops and pubs — everything — treat every day like any other day. Cinemas, theatres, night-clubs, discos — the lot — seven days a week, with not a scrap of difference between one day and the next. Football matches, cricket matches, race meetings — any and every sporting activity — not always *Saturday*. Not always at the so-called weekend. Smash the infernal seven-day cycle. It adds nothing but inconvenience. And the churches? Fine, let *them* treat every day like every other day. Keep the parsons and priests busy. Communion, Matins, Evensong, *every* day.

Link that with a three-shift system — morning, afternoon, night — in order that maximum advantage can be taken of rates, overheads and machinery.

God! Done properly — done well — production would rocket, unemployment would plummet, and we could become the richest nation on earth, with leisure time to spare. Sunday and all it stands for — the crazy seven-days-a-week anachronism — the single biggest wall between poverty and prosperity.

The idle thoughts of an idle man on a lawfully-enforced idle day.

Then, at just before two o'clock, Mary Sullivan visited.

To argue with a woman you admire, with a woman whose husband you respect, is not easy. However hard you try, however carefully you choose your words, it tends to make you feel unclean. I do not mean polite persuasion. I do not mean smiling disagreement. I mean a toe-to-toe slugging match, with a good and honourable woman who, quite genuinely, believes she is fighting for the future of a man who is the most important part of her life.

It isn't easy. Had she been some sexless, political virago bawling dogmatic piffle from brass-bound lungs I could have traded punch for punch and delivered a knock-out within the first few minutes. But she was Sullivan's wife. A fine woman, married to a fine man. A friend of long standing whose friendship I treasured and didn't want to lose.

But she'd come to fight . . . and fight she did.

It started courteously enough. Despite the gleam in her eye, she settled in the proffered armchair. She accepted the hospitality of tea and biscuits. She lighted a cigarette and gave a quick, tight smile of acquiescence when I politely asked her permission to smoke a cheroot.

Then, having tasted the tea, nibbled at a biscuit and inhaled cigarette smoke, she said, 'It's got to stop, Lenny.'

I waited. I knew what she was talking about; I couldn't bring myself to insult her by pretending not to know the reason for her visit. Nevertheless, I allowed her to make the first running.

'Dick told me what you did last night,' she said.

'I see.'

'It's mentioned in the Sundays. Just mentioned, it was too late to get a spread. But tomorrow morning there'll be headlines.'

'I suppose so,' I agreed.

'And it *has* to stop.'

'Did Dick send you?' I asked gently.

'No.'

'In that case . . .'

'He thinks I left something at the Raffs. That I'm collecting it.'

'That's not very honest of you, Mary,' I chided.

'I'm not committing a crime,' she said harshly. 'I've yet to sink as low as the tearaways.'

'You think that's what we did?' I asked carefully.

'What else?'

'Counter-terror against terrorists?' I suggested mildly.

'It's an argument. I don't subscribe to it.'

'Talk to them, perhaps? Appeal to their better nature?'

'Don't treat me like a child, Lenny.'

96

'All I'm doing is . . .'

'I've been with it as long as Dick. As long as *you*.'

'In that case . . .'

'Would *you* have tolerated it? Differentiated?'

'Maybe not.' I made the admission grudgingly.

'Two o'clock this morning.' Her eyes shone; a hint of tears, but a lot more anger. 'He hadn't come to bed.'

'I don't see why . . .'

'In the kitchen. Drinking coffee. Chain-smoking.'

'It's — it's a reaction.'

'The hell it's a "reaction"!' she blazed. 'Fastening men to lamp-standards with barbed wire.' She quietened a little, then added, 'Lenny, my husband doesn't enjoy being an animal. He's too good for that.'

'We could have done more,' I growled. 'A lot more.'

'More shame on you for even suggesting it.'

She was winning. Damn it, I *knew* she was winning. That was, in effect, the end of the first round and already I was in a corner. Not defeated, but backing away a little. I allowed time for her to smoke more of her cigarette, sip more of her tea, munch more of her biscuit. I drew deeply on the cheroot, then tried again.

'Mary, it's not the same force.'

'It never was.' Her lip curled slightly. 'It never *is* with anything. Old men . . .'

'Dammit, we're not yet "old men".'

'Recalling the days of their "virility" . . .'

'That's damn all to do with it.'

'When Gods walked the earth and *they* consorted with Gods.'

'Mary, that's not fair,' I pleaded.

'Growing old gracefully,' she mocked.

'We try.'

'Complete with barbed wire, fish-hooks and coshes.'

'Mary!'

'Silly old men, playing a grown-up game of cowboys and indians in the hope that . . .'

'If we're "old men",' I said harshly, 'what the hell does that make *you*?'

Okay, it was hitting below the belt. It wasn't gentlemanly. But I'd allowed her to make the rules, and I was damned if I was prepared to let her have it *all* her own way. Then, having said it, I almost apologised, but stopped myself in time.

She drew on the cigarette, looked me straight in the eye and, very calmly, said, 'I'm an elderly woman, Lenny. I'm not ashamed of my age, but I try to retain some degree of dignity.'

'You're not an "elderly woman",' I muttered. 'you're only . . .'

'Because if I *am*.' She even smiled. 'To use your own words, what does that make *you*?'

Women! Judas Christ, who can argue with *women*? They won't *listen*. They won't even concede the simple fact that there *might* be another point of view. All blacks, all whites, no grey areas. Think about it. From Catherine the Great and Maria Theresa all the way down Indira Gandhi and Margaret Thatcher . . . they eat men alive, before breakfast. And some lunatics argue there wouldn't be wars if women ruled the world!

Her cup was almost empty. I pushed myself from the chair, went to the kitchenette and returned with the cosied teapot. I refilled her cup and added sugar and milk, and she nodded polite thanks. Then I returned to my armchair and tried sweet reason.

'Mary, we're hurting each other.'

She nodded agreement as she lighted a second cigarette.

'You . . .' I hesitated. 'You didn't come here for that, surely?'

'If necessary,' she said gently.

'Not even to listen?'

'So far I've heard nothing worth listening to.'

'*Will* you listen?'

She was still stirring the tea. She continued to stir as she nodded.

'Collins,' I began. 'Henry Collins. Never forget Henry Collins.'

'I was here when it happened. You *weren't*. You were . . .'

'Dammit to hell, listen!' I exploded. 'Hear the *other* side. Henry Collins was murdered. That above all. Nothing else matters. That two young yobs felt barbed wire for a while. That

98

one of 'em had fish-hooks in his thieving hand, that they were smacked around a little, what the hell's *that*, compared with the fact that Henry Collins was hammered, took weeks to die, and that whoever killed him still has the freedom of the streets?'

'Kid yourself, Mary. Kid yourself as much as you like. But don't kid *me*. And don't kid Dick. The force isn't the same. It's gone soft. It's lost its bottle. Well, *we haven't*. If necessary I'll use barbed wire to flay the hide from every tearaway in Bordfield and Lessford, but before I'm through I'll have a name. *The* name. I'll have it, even if it's screamed at me.'

'And *that*,' she breathed, 'is old-fashioned policing?'

'No, it's not.' I quietened my emotions a little. 'Not policing, because we aren't coppers any more. The only authority we have is what we can claim. We can't lock 'em up. We can't interview 'em, till we fanny the truth into the open. The only thing we have left is the other thing . . . like last night.'

'Vigilante authority.'

'It's a name,' I grunted.

'Mob rule.'

'Hell's teeth!' The woman's blind stupidity shocked me. 'The mobs *do* rule. That's the pity of it. That's what it's all about. The mobs, the hooligans, the animals. After dark, *they* rule the streets. Decent women — aye, and decent men — daren't venture out at night. Parts of this city — parts of Lessford — they're "no-go" areas from dusk to dawn *and* during the day, too, sometimes.' I paused. I was, I thought, getting through to her. Her face was set and expressionless, but this time she *had* to be seeing things from our point of view. In a gentler voice, I continued, 'Mary, think back. Remember what it was like twenty years ago. Even ten years ago. Sure we had crime. As much crime as we could handle. More than we could handle, sometimes. But it was different. A different sort of crime. Less violent. Less disgusting. The thugs weren't as thick on the ground. We knew 'em. We could monitor 'em, and keep 'em in check. Bastards they might have been, but they didn't *enjoy* inflicting pain. That to their credit. But today? It's sick. It's rotten. Injury for the sake of injury. Violence for kicks.

99

'It hasn't come suddenly, Mary. It hasn't happened overnight. That's the hell of it. Slowly. A steady increase each year. Like a cancer creeping across the face of society. Dammit, unwarranted violence is accepted as *part* of the society. That's how far down we've slipped. That's how foul we've become.

'God knows why.' I moved my shoulders. 'Television. Cinema. Maybe this do-your-own-thing theory we've had rammed down our throats. Drugs, for sure. That's part of it. But, my oath, the coppers have let it happen. Corruption, maybe. Busting a gut to be "popular". Chief constables whose real place is inside a bloody monastery. Apologising for Christ's sake! Forever apologising for doing their job. It starts at the top and it works down. It always did, it always will. The Big White Chief gets wet feet, the copper on the beat loses his guts. And we end up with *this*. Somebody had to do something. *Somebody.*'

'You?'

'Somebody,' I repeated.

'"The Citizen Vigilante Committee"?'

'It's a start.'

'Silly old men who aren't satisfied to know they've done their share, and more than their share?'

'Mary.' My voice hardened. 'Don't belittle . . .'

'That's what you are,' she said bitterly. 'That's all you'll ever be. And you'll get hurt.' . . .'

'Henry Collins . . .'

'Damn Henry Collins! The only person I'm interested in is Richard Sullivan.'

'You don't mean that.'

'Look . . .' She moistened her lips. 'I don't want my husband to end up where you've been.'

'It won't happen,' I promised.

'I won't let it happen.' She bent and placed the cup and saucer on the tiled surround of the fireplace. She drew on the half-smoked cigarette. There was harsh determination in her voice as she said, 'Don't think I'm bluffing . . .'

'I don't.'

'I'm here to protect my husband's future. He doesn't seem to care.'

'Of course he cares. That's why . . .'

'But *I* care. I want your word — your solemn promise — that this madness stops. Here. Nothing else. Nothing else even planned.'

'I can't give you that promise. I'd be . . .'

'In that case . . .' Again she drew on the cigarette, then stared at me with hard uncompromising eyes. 'In that case, I go straight to the police. From here, straight to Bordfield Divisional Headquarters. And I tell the most senior officer I can find that *you* planned and executed the abomination outside the Star Bingo Hall last night.'

I was (and I probably fully realised it for the first time) dealing with a very desperate woman. The female of the species, as Kipling once put it. Driven into what she saw was a corner, and prepared to fight with every weapon she could lay her hands on.

I stood up from the armchair, walked to the window, stared down into the street and digested the truth. It wasn't an argument. It wasn't even a fight. It was a *war*. I spoke slowly, with my back to her. 'What about Sykes?'

'Sykes isn't my concern.'

'Butterfield?'

'Nor is Butterfield.'

'All right, Dick Sullivan?'

'He wasn't there.' Her voice didn't quaver. 'He was with me. We were at the Raffs. We stayed there until after midnight. I'll go into any witness box on earth and swear to that. So will Gwen Raff.'

'So, you've been to the Raffs?'

'Of course.' There was a moment or two of silence, then she added, 'I'm not bluffing.'

'That thought never crossed my mind.'

Down in the street, two kids were sharing a bicycle. One sat on the seat, one sat on the cross-bar. They were racing like young maniacs along the pavement and people — decent people going about their ordinary business — were having to leap aside. A small thing; a minor law-infringement. But where were the coppers? What the hell sort of enjoyment did kids get from deliberately frightening people? A nothing, but it typified *everything*.

'Put me in the dock.' I turned as I spoke.

'Don't ever think I won't.'

'Stand Sykes and Butterfield alongside me.'

'They'll be there. Don't even doubt it.'

'Woman,' I snapped, 'you don't even know your own husband.'

'I know . . .'

'Not you — not Gwen Raff, not a hundred like you — could prevent Dick Sullivan from joining us. He'd be there. He'd refuse *not* to be there.'

'I think you're . . .'

'Loyalty,' I said harshly. 'The brand of loyalty we learned in the old days. Bigger than what you care to call "love". Personal honour. I know. I'd do the same and he's no less a man than I am.' The steel — the ruthlessness I'd had driven into me by three years inside — surfaced and made my tone as ugly as my expression. 'You puny, insignificant creature. You don't deserve the man. You come here and debase him. You think — you honestly *think* — he'd hide behind *your* skirts, while you play informant in order to make him a pipe-and-slippers lap-dog? Go ahead. Do it.' I waved a hand. 'There's the phone. Use it. Save yourself a journey. But when you've telephoned the police, *I* telephone Dick Sullivan and tell him what you've done. And why. And, lady, I'll have a small wager with you. Five gets you ten he'll be back at the nick before *we* are . . . *and* under his own steam. Evens — and what the hell happens to us — this day sees the end of your marriage.'

Ten years before — *five* years before — I'd have had my tongue cut out before I'd have used those words and that tone to Mary Sullivan. But things happened. Terrible things. I'd learned the meaning of hatred; deep-down, gut hatred. I wasn't going back to that place alone. More. Nobody was going to *send* me back, without living to regret it right up to their last breath.

I make no apology. Apologies are empty excuses at the best of times and the way I felt — the way I still feel — I needed no excuse. What we'd done the previous night was legally wrong; legally wrong, but morally right. The bastards now knew what it felt like to be at the receiving end of bastardy. They'd tasted what they enjoyed dishing out. They'd think twice. Maybe, in the long term, we'd prevented some poor innocent from suffering anguish in a hospital bed.

That . . . and prison . . . and Henry Collins.

What the hell had the woman hoped to achieve by visiting me behind Dick Sullivan's back?

She'd lowered her head, lowered her eyes. All colour had left her face and the cigarette trembled as she raised it to her lips.

'Anything,' she whispered. 'Anything at all.'

I stared at her. I hoped to God she didn't mean what I thought she meant.

'You've . . .' She choked, and the cigarette made another trembling journey to her lips. 'You've been in prison.'

'I have a good memory,' I rasped.

'Not Dick . . .' She was floundering. Drowning. Grabbing at any words, in the hope they might be the right words. 'I — I don't want him to go to . . .' She raised her eyes and stared at me. 'Anything, Lenny. Name it. Just don't use him again.'

'I didn't twist his arm.'

'I know. I know.' She closed her eyes, opened them, then in a cold emotionless tone said what she'd decided to say. The last card she could play. The last card a woman like her could ever play. 'You're a man. You — you have feelings. Natural feelings. A woman. You — you won't have had a woman for a long time.' She dropped the cigarette, still smouldering, into the ash tray. She pushed herself wearily from the armchair and, as she continued speaking, began to unbelt and unbutton her mac, very slowly. 'Just tell me what. *Anything*. Just say. Not love . . . not *that*. But the other thing. Whatever pleases you. Now. Any time. It's the only thing I can offer, but . . .'

'Get out of my house, slut!' I snarled. '*That* I can get — if I want it — from any whore in the street. Not from Dick Sullivan's wife. *Get out of my house!'*

Before those who subscribe to the beliefs and fictions of the average romantic novel nod their eager approval, let the truth be dredged and made known. I was angry; so angry I was physically trembling with rage for some few minutes after she'd left. But angry at what? Angry at who?

In the Victorian melodrama it would have been a different brand of anger. An outraged anger. A puritanical anger. But it *wasn't* and I knew it wasn't. We live in a real world, not a world of clean-cut heroes and black-hearted cads and bounders.

Certainly my anger was directed at Mary Sullivan. But not all my anger, and what *was* directed at her was based not upon what she'd done — not upon the invitation she'd extended — but rather upon the realisation that *she* knew I'd been tempted. Dammit, she *knew!* It had been there in her eyes as she'd silently re-fastened the mac and walked with a steady step from the room. The mockery. The certain knowledge that I wasn't only fighting her. I was also fighting myself.

A handsome woman, you understand. A woman who had once been almost beautiful. No gawky virgin, this. No fumbling, frightened teenager. A woman with years of carnal experience behind her and yet — and of this I was certain — a woman who'd only been touched by one man. That's what she'd offered. That was the prize: the price she'd been willing to pay.

And, dammit, I'd almost accepted. The truth is, I *would* have accepted, had I known the right words to say. The right moves to make. Maybe because I hadn't known the words — hadn't known the moves — maybe *that* was why I trembled with anger. Maybe it wasn't even anger. Maybe it was frustration, masquerading as anger.

And the hell of if was, she knew. She hadn't just guessed. She was a married woman, Sullivan was a normal, red-blooded man, therefore, she *knew.* Which meant she'd licked me. That last card. She'd played it, quite deliberately. Knowing that I might have picked it up, then told her to go to the devil . . . but also knowing men. Men who, all their adult lives, have been buddies. She'd played the card, unbuckled and unbuttoned her mac and forced me to either pick it up or discard it. Either way. It could have gone either way and she'd known that, too. Well, it had gone *her* way. And because it had gone her way I knew I'd never use Sullivan again. Never!

Women . . . especially truly good women. Blast their eyes! They know too much. They're far too wise.

That evening, having telephoned and been invited, I sought sanity and peace of mind with Chris and Susan Tallboy. I stayed late, drank little and talked hardly at all. No questions were asked. No probing was indulged in. They knew something was wrong — it didn't need to be explained — but they were conscious of my need for quiet company, and that's what they gave me.

I drove back via the Tops. I was sad; very sad. To lose two friends — Sullivan *and* Mary Sullivan — in a single day is a bitter pill to swallow. The great mix of my previous emotions were forgotten. Richard and Mary Sullivan. They'd gone, as surely and as finally as had Henry Collins. I was losing friends at a rare rate of knots.

Eventually, I reached my bed, but I slept little that night.

The next morning (Monday, March 8th) *The Lessford And Bordfield Tribune* carried banner headlines. CITIZEN VIGILANTE COMMITTEE TAKES LAW INTO ITS OWN HANDS. Lesser headings spoke of "public lack of confidence in police", "a new anger at rise in violence" and "a halt to the law of the jungle". All hot stuff. The two young tearaways were named as Broadbent and Guff and, from somewhere in their files, *The Tribune* had unearthed photographs which showed them as first cousins to the Neanderthal Man. Badger had been interviewed and Badger was quoted as saying, *As a police officer, I must deplore unlawful violence of all kinds. Nevertheless, while not condoning what happened, I can well understand the outrage felt by members of the public at the unacceptable level of hooliganism in present day society.* Clever stuff, in effect saying, 'Go to it, boys. But if you get caught you'll have your fingers trapped.

Even the editor moved in on the act. His leader devoted itself to a sly, ten-syllable dig at police incompetence, and an equally sly, equally long-winded nod of approval in the direction of *these, some would say foolish, citizens who have risked prosecution in an attempt to bring the Rule of Law back to the streets.*

I'd checked the cleaners, returned to the flat and was relaxing with mid-morning coffee as I gave the journalistic splurge my undivided attention. Sullivan would read it. So would Sykes and Butterfield. So would Mary Sullivan. I found myself wondering if their feelings were on a par with my own. With the exception of Mary, we'd all hit the headlines at various times in the past, but never quite like this. This time we'd broken the law, and couldn't be named, and never before had we been given as many column-inches. Therefore, satisfaction and disgust. Satisfaction that, in one go, we'd let the world know we were around. Disgust, in that we'd had to go in at the back door and do what good coppers should have been able to do via the front.

The telephone rang. I answered it, and held a very guarded conversation with Badger.

'Lenny, old-timer.'

'Who is that?'

'You making out you don't know?'

'Are we playing guessing games?'

'Okay. Okay.' A gentle chuckle came over the line. 'Badger. That satisfy you?'

'I like to know who I'm talking to.'

'You read the headlines?'

'Uhu.'

'Some story, wouldn't you say?'

'Somebody made a name for themselves on Saturday night,' I said carefully.

' "Somebody"?'

'Whoever they are.'

'Yeah, whoever they are.' There was a pause, then, 'Get the handcuffs?'

'Which handcuffs?' I said flatly.

'Lenny, don't be coy.'

'I don't know what the hell you're talking about.'

'Up a duck's arse you don't.'

'I don't even know why the hell you've telephoned.'

'Just that I think we should get together again.'

'Again?'

'We should get together,' he repeated heavily.

'You know where I live. You should. You got me the job, and the flat.'

'Not there.' He said it a little too hurriedly.

I smiled and said, 'It's a small world,' and hung up.

A very short exchange. Too true! Telephones can be tapped; conversations can be recorded — from either end. I, you must remember, was the nerk who hadn't pulled down his mask. Badger, on the other hand, was the guy who could organise an identification parade. All he needed was an excuse. He might even try it *without* an excuse, but that was something I was prepared to risk. Badger didn't want me caught, but he yearned to have his thumb on my throat. That for starters. That plus any other plain and fancy gag he could pull. Hence the return of the handcuffs; to link yours truly with the Queen's Street episode. But I hadn't *received* the handcuffs ... not officially. Just a parcel, and I'd unwrapped the parcel in the privacy of the flat. No receipt. No acknowledgement. I hadn't even returned the handcuffs to their rightful owners.

Friend Badger, I was not left on the doorstep with this morning's milk. I was playing catch-me-if-you-can games while you were figuring out which end of your whistle went into your mouth. No way — no way at all — are you going to jockey *me* into a position where *you* can turn the screw. For three long years I have consorted with past-masters in the blackmail caper. Whatever I didn't know before, as sure as hell I know now. One day — with luck before the turn of the century — it will get through to you that my backside warmed that chair before yours did.

I returned to the armchair and resumed my reading of the newspaper.

There was a tap on the door and, when I called, Stowe, the

bank manager entered the flat. I lowered the newspaper and nodded a welcome.

'I thought I'd call,' he said apologetically.

'Please, sit down.' I waved a hand.

He lowered himself into the spare armchair, fished a pipe and pouch from his jacket pocket and made a gesture which sought permission.

'Go ahead,' I smiled. 'I like the smell of pipe tobacco. I just don't like the taste of it from the mouthpiece of a pipe.'

He talked as he fingered dark shag into the bowl.

'Just a politeness,' he said. 'To ask if things are working out satisfactorily.'

'Fine,' I assured him.

'You like the flat?'

'Couldn't be nicer.'

'Not too small?'

'For one person, it's ideal.'

'Good.' He continued filling the pipe, glanced at the newspaper I'd dropped alongside my chair, then said, 'You'll have read about Saturday night?'

'Evil versus evil,' I countered. 'It only adds to the sum total.'

'You talk like a banker,' he smiled.

'I talk like an ex-policeman.'

I didn't trust the timing. The telephone call from Badger, then the sudden arrival at the flat of Stowe. I was in no mood to accept coincidences.

He lighted his pipe. Slowly. With what can only be described as careful precision; an even burn across the whole surface of the tobacco, combined with a steady, rhythmic draw. Despite his smiled remark, the sadness was still in his expression. The sadness I'd noticed when we'd first met. The final, accepted sadness of a broken man.

Very quietly, very sombrely, he said, 'I'm biased.'

I waited.

'My son was blinded. Acid, thrown in his face. I understand — from Detective Chief Superintendent Badger — a man called Kendal.'

'I've heard of him,' I admitted.

'A bank raid. One of our branch offices in Lessford.' He seemed to be talking to himself. Reminding himself. A form of gentle self-torture as he painted word-pictures. 'James, my son, he was a teller. Behind the counter when it happened. He did a foolish thing. A brave thing. He pulled a mask away and saw a face. He — he shouldn't have done. He worked in a bank. I'm his father — I'm a banker — money isn't so important.' He paused, stared into the past, then continued, 'They — they could have shot him. Killed him. That, at least, we must be thankful for. They didn't. They — they took him with them when they left. A hostage, in case they were followed. Then . . .' Another pause then, in a slightly stronger voice. 'A passing motorist found him out in the country. Crawling on his hands and knees. They'd thrown acid in his face. Blinded him. Safety, I suppose. And as a warning to others.'

I murmured, 'I'm sorry.'

'Like that.' He nodded towards the newspaper. 'A lot of headlines, for a few days.'

'I — er — wasn't around.'

'No.' The sad smile came and went. 'Two years ago. Thereabouts. People tend to forget very easily.'

'I was otherwise engaged.'

'No.' Again the quick smile. Almost apologetic. 'I didn't mean you. People generally.'

'You mentioned a man called Kendal,' I reminded him.

'According to Badger.'

'Your son saw Kendal? Could describe him?'

'Oh, no.' He moved the stem of the pipe. 'Not *that*. That this man Kendal was *behind* the raid. Organised it, if that's the right word.'

'Is it?' I asked innocently.

'What?'

'The right word?'

'According to Chief Superintendent Badger.'

'You have,' I mused, 'a remarkably high opinion of Badger.'

'He's a very high-ranking police officer. He holds a position of trust.'

'Uhu, so did Judas.'

'You think . . .' He looked genuinely shocked.

'I don't think anything,' I sighed. 'On the other hand, I think too many things. I think, for example, that you're here because Badger sent you here. After I'd hung up on him.'

He made believe he didn't know what I was talking about. Maybe he was telling the truth. Maybe not. Either way, it didn't matter; either way he'd mention my suspicions to Badger, and Badger would know he wasn't handling *quite* the lemon he might have in mind.

Reginald Stowe returned to the business of counting other people's money, and I was left to mull things over on my own. We'd hit the headlines, we'd made the first turn of the screw. It seemed stupid not to keep up the pressure. Increase it, if possible. But this time *my* way and without any under-the-counter assistance from Badger.

I flipped a mental coin, and decided upon Houseman.

William Andrew Houseman. Go to any sewer, loosen a brick and the chances are you'll find a "Houseman" ready to scurry into the nearest patch of darkness. A born hare-and-hounds type; chances are he tried to nick the midwife's ring when she was delivering him. When it paid him he was a grass; like every other grass, he'd sing if the money was good; he'd also sing to save his own hide or even to do the dirt on somebody he didn't like at that moment. Coincidence being what it is, I'd used him as an informant in the old days, and I'd met him inside while he was doing a short stretch for shop-lifting. At a guess, he was one of the snouts Badger used, but no matter. I had the edge. I'd known Willie Houseman longer. More than that, I knew him coming and going from both sides of the law.

Having decided, I contacted Sykes and arranged a meeting outside a certain billiard hall.

'Be ready for some heavy leaning,' I warned.

'Do I know what we're leaning against?'

'Willie Houseman.'

'No, it doesn't ring bells.'

'In that case, you don't know him.'

'Big?' Curiosity, not fear, prompted the question.

'He claims to have muscles.'

'They make these wild assertions,' he chuckled.

'Half-past four.'

'I'll be there.'

The billiard hall was above a parade of shops in one of the run-down areas of the city. Six tables, out-of-true cues and enough dust to fill a council refuse cart. It was a sort of meeting house. A very minor thieves' kitchen. On one never-to-be-forgotten occasion, a few years back, I'd strolled into its dimness and interrupted half-a-dozen would-be great train robbers huddled around one of the tables planning a very involved wage-snatch, with the whole lay-out drawn in billiard chalk on the green baize. One of the moments of my life. The proprietor — one Robert May — had sworn whiter-than-white innocence and, although I'd know him to be a black-hearted liar, I'd pretended to believe him when he'd insisted that he hadn't realised that one of his tables was being used as a makeshift blackboard. As of that moment May had been my man. A little extra pressure here, a little arm-twisting there. By the time I'd stood in the dock and faced the murder/manslaughter charge Robert May figured me as the perfect mix of God and Old Nick. No doubt — no doubt at all — he'd heaved a sigh of relief when I'd gone down. The odds are he'd gone out and got himself plastered.

Well, although he didn't know it as we climbed the dimly-lit stairs, now I was back.

On the landing, I risked a quick glance into the main hall. Two tables were in use. The rest of the hall was a gloomy, echoing cavern. We turned into the office. Office! It would have needed a Rubic Cube expert to work out a way of fitting two telephone kiosks in the ground space. May looked up from the girlie magazine he was goggling at, and his eyes opened even wider.

'Robert,' I greeted amiably.

'Mr — Mr Lennox! I thought . . .'

'Don't. You'll strain yourself.'

'What?'

'Think. Close shop for the next hour.'

'Eh?'

'Houseman.' I jerked my head. 'He's on the far table.'

'Sure. He's . . .'

'He's a creature of habit, Robert.'

'Yeah. He usually . . .'

'He *always*, when he's not inside. That's why we're here.'

'Shut shop, May,' rumbled Sykes.

'Who the hell . . .'

'Sergeant Sykes,' I explained. 'A hard man. Don't upset him.'

'Look, you're not a . . .'

'No, but *he* is,' I lied. 'I'm just here to guide him along the right lines. List all the little naughtiness you've indulged in, if necessary.'

'Christ!' May's lip curled. 'Once a pig . . .'

'Always a pig.' I ended the sentence for him.

Sykes said, 'Shut shop, May. Get those two on the near table out of here.' He glanced at the girlie magazine May had dropped on the floor. 'Then go out and buy yourself a new comic. Unless, of course, you want to be part of the forthcoming fun and games.'

'No. No. I'll — er . . .'

'We'll drop the latch, when we leave,' I promised.

It was pure, red-neck copper-talk. Get 'em off balance, then keep 'em rocking. The old way. The only way worth a damn with scum like May. Sykes was a past-master at it and, secretly, I was delighted I hadn't lost the touch. Less than five minutes later we strolled the length of the otherwise deserted hall, to where Houseman and his partner were playing snooker.

The partner was taking careful aim at a red. Sykes lifted the red, tossed it in the air and caught it.

'Police,' he said flatly. 'Let's say you've won the frame. Now, blow.'

'What the . . .'

'Blow!' snapped Sykes.

Houseman was watching me through narrowed eyes. I beat

him, before he could say anything.

'Keep out of it, Houseman. You've more trouble than you can handle as it is.'

The partner was a youngish man; early twenties, if that. At a guess, not yet wholly bad. Maybe one of the unemployment statistics. On the downhill slope, but not yet gathering speed. For a moment he looked as if he might argue, but Sykes tossed and caught the red again, and the partner had second and wiser thoughts. He shrugged, placed his cue alongside one of the side cushions, then slouched from the hall.

Houseman, on the other hand, did not intimidate too easily. Not that he was armour-plated, you understand. Nothing like that. But he had size — he topped the six-foot mark — and, although he had a gut, he also had muscles. He could be tamed; I'd tamed him in the past. But on the other hand, he'd been through more than one threshing machine, and didn't bluff readily.

'What's the game, Lennox?' he growled.

'*Mister* Lennox,' said Sykes quietly.

Houseman ignored Sykes, and sneered, 'You still with the law, then?'

'I never left the law, Willie.' I smiled into his contemptuous eyes. 'Merely a prolonged vacation.'

'Lennox, I don't give a monkey's toss whether . . .'

Sykes was still holding the red snooker ball. Houseman's hand was resting on the wooden surround of the billiard table. At a conservative estimate two fingers went as Sykes smashed the ball down on the exposed knuckles.

Sykes repeated, '*Mister* Lennox,' as Houseman screamed, jerked the hand away and tucked it under his left armpit.

'You're bloody crazy!' he yelled. 'You've lost your bloody . . .'

'The mouth next time.' Sykes drew back the hand holding the snooker ball. 'Watch your lip, Houseman, while you still have teeth.'

It had been quick. It had been professional. As far as Houseman was concerned, it had been very painful. But, as both Sykes and I knew, it had been very necessary. Men like Houseman can be made to jump through hoops, but they can't be coaxed through.

I picked up the cue the youngster had placed on the table. In a slow but pointed rhythm I slapped the thick end into the palm of my free hand.

'We aren't playing puss-in-the-corner, Willie,' I said. 'Or if we are — if you insist — it's going to be *you* in the corner, and *your* puss that gets re-arranged. A few questions. A few answers. That's not asking too much.'

'You can't *do* this.' The pain from his broken hand almost made him sob. 'You can't . . .'

'Don't be bloody stupid,' said Sykes calmly. 'We already *have*. And that's only hors-d'oeuvres.'

The truly professional fighters can always tell. The ring-wise champ, the crack fighting corps, the barrister who's cross-examined more witnesses than he can remember. They know when the honey-pot is theirs for the taking; when the opposition is buckling at the knees and things are right for a complete take-over. It is there, in the eyes. In the barely controlled panic. In the very slight muscle-tremble at the mouth corners. I'd warned Sykes of "heavy leaning", and Sykes had gone out on a very long and slender limb. No messing, no threatening, no big talk. Just pain, and the simple promise of more pain, followed by even more pain unless and until Houseman called a halt and was ready to answer questions. And Houseman was nearly ready.

I dug him hard in the gut with the thick end of the cue and said, 'How do we play, Willie? Rough or smooth?'

'I — I dunno what . . .'

'I'll tell you "what",' I assured him.

He gripped his broken hand between his side and his upper arm, winced, then muttered, 'I've helped you before Le . . . Mister Lennox.'

'A little.'

'What makes you think I don't . . .'

'This time, a lot.'

He waited. Watching me most of the time, but flicking glances of apprehension at Sykes, who stood close and held the snooker ball ready.

'Collins,' I said gently.

'I don't know anybody called . . .'

'He was a chief superintendent. Hallsworth Hill Division. Retired.'

'Oh!' Houseman's memory returned with a rush.

'Mugged, while I was inside.'

'Yeah. I . . .'

'Murdered. He died in hospital.'

'Look, I dunno what . . .' He cringed as Sykes weighed the ball in his hand and gabbled, '*I* didn't do it, Mr Lennox. Honest. I swear, *I* wasn't . . .'

'If not you, *who?*' rumbled Sykes.

'I dunno. I . . .'

'Kendal?' I suggested.

'No . . . not Kendal.'

'Not Kendal?' I purred.

'No. Kendal doesn't *do* things. He arranges 'em. *Allows* 'em.'

'Why should Kendal want Collins mugged?'

'No. You've got it all wrong. Honest, Mr Lennox. It's not that way at all. The big man, see? If he says not, it don't happen. But, okay, if Kendal *doesn't* pull the blind . . . okay. He gets his cut. An understood thing.'

'He's asked?' I said.

'Well — y'know — sometimes.'

'If he isn't asked first, how the hell can he blue-pencil anything?'

'Well — y'know — the big things. Nothing big without his say-so.'

'Murder isn't "big"?' I mocked.

'No, it wasn't murder, Mr Lennox. Not *meant* to be. Just a mugging. It went wrong, that's all.'

'That's all?' I said flatly.

'A mugging. Christ, you don't have to ask Kendal about a *mugging*. Just so he gets his cut.'

I was learning things. For example, how crime had been firmly planted on a multiple-branch basis. How the head office, in the person of this Kendal character, controlled things. How the coppers had been elbowed completely out of the field of play. Why Badger was prepared to condone tacitly just about *anything* to regain the initiative.

Sykes muttered, 'Crap,' and I sympathised with him.

But he was wrong. I'd been inside, Sykes hadn't. And always inside those walls there's talk of some "Mister Big". Somebody who's trying to do for the UK what the' Mafia and the Syndicate have done for the United States. Not from the Big City. That's the wrong way; the stupid way; the way that's *never* going to succeed. In America it didn't start in New York, it started in other places. More than one place. The Black Hand. The Cosa Nostra. Fancy names that began to *mean* something. Then it grew and coagulated, then it spread to New York. By which time it was too late. One day it will happen here; the "Mister Bigs" will each have created his own little empire of crime and terror; then they'll fight it out for supremacy — a re-run of "The Roaring Twenties" — *then* London will be taken. Plucked like a ripe plum within easy reach on a lower branch.

I rested the ebony butt of the cue on Houseman's shoulder, and said, 'My friend thinks you're talking crap, Willie. *Are* you talking crap?'

'No, Mr Lennox.' I tapped the shoulder, and he sucked in air as the extra pain hit him. 'Honest, Mr Lennox. I swear it's the truth. Kendal . . .'

'Because if I thought you *were* talking crap — if I even *suspect* you're talking crap — God help you, Willie. This thing . . .' I tapped his shoulder again. 'Applied vigorously and with great enthusiasm — applied in the right spot — could break that neck of yours like a rotten twig.'

'You — you wouldn't . . .'

'Don't tempt me, Willie,' I breathed. 'Don't be foolish enough to "dare" me. We've both been inside that horrible place. You know. What you didn't witness, you heard about. Hard men. Men who could end your miserable existence with one hand tied behind their backs. Five times they tried to take me. Five separate times. *I'm still here.*' I shook my head slowly. 'I'm not the same fat, jolly, friendly policeman you used to know. The granite wall rubbed all that away. I could kill you. Smash you to pulp. Then step over you and enjoy a good fish-and-chip supper. I could . . .'

'Sir!'

Sykes's exclamation stopped me. It was a little like surfacing from deep water; I even shook my head, as if to clear the moisture from my eyes. For the moment, I'd been . . . somewhere. Somewhere terrifying. A strange land of dark shadows and limitless hatred. I moved my lips into what I hoped was a smile, then swallowed in order to moisten my dry throat.

'Keep it going, Willie,' I said in a more normal voice. 'Keep answering questions.'

'Y-yes, sir.'

His knees were trembling slightly. For a moment I thought he was going to drop to a kneeling position. The front of his trousers were stained where he'd been unable to control his bladder.

'Not Collins,' I said heavily. 'I'll accept that another man must be asked about Collins . . . eventually. Let's talk about a bank raid. A young man called Stowe who had acid thrown in his face. A blind man . . . and the bastard who blinded him.'

There is a level of fear — a sort of melting point — at which all so-called iron resolve disappears. Loyalty, friendship, every promise ever made becomes so much mush and dissolves in a single puddle of self-preservation. The melting point varies with each man, with each woman and, with men like Houseman, it is reached without too much trouble. They are curs of the human race — treacherous animals at the best of times — and if the whip is cracked across their hides a few times, they come to heel and hurriedly whimper whatever answers they know.

Sykes and I left a broken wreck in the billiard hall, but we came away with a name. James "Spud" Murphy. The so-called "wheel-man" of the bank-robbery team. It was enough. It was the crack into which the wedge could be inserted and, assuming the hammer-blows were hard enough, the edifice would crumble. Kendal could be made to realise that he hadn't cornered the market in terror.

Sykes was silent as we walked towards where we'd parked the

car and van. A slightly unusual silence, perhaps, but I thought little of it until, instead of walking across to his own vehicle, he waited until I'd climbed into the VW and leaned across to unlatch the nearside door and allow him access to the front passenger seat.

He lighted a cigarette, held the opened packet towards me, but I declined. There was, perhaps, a quarter-of-an-inch of cigarette-smoking silence before he spoke.

'You'd have killed him, sir,' he said gruffly.

'What?' The question (and it was part-statement part-question) surprised me.

'When you threatened to break his neck. You weren't bluffing.'

'I think you broke his fingers, sergeant,' I reminded him gently.

'Not quite the same thing.'

'A matter of degree, surely.'

'No, sir.' He was having difficulty in leading up to what he wanted to say.

'No?'

'A pea-shooter and a naval bombardment. That's not "a matter of degree". That's . . . a different thing altogether.'

'You — er . . .' I raised a sardonic eyebrow. 'You seem to have had a change of heart since Saturday night.'

'No, sir,' he said stiffly.

'That's the impression *I* get.'

'I never had killing in mind,' he muttered.

'Only barbed-wire and fish-hooks and coshes. And snooker balls,' I said sarcastically.

'They don't *kill*,' he insisted stubbornly.

I controlled my rising impatience, and in a quieter tone said, 'That offer of a cigarette . . .'

Before I could complete the sentence the packet was out, opened and held towards me. He seemed to be anxious to make it plain that our friendship wasn't at risk. I took a cigarette and lighted it from the match he scratched into flame.

'You're troubled,' I said soothingly.

'Yes, sir,' he admitted.

'About what?'

118

'The limits.'

'Limits?' I truly didn't understand.

'How far this "Vigilante Committee" thing is going to be allowed to go.'

'As far as necessary,' I said.

'*No* limits?' He frowned as he asked the question.

'*They* determine the limits.'

' "They"?'

'Kendal. His kind. Whoever killed Collins.'

'We're not like them,' he argued desperately. 'We never were. Even in the old days . . .'

'We aren't coppers any more, sergeant. What authority we have we *make*. By definition outside the law. Did you think otherwise?'

'No, sir.' He drew on the cigarette. He exhaled the smoke, then took a deep breath — almost a sigh — before continuing, 'Mr Lennox, I can be hard. I can be as big a bastard as the next man . . .'

'You've just proved it.'

'But I won't kill. Not even for you. And — I'm sorry — I won't stand by and watch *you* kill.'

'I haven't yet asked you,' I fenced.

'You bloody-near did today!' he exploded. He closed his mouth, then, in what was almost a groan, said, 'You *did*, sir. You'd have killed Houseman, and expected me to stand there and watch.'

The hell of it? He was right, and I knew damn well he was right. I was neither proud nor ashamed. It didn't seem important enough to be either. Houseman dead, Houseman alive? What the hell difference did it make? I was after Kendal, and from Kendal to the man who'd killed Henry Collins. That's where I was going, and to get there I was prepared to step over a hundred Housemans. The one thought — the *only* thought of any consequence — but Sykes didn't seem to understand.

In as steady a voice as I could manage, I said, 'You're forgetting Chief Superintendent Collins.'

'No, sir. I'm not.'

'He was smashed to an early grave.'

'I know that too, sir.'

'He took a long time to die, sergeant.'

'He was an old man, sir. Older than you. Older than me. That's one reason why he couldn't take the beating.'

'Dammit, you're making excuses!'

'No, sir. I'm not making excuses.' The voice was tight and hard. 'I'm not making excuses,' he repeated. 'But I'm not judge, jury and hangman. If that's the game we're playing . . .'

'That's *exactly* the game we're playing.'

'In that case, I want no part.'

'In hell's name, what did we do on Saturday night? You were keen enough then.'

'We *saw* them. We *knew*. All we did was punish. Make 'em think twice next time.'

'You have a peculiar conscience, sergeant,' I mocked.

'You don't see the difference?'

'If there *is* a difference, it's so small as to be invisible to the naked eye.'

'Or to a blind man.'

We were hurting each other. Deliberately. Savagely. The atmosphere inside the VW seemed to crackle with mutual disgust.

I snapped, 'Sergeant, you're suspect. In a tight corner that so-called "conscience" of yours isn't to be trusted.'

'Don't lose sleep. There won't be any more "tight corners".'

'*I'm* telling *you*.'

'I won't wish you luck.' He opened the door as he growled the words at me. 'You don't deserve luck. You've changed, Lennox. You've changed for the bad. You deserve what you'll eventually *get*.'

And that was that. He slammed the door and walked away towards the parked van. First Sullivan. Now Sykes. What the hell sort of men had they become? Sullivan couldn't control his wife. Sykes's guts were leaking like water from a punctured can. What the hell sort of *men*?

Back at the flat I steadied myself a little and took stock of things.

Sullivan gone. Sykes gone. I still had Butterfield and in the background, according to Sullivan's list, Bear, Cockburn and Evans were waiting to be contacted. There'd also been mention of Greenapple. And the hint of others. As a so-called "Vigilante Committee" we were still a viable concern, but I needed a little time to make sure no more carpets were likely to be pulled from under me.

Meanwhile, a name had been given and, pending the reorganising of *real* coppers, something had to be done in a hurry.

I telephoned Badger. His office, on the chance he hadn't yet gone off duty. He was still there.

'Lennox?' There was suspicion in his tone.

'Can't you recognise the voice?'

'Hang up. I'll ring back.'

'Why should I . . .'

'You at the flat?'

'Of course I'm at the flat. Where . . .'

'Just drop your receiver back on the hook, pal. I'll buzz you straight back.'

'Look, I don't know what . . .'

'As a personal favour.' There was a hint of hard sarcasm; a side of Badger I hadn't previously encountered.

I lowered the receiver onto its rest. In less than a minute the bell rang and I returned to handset to my ear.

I said, 'All right. Presumably there's a reason.'

'Yeah, there's a reason.'

I didn't want to waste any more time on "Badgerisms", therefore I said, 'Murphy? James "Spud" Murphy? One of the bent brigade. He can drive a car. Know him?'

'He's been through the machine,' he admitted carefully.

'A bank job. Your pal Stowe's son had acid thrown in his face. Was blinded. Are you still with me?'

'I'm still alongside you, pal.'

'Murphy was the wheel man,' I said bluntly.

'You have that on authority?'

'I have it on *excellent* authority. If you know your job — if you're worth that office — that's all you need to know. Pull him in. Sit him in an interview room. If you *do* know your job, he'll name the others.'

Very softly he said 'I owe you, old-timer.' There was a pause, then he continued, 'Your buddies?'

'What "buddies"?'

'Okay, we play dumb.' The sigh came plainly over the wire. 'This is not being taped, Lennox, but I don't expect you to believe that.'

'Does it matter whether it's being taped or not?'

'I rang you back to double-check. That you were at home.'

'Does that matter, either?'

'Yeah, it matters. Short of having a Harrier Jump Jet in your hip pocket, you're in the clear. *You* . . . personally.'

'You like riddles, Badger.'

'Could be.' The voice became flat and expressionless. 'What I *don't* like are public executions.'

Something about the words made me wait.

'Twelve-bore shotguns,' he said gently.

'Twelve-bore shotguns?' I turned the sentence into a question.

'Okay, let's play games. Let's assume you *don't* know. Lessford, less than thirty minutes back. Two of Kendal's known soldiers . . . they don't have heads any more. Four men wearing stocking-masks. A visiting card, reading "With the Compliments of the Citizen Vigilante Committee". Not you, you couldn't have made it back in time. But — old pal, old pal — that doesn't get your buddies off the hook.'

I took a deep breath, then said, 'Would it help if I said, *not* my buddies?'

'Like you've already said, Lennox, *what* buddies?'

A thing like this happens. What can you do? You can't take a patent out. There is no right of ownership. Copyright doesn't apply. So, what can you do?

Having asked all the questions and believed some of the answers, I hung up, sat in an armchair, smoked a cheroot and tried to work out all the reasons. Facts. Four men wearing stocking-masks had taken up the torch we'd lighted in Bordfield and carried it to Lessford. They'd bundled two of Kendal's tearaways into a deserted warehouse, pointed two twelve-bore shotguns at their faces and pulled the triggers. They'd done it within easy hearing distance of a fairly busy street, and at a time of day — early evening — when people would be around to hear. They'd even been *seen*; racing from the scene, then driving away in a fast car, make and number not known. They'd left a pasteboard alongside the corpses, with the words "With the Compliments of the Citizen Vigilante Committee" printed across its face.

Those were the facts. The facts *I* knew. Maybe Badger had a few facts I *didn't* know, but somehow I doubted it.

Which left the reasons . . .

I could find reasons galore. Because Kendal and his crowd had been allowed to run riot. Because the coppers weren't on top. Because the man-in-the-street had had a gutful. Because we, in Bordfield, had shown the way. Because the media — especially the local media — had given the Saturday night episode a lot of coverage.

Those were the obvious reasons. The basic reasons. But other more subtle reasons suggested themselves.

As an example, take suicide. Ask any working copper. Suicides rarely come singly; usually three on the trot and sometimes more. As if, in a given area, a group of people are all tottering on the verge of self-destruction. One of them takes the plunge and, within days, the others follow. Shop-lifting, house-breaking, sexual assaults. Like bananas and grapes, they come in bunches; the overall annual figure gives a false picture; this so-called "steady rise". Not so. They come in peaks, but over the year the troughs don't average out as low as the previous year.

Okay. Now it looked as if we were entering a peak-period of "Citizen Vigilante Committee" activity. It would worry Kendal. And whatever worried Kendal pleased me.

That evening I treated myself. I went out for a meal. On the way to the restaurant I bought an evening newspaper and for the first time I saw it in print. In headlines. "The Time of the Vigilantes".

Tuesday, March 9th. I used Tuesday to contact Butterfield. Without giving too much away, I explained that Sullivan and Sykes were no longer available. He seemed surprised, but not too worried. His main concern centred around the possibility that we'd been in action at Lessford without including him in the party. I don't think he *quite* believed me when I told him that the Lessford killings had been carried out by a copycat group.

'You'll count me in on anything else, sir?'

'That goes without saying.'

'I won't let you down.'

I grunted some sort of reply. Sykes had said pretty much the same thing.

'What d'you think about the Lessford do?' I asked.

'Why not? Two less to worry about.'

I changed tack and said, 'Remember Sergeant Evans?'

'Yes.'

'Sopwith. As I recall that's where he retired to. Is he still there?'

'As far as I know.'

'D'you know the address?'

'No, sir.'

'Never mind, he'll be in the directory. Mr Bear. Remember him?'

'Yes, sir. He's at Lessford. Park View area somewhere.'

'That's near enough. They can be traced.'

'Are we going to . . .'

'I'll ring you tomorrow,' I interrupted. 'Keep yourself ready.'

'I'll be ready, sir. Anytime.'

'Fine.'

Then, having knocked myself up a scratch meal, I left the flat and walked the streets. It was still something of a novelty; to walk where I liked, when I liked. No bars, no walls. Freedom. No screws playing "big man" and throwing their weight about. No fellow-cons, hustling and elbowing as I passed. Just Bordfield. A nice city. A very independent city. It had once worked hard for its living and as a result had been a very wealthy city. A reputation as a "muck-and-brass" community, but it had deserved a better reputation. It had produced artists; musicians, writers, painters, sculptors; men and women who'd won world-wide recognition. As long as I could remember its football team had retained a place in the first division. The county cricket team played regularly on its magnificent ground throughout the season. Its theatres catered for top-class ballet and opera and, more often than not, any plays produced included in their casts West End stars. Its concerts halls had played host to the finest orchestras and instrumentalists in the world. A proud city, then. Perhaps even a great city.

But a maggot had entered its flesh. Something far and beyond the normally accepted "criminally-minded percentage". Something which could — which *would* — eventually turn the whole city rotten. Something that had to be stopped.

The mugging and killing of Collins was merely a personalisation of this something. This combination of evil and the inability of the present police force to combat that evil. This flaw — this weakness — which some Whitehall clown had created when he'd approved "amalgamation". In the old days, with its own force, Bordfield had been a law-abiding city. The criminal activity had been pegged below a certain, acceptable level.

But now . . . The law was being laughed at. At this very moment, Badger and his underlings were seeking out not the criminals — not those basically responsible for the foulness — but, instead, four unknown citizens whose outrage had moved beyond the threshold of tolerance. Who'd had the simple guts to take the war into the enemy's camp. Therefore, the law was being laughed at, and would continue to be laughed at. And why? Because the law limited its concern to motoring offences, and piffling thefts and the like. Not murder. Not terrorism. Not to the smashing of Kendal and his loose-knit organisation which *really* controlled the district.

I found myself wondering about this man Kendal. This self-proclaimed "king". What was he like? I could guess the sort of man he was; amoral and immoral; a lout with something resembling a brain. I'd seen the type too many times. For three years I'd shared a prison with their breed. The "landing bosses".

The "block bosses". Men who claimed power, then went mad. Not, then, the sort of man he was, but his physical characteristics. Big framed? Yes . . . that for sure. Some of the weasel-like creatures had been hateful and perverted, but their size had always denied them the place on top of the heap. A big man, then, and probably carrying the marks of his battle to the position he now held. Knife scars, perhaps. A smashed nose. Beetled-browed . . .

Hold it, Lennox!

All wrong. Monumentally wrong. Men with faces like angels: multiple-murders and child-ravishers. That old word-weaver, Dickens, created Bill Sikes. He didn't make many mistakes, but that was one of them. If there is a "Sikes" — anything approaching a "Sikes" — he's inside. So obviously bent, so obviously a wrong 'un and so obviously as thick as two short planks . . . for every day of freedom he lives a month behind bars.

That being the case, what the hell *does* Kendal look like?

I walked a long way. I needed the exercise, I needed the fresh air. It was closing up to seven when I made my way back to the flat and on the way I passed the garage. Lights shone from the dirtied windows, and, when I turned in, I saw Alf Black, still in dirtied boiler-suit crawling from under the front of a new Vauxhall.

'Mr Lennox,' he greeted with a grin.

'Working late,' I observed.

'Bloody aerials.' He wiped his hands on a piece of cotton waste. 'I keep telling 'em. They won't *be* told.'

'Motorists?' I leaned my backside against a stack of used tyres.

'Get a collapsible aerial.' He took a half-smoked cigarette from the edge of the workbench. Struck a match and blew smoke. 'Not much more. Then when you leave the car, shove it in. It's the only way.'

'And if they don't?' An idea was forming itself at the back of my mind.

'The buggers snap it off.'

'The hooligans?'

'I tell you.' He drew on the cigarette. 'Four, six, sometimes

126

eight a week. Park the bloody car. Leave the bloody aerial stuck up there. It's a bloody invitation. When you come back, it's snapped off. That or bent to buggery.'

'As regularly as that?'

'Every bloody time.'

'Any particular area?' An idea was fomenting in my mind.

'Any bloody area.' He held the short length of cigarette between the tip of a forefinger and the tip of the thumb. Drew on it, with an in-sucking of cheeks. 'Round Bank Street. The parade of shops. Park on the frontage, nowt surer. Unless you've a telescopic aerial — unless it locks in the down position — it'll go.'

'Why?' I asked with mock innocence.

'Eh?' He used the ball of the thumb and his fingers to shred the smouldering ash, the tobacco and the paper into safe mush, then dropped the mush on to the floor of the garage. He dusted his already greasy hands.

'Why pinch car aerials?'

'A bloody sight better than whips,' he growled. 'You catch a clout across the face with one of *them* things. You're marked for life.'

'Gang fights?' I suggested.

'Owt.' He began collecting tools from the bench and storing them in a steel tool-box. 'Terraces, at matches. A folded down telescopic aerial fits into a pocket, see? Fit a decent handle. Y'know — electrician's tape — the handle from an old fishing rod. Pull it out when the trouble starts. Christ! You can put a man's eye out without even trying.'

'It's been done?'

'God.' He clicked his tongue in disgust. He turned and, very sombrely, said, 'Mr Lennox, this used to be a nice town. Y'know, a *nice* town. Nowt flashy, but if you said you came from Bordfield — or Lessford come to that — you could hold your head up. Nowt to be ashamed of. Today?' He shook his head slowly. 'You don't tell anybody. You keep quiet about it. Kendal's kingdom, see? Tell you what it's like.' He waved a ring-spanner he was holding to emphasise the words. 'I'm not an educated man. Never made out to be. These things — motor cars and such — I seem to have a natural flair. But other things, I'm a bit thick. Don't read much. Don't watch much television. But Westerns, see? I like Westerns. Books, television, pictures . . . ⁣wt. And its like *that*. Bloody outlaws. Cowboys and indians. And we haven't a bloody sheriff worth a pint of piss.'

'A posse, perhaps,' I murmured with a dry smile.

'It's what we need.' He took the remark very seriously. 'This vigilante crowd, they have the right idea. Making 'em hop, skip and jump on Saturday. Blowing two of the bastards to hell last night. It's what's been needed for a long time.'

And yet — and yet — and yet . . .

Make no mistake, I lost no sleep about the Lessford episode. Two dead villians caused *me* no heart-ache. And yet I was still copper enough to know that if caught (and there was a fifty-fifty chance they would be caught) the shotgun artists would find that "vigilante" would cut no ice in a court of law. I was still copper enough to give them a bare fifty-fifty chance of getting away with it. I was still copper enough to . . .

No! The hell I was.

That was the evening I stopped kidding myself. I wasn't a copper. I wasn't even part-copper. Not even *ex*-copper . . . any more than I was ex-schoolboy or ex-baby. I'd been a copper. No more than that. But since then I'd changed, I'd become a realist. I was prepared to *use* ex-coppers for my own ends, but I wasn't one of them. I was a killer and, if I was ex-anything, I was ex-con. That and nothing more.

By grabbing the truth and accepting it, I cleared a lot of dross from my mind. It depressed me a little. The stark realisation that I was something other than what I'd thought I was. But (hell!) depression had become part of my personality. I ⁣rarely smiled and hardly ever laughed. In God's name what was there to laugh about? A crazy world, peopled by louts and fools, what the hell *was* there to laugh about?

I was here for one thing; to tame one man and, in the taming thereof, hear the name of another. Who the hell was hurt or blown away didn't matter too much. Didn't matter at all. Nobody

128

— *nobody* — was going to kill Henry Collins with impunity. Not just because he'd once been a copper; once been my friend. Not that. But because he'd been *Henry Collins*. Unique. Peerless. The only flawless human being I'd ever known, and not to be smashed like an old and useless piece of crockery: not without all hell being let loose.

Night is a strange time. It has a magical, unknown quality. Our ancestors, who were far wiser than we ever give them credit for, knew this; they knew that with the coming of darkness mysterious and unexplained forces take over. With sleep the brain claims a life of its own. Thoughts gather and travel along corridors crowded with emotions and passions beyond recognition of waking hours. They fatten; they become more than thoughts; they become ideas, then certainties. In the course thereof, they spawn dreams. Sometimes good dreams. Sometimes bad dreams. Sometimes nightmares. Often dreams beyond recall.

But with awakening there comes a knowledge which was not there with the closing of the eyes.

On the morning of Wednesday, March 10, I awoke with the knowledge that I was mad. Not crazy mad. Not straw-in-the-hair mad. Not even certifiably mad. But, nevertheless, enough out of plumb to need to watch myself; to acknowledge the undoubted fact that those three years inside, plus all the keyed-up nervousness which comes with the certainty that you're surrounded on all sides by enemies, had marked me.

Strangely, it was quite a relief. This knowledge that I was a little unstable. That nobody — not even myself — could be absolutely sure of what I might do in any given circumstances. In an odd way, it eliminated fear. Or, to be strictly accurate, it explained why I'd never *experienced* fear. In Cross King Street in the billiard hall personal fear — even a feeling of trepidation — had been absent. That the albeit unplanned killing of the two men in Lessford, and the possibility that I might not have had an alibi acceptable to Badger had caused me no real concern. The ultimate *was* death. The only real — the only real logical — answer to Kendal, and the stranglehold he seemed to have on the district, was elimination. And, by the same token, elimination was the only acceptable price to be paid for the murder of Henry Collins.

I was not, therefore, unduly perturbed when an agitated Badger telephoned me and demanded impossible answers to ridiculous questions.

'Last night, Lennox. Where were you?'

'Last night?'

'As near as we can estimate, three o'clock this morning?'

'In bed. Asleep.'

'Alone?'

'Is it important?'

'You bet your damn sweet life it's important.'

'Quieten down, Badger,' I warned. 'I'm not some grass-green recruit you're trying to impress.'

'Lennox, I'm in no mood for . . .'

'Nor am I. Cool down or this receiver goes back on its rest.'

There was a moment's silence. Presumably he was re-stacking his cards a little.

In a low, hard voice he said, 'Lessford. Last night, we estimate at about three o'clock. Two more were killed. Hanged.'

'Kendal's "soldiers"?' I almost chuckled.

'Another visiting card. The usual "citizen vigilante" crap.'

'People seem to have had enough,' I observed.

'*I've* had enough.'

'So?'

'I want to know where *you* were, Lennox.'

'I've already told you.'

'You can prove that?'

'I don't have to prove it, Badger,' I teased. 'That's your job. If you don't believe me, you have problems.'

'A get-together,' he snarled.

'I beg your pardon.'

'You and me. Off the record.'

'What good would it do?'

'Lennox, I don't go for having goddam streets littered with stiffs. All this vigilante crap. No way am I gonna . . .'

130

'Shove it, Badger,' I said gently.

'Look . . .'

'No, *you* look. You had me tabbed as a ready-made patsy. This job. This house. Collins and what happened to him. Kendal's too big for you. Somewhere you put a foot wrong, and *allowed* him to grow. *Allowed* him to become too big. I was a possible answer. Feed me enough moonshine, come the old-timer talk often enough and *I'd* shove a hand in the fire and try for chestnuts. Now even that's scaring you.' I paused, then very quietly said, 'Don't get together with me, Badger. Get together with Kendal . . . at a guess, he's as scared as you are,' then I rang off.

That telephone conversation had been all I needed. Now I knew. I'd started something big; something big enough to topple Kendal and if, at the same time, it toppled Badger, who the hell cared? For the moment I was king of the castle and if I watched my step I'd *stay* king of the castle until *I* decided to step down.

That evening Butterfield and I worked together.

During the day I drove south as far as Huddersfield and made the purchases I needed. I collected Butterfield as he left the office where he worked. Out in the country, on a deserted lay-by, we spread sacking under the offside wing of the VW and went to work. We worked carefully and slowly by the light of the torch. We both knew enough about electricity to know we didn't know it all, therefore we had to be damn sure of each step.

'That's it, then,' said Butterfield as he pushed himself upright. 'The socket's marked. Make sure we only use brown wire — with red if it's old wiring — it *must* work.'

We drove back to Bordfield, I parked the car and waited while Butterfield scouted the rear of the parade of shops in Round Bank Street. He was away all of twenty minutes, and I began to worry. I'd have been happier with Sykes, but Sykes had developed a belated conscience. Dick Sullivan was wife-dominated, so I had to be satisfied with Butterfield, and at least Butterfield had enthusiasm.

I was tetchy when at last he returned and climbed into the VW.

'You've taken your time,' I complained.

'It's fitted up and ready.' He seemed unaware of my irritation. 'There's a hardware shop. Round the back — in the yard — there's a window. It didn't take much forcing and I've been inside. The main switch — junction-box, fuses, everything — about head-level on the right by the front door.' He grinned his delight. 'All the tools — everything — there at hand. I've switched off the juice and left the wire ready. A pair of pliers. I've left them on the floor behind the door. All you have to do is twist the two ends together.'

'How do we get the wire out?' I asked.

'Letter box. Low down in the door. I've carried some old cartons round from the yard. Stacked in the doorway, they'll hide the wire.'

I put some more questions to him. Some necessary, but most of them unnecessary. The truth is, I sought fault. Even small fault would have satisfied, but I could find none. It annoyed me. Made me cross and a little sulky. Don't ask me why. I should have been satisfied. Delighted. I wasn't . . . that's all.

I was scowling unnecessary irritation as I drove the car to the parade of shops; as I reversed it across the pavement and onto the tarmac apron in front of the hardware shop; as I parked it firmly in position and carefully locked both doors. The aerial was there on the front mudguard swaying gently and catching the reflection from the street lamp less than twenty yards away. It was a perfect lure. Perfect! And some of the annoyance left me.

I kept watch on the deserted street while Butterfield bent, plugged the socket in beneath the wing of the VW, tossed the wire towards the rear of the car, squeezed into the space between the rear bumper and the shallow entrance, coiled the wire and threaded it through the low letter box, then arranged cartons to hide the short length of wire between the rear of the car and the door. His slight breathlessness was proof of his mounting excitement.

'Easy,' I warned. 'We're here early for a purpose. We may have to wait for hours.'

'I'm okay.' He nodded towards the maw of an unlit alley at an angle across the street. 'I'll be in there. There's an unoccupied house. First one on the right. Condemned, I think. I can get in through the window.'

I estimated the sight-line between the alley and the door of the hardware shop.

'You'll see the torch, sir,' he assured me. 'And I've a good view of the car.'

I grunted approval and made my way towards the rear of the shops. As promised, there was a window open and I had no difficulty in climbing into the store-room. It had a faint smell of detergent and carbolic soap and, from some unseen corner, I heard the tiny scurry of mice hurrying for cover. I wore gloves — I'd snapped them on as I'd sought the correct yard — black leather gloves, well-fitting enough to give me free movement of the fingers without being clumsy. I waited for my eyes to become accustomed to the near-darkness, then I moved a few boxes and cartons to give a clear and speedy path back to the window.

In the front of the shop I found the main switch-box, as Butterfield had promised. The thick, scarlet-covered wire leading from the switch and disconnected from the fuse-box. There was only one main switch; an old-fashioned, black metal affair with the lever in the "Off" position.

Odd. I felt no excitement. Neither satisfaction nor dissatisfaction. A job to be done. No more than that. One more step to be taken, before a determined goal could be reached.

I touched the pliers with the toe of my shoe. They were where Butterfield had said. I uncoiled the heavy wire he'd threaded through the letter box, picked up the pliers, took the bared end and twisted a firm conncection with the bared end of the wire leading from the meter. For a moment — for one split-second — I hesitated. What if the wire from the meter was still live? What if . . .

The touch of fear lasted no time at all. Butterfield had already handled the wires. They *had* to be dead, otherwise he would have been. The thought — the realisation — made me chuckle quietly. A play of words. A gentle joke. The exposed wire; the wire or Butterfield had to be dead, and Butterfield was still alive and waiting for my signal.

I tapped gently on the glass of the door to indicate that I was ready then, from the gloom of the shop, watched him cross the street and disappear into the alley opposite.

From then on, it was a waiting game. What else? It *had* to be. We might not even be lucky. Black, the garage proprietor, had named Round Bank Street and its parade of shops as a place where car aerials were regularly stolen and, other than the VW, at least four cars were parked on the tarmac apron fronting the shops. None of them had aerials showing, therefore if an aerial was to be stolen this night it would be the one on the VW. Nevertheless, there was no guarantee. We'd baited the trap. All we could do now was wait and hope.

At around nine o'clock the weather eased itself into a steady drizzle. Typical March weather. None of the "in-like-a-lion-out-like-a-lamb" garbage, so beloved of weather-lore experts. March is a miserable month; a dark and damp month. The dog-end of winter, with yet no real promise of spring. Like that evening, with the fine rain coming down in lazy clouds, soaking everything and yet without the slight saving grace of the hint of exuberance which accompanies a genuine downpour. Creeping, secretive weather. Gutless. A scavenger, crawling from its hiding place to pick the bones left by the furies of true winter.

People and vehicles passed. It wasn't a particularly busy road, nevertheless cars and vans drove by and their tyres hissed on the damp road surface. Pedestrians, too. Sometimes singly, sometimes in pairs, sometimes in small groups. Hurrying to hide themselves from the weather, but never pausing or even glancing at the cars parked on the tarmac apron.

I remembered the old days. The days before the terrible days. It had gone under the official title of surveillance. Some tip-off. Perhaps genuine, perhaps a minor con, in order to tease the price of a few drinks from a gullible detective. Perhaps even a deliberately planted snippet of false information, in the hope of drawing the police to a spot well away from the planned crime. It mattered not at all. Surveillance had been necessary . . . just in case. And some of the places we'd watched from! I remembered a railway tunnel, one end of which flanked a tiny station. December

134

and a wind with filed teeth funnelled through the tunnel and damn near freezing us to death. Four of us — two men from the railway police and two miserable detective constables from the county constabulary — huddled in the darkness, watching for some light-fingered porter to nip from the warmth of the staff room and heip himself to the contents of a handily-placed packing case. Or another time, hidden in a workman's hut, way and gone to hell . . .

I heard them before I saw them. Shouting voices approaching. Noisy, argumentative voices raised by young men or youths, obviously out for trouble. I glanced at the luminous dial of my watch — one more automatic reaction from the old days — and saw that it was a few minutes after ten o'clock. The time did much to verify the opinion. Booze-noise. Young louts carrying a skinful and out for trouble. At a guess, on their way to some other public house, having already ruined the evening at others.

Then I saw them. Skinhead types, complete with drainpipe trousers and bovver boots. Yelling and weaving their way nearer. Grabbing and drinking from what seemed to be a bottle of whisky. The type . . . *exactly* the type we were waiting for.

I raised my gloved hand to the lever of the main switch.

As they drew level with the window of the hardware shop one of them bent his head back and tipped the last drop of booze down his throat. He staggered a little, then deliberately hurled the empty bottle at the hardware shop. The plate glass shattered, and a companion weaved across the tarmac apron and heeled the broken glass into needle-pointed, razor-sharp teeth. A third spotted the aerial and broke into a staggering run.

I watched the darkened alley and, as the torch flashed, I slammed the main switch lever to the on position.

It was horrifyingly beautiful. What they deserved. *Exactly* what they deserved. The fuse-box seemed to explode with blue-white light and, at the same time, I heard a lout scream. What killed him I don't know. In effect, he was killed twice. The surge of electricity, as he grasped the aerial *must* have killed him, but it also threw him backwards, turned him and he fell face-forward into the smashed window. The point of one of the shards penetrated his neck, and as he flopped the edge of the plate-glass damn near decapitated him.

That was as much as I allowed myself to see. I looped the wire around my hand and tugged the bare ends free from each other. Then the other end; yanking the wire in through the letter box, and at the same time pulling the plug from the socket beneath the wing of the VW. Then, with the wire in an untidy bundle under one arm, out of the shop, across the store-room and through the open window. The thought passed through my mind that, with the sudden voltage of electricty which must have ripped through the metal of the car, damage might have been done to the engine. I didn't know. My ignorance, as far as motor mechanics was concerned, was just about absolute. But, strangely, it didn't seem to matter. Not even day-at-a-time. Minute-at-a-time was my present time-scale and if the car wouldn't start that was something we'd handle when that minute arrived.

Other than Butterfield, standing ready alongside the VW, Round Bank Street was deserted. The undoubted corpse sprawled in and out of the window and blood was spreading like a miniature lake around his twisted, jeans-covered legs. I touched the metal of the car, experimentally. Nothing. Not even a tingle. The aerial was twisted and discoloured.

In a remarkably calm voice, Butterfield said, 'I've left the visiting card.'

'Good.'

I unlocked the door of the car, climbed inside, leaned over to unlock the nearside door, then pushed the key into the ignition and turned. The engine burst into life, as if it was as eager to leave the scene as we were. I tossed the wire into the back and, as Butterfield climbed aboard, reversed onto the road and drove away.

We used the same lay-by. Having disconnected the socket and removed the ruined metal, we twisted everything — socket, plug, aerial and wire — into as tight a ball as possible, then shoved it well into the hedge-bottom alongside the lay-by.

Back in the car I checked my watch. Not yet eleven o'clock. I took out my wallet and peeled ten five-pound notes from one of the compartments.

'Married?' I asked gruffly.

'Separated.'

'Take this.' I handed him the notes as I turned the ignition key. 'I'll drop you off. Find yourself a whore . . . fast. I'll drop you off. You've been with her since just before ten.'

'Look, I . . .'

'Fifty quid. Give her a night she'll remember . . . and make sure she *does* remember. And that it started before ten o'clock. Get the details and the timing right. Everything! Then enjoy yourself.'

'Because . . .' He took the money and stuffed it into an inside pocket. He moistened his lips and said, 'Because it's murder?'

'Murder be damned.' I wound the VW up to a steady fifty-five/sixty and headed for the city centre. 'Suicide, what else? If he'd kept his thieving hands away from that aerial . . .' The rear-mounted engine hammered its throb into my brain. 'Then there's the bottle. Fingerprints galore. Badger should have a bean-feast.'

'You — er — you don't like Badger, do you, sir?' he ventured.

'Don't call me "sir". I don't hold the rank,' I fenced.

'Nevertheless . . .'

'Butterfield, I neither like him nor dislike him.' I braked and waited for traffic lights to change as I continued, 'He isn't important enough. To like a man — to *dis*like a man — there has to be a sense of communication. You have to care one way or the other. I don't.' The lights switched to green and I eased the VW forward. 'If Badger could do his job — if he'd ever been *able* to do his job — tonight's episode wouldn't have been necessary. To me, therefore, Badger is unimportant. Insignificant. Beyond notice . . . *below* notice. He is certainly far too unimportant to either like or dislike.'

'Oh!' He gave a quick, nervous laugh. 'Still, as you say, he'll have fun and games with those fingerprints.'

'Quite,' I grunted.

And other fingerprints. (Although I thought it unwise to remind him of this fact). Fingerprints inside the shop.

Fingerprints on the frame and glass of the forced window at the rear. Fingerpriints in and around the main switch complex. Lots and lots of fingerprints . . . all of them Butterfield's.

I hoped he'd find some street-walker ready to co-operate.

I think it was Wilde who remarked that there is no sin except stupidity. I tend to agree. Mere ignorance is something which can be rectified. Stupidity is part of a man's nature. And for an ex-policeman — even for an ex-policeman who couldn't stand the pace — Butterfield was stupid. Mcnumentally stupid.

Fingerprints, for God's sake! Even a man or woman whose relationship with real crime stops short at the puzzles of the excellent Miss Christie knows about fingerprints. Fingerprints are more certain that handwriting. They are more absolute than any signature. They are identification, free of all doubts or restrictions or conditions.

Butterfield had left his fingerprints. He *must* have left his fingerprints. And whatever else he was or was not, Badger had sense enough to search and eventually find.

Oh yes, I had given Butterfield the money with which to buy himself an alibi of sorts. But the ladies of the lamp-posts are notoriously weak when subjected to interrogation (another fact any half-competent ex-policeman knows), and once an alibi is broken it rebounds with devastating results. I therefore quite genuinely wished Butterfield luck . . . with the proviso that I doubted whether there was that amount of luck available.

For myself?

A trick, for what it is worth. No alibi at all is as good as (and often better than) any alibi on earth. It is no crime to be alone. It is not even suspicious. Man often prefers his own company to the company of others, and if you *are* alone — or even claim to be alone — the police have a near-impossible task on their hands. Their job is still to prove you are a liar, but who do they use and how do they nullify that first, formidable anti-conviction barrier, the presumption of innocence?

I was, I suppose, the perfect example of gamekeeper-turned-poacher and, that being the case, I acted accordingly.

138

Having dropped Butterfield, I parked the VW in the main municipal car park. Thereafter, I walked. I walked in well-lighted streets, paused occasionally to stare into the display windows of large stores, bought asprins at an all-night chemist's as a useless counter to my throbbing head, found a quiet café still open and, in a secluded corner, sipped tea-bag tea and munched a mass-produced scone. Then I continued walking. The passing pedestrians gradually changed their type. From evening-people to night-people. From noisy, but in the main innocence, to rowdy and trouble-seeking, to silent and in the main evil. The change in the people abroad brought about a subtle change in the streets. From city to jungle; from occasional nuisance to more-than-occasional menace. This had once been my patch. I knew it; knew its every mood. Given the right trigger, it could laugh, hold street parties, celebrate in great, noisy innocence. Given national tragedy, it could mourn with quiet dignity and without melodramatics. Equally, and if its unclean elements were not kept in check, it could be a killing ground; a dark place of hurt and heartbreak.

That night I walked my city until I was dog-weary. I heard its heart quieten; the traffic leave the streets; the good people leave the pavements. I saw it gradually transform itself into a shadowy, quietly pulsating creature of potential foulness. My city! Gone rotten from lack of real supervision. Gone rotten, because of men like Badger.

A thought worthy of careful consideration. Badger (along with his kind) were responsible for the overcrowding of those terrible places in which I'd spent the last three years. As responsible as any gardener who, because he doesn't spot and take action against some common pest, is responsible for a crop failure. As simple as that. Criminals may be made. They may even be born. But above all else they're allowed. The long-stop against anarchy. Not so-called democracy. Not even the army . . . by that time things have gone too far. The police. Who else? A force capable of drawing a line, then saying to the criminals, 'So far. But take one step beyond and the text-books are burned, and it becomes all-out warfare until you're back *behind* that line. That line is your boundary. Trespass beyond it and you'll be pulped into nothingness.' But where were the coppers still capable of taking that stance? Where *were* they? Organising youth clubs, perhaps? Teaching school-children the rudiments of road safety? Or, like Badger, sitting in fancy offices, content to draw their cheques while men like Kendal ran riot?

Thoughts. Possibilities. Conclusions. A whole bubbling broth of ideas, and it was closing up to three o'clock in the morning when I eventually reached the door leading to the flat. I was tired. My head felt as if a pile-driver had been installed inside my skull and was gently and rhythmically pounding my brain into mush. The drizzle was still falling and I was soaked to the skin; my shoes were squelching water; the moisture had run from my near-bald head and saturated the collar of my shirt. I was also very cold. At the moment, neither physically not mentally, was I a man to be trifled with.

As I slid the key into the lock, a voice said, 'Lennox.'

I turned. The squad car had obviously been parked within sight of the bank, waiting. It had eased up behind me, and braked at the kerb.

The peak-capped motor-patrol officer was opening the door as I turned, and he repeated the name. This time he made it a question.

'Lennox?'

I remained silent. An old ploy. Silence is something policemen are not trained to handle.

'Are you Lennox?' he asked hesitantly. 'Is your name Lennox?'

'No.' I shook my head.

'In that case, what are you . . .'

'My name is *Mister* Lennox, constable. I tend to be touchy on these small matters.'

'Oh!' He managed a quick, embarrassed smile. He was a young officer. Obviously a decent enough person, but not yet wise in the various approaches required when confronting ill-tempered old men like myself. He tried to rectify matters. 'I'm sorry sir. I wasn't meaning to be rude.'

He'd been joined by his colleague. An older man. A man who fancied himself as a no-nonsense boyo. Perhaps even of the mould

140

of which I'd been thinking.

'What's happening?' he demanded.

'Mr Lennox.' The younger officer moved his hand in a vague gesture.

'Oh, aye.'

The younger man said, 'Would you mind coming with us to the station, sir.'

'Yes.'

'Thank you, sir.' He opened the rear door of the squad car invitingly.

'Yes, I *would* mind,' I amplified.

'Why?' asked the elder man.

'Do I need a reason?' I countered.

'If you're innocent . . .'

'Innocent of what?' I snapped.

'We — er — we'd like your assistance, sir,' said the younger man.

' "*We*"?'

'Detective Chief Superintendent Badger.'

'Ah!'

'So, if you'll . . .'

'It's three o'clock in the morning, constable. I'm wet and I'm tired. I'm going to bed. My compliments to Detective Chief Superintendent Badger . . . and give him that message.'

'No way,' growled the older man.

'I beg your pardon?'

He took a step towards me and said, 'You're coming with . . .'

'Shouldn't you caution me, first?' I warned.

'Eh?'

'Then shouldn't you tell me *why* I'm being arrested?'

'You're not *being* arrested.'

'Constable,' I kept my voice low and hard. 'I was playing these games when the original Motor Patrol Unit was using open MG sports cars. I know all the gags. All the "Ways and Means Acts" you've ever learned . . . *and* a few you've never even heard of. I am *not* getting into that vehicle. I am going to bed. Now. And if you make a move to stop me — if you physicaslly force me into

141

your shiny motor car — you'd be well advised to remember that *that* constitutes an arrest. And in the event of you not having good and sufficient cause for arresting me, *and* notifying me of that cause, you — *you personally*, not the Police Authority — will be sued off the face of this earth for Wrongful Arrest. That is not a threat, constable, it is a solemn assurance. Accept it as such and be grateful. Then go back to your Detective Chief Superintendent Badger and suggest he tries more subtle, and more lawful, methods of encouraging any co-operation he thinks I might be able to offer.'

I swung on my heel, turned the key and entered the flat. And nobody made a move to stop me.

Oddly enough, I was sorry. Disappointed. Like hell I'd have sued anybody. All I'd really done was meet bluff with counter-bluff and in the old days. . . .'

But these weren't the old days, and it saddened me.

I didn't enjoy doing it. Make no mistake. As I closed the door — as I climbed the stairs to the flat — I'd have given ten years of what life I had left to have heard a hammering on that door. A hammering, damn near capable of splitting those panels, solid though they were. It's what should have happened. Hell's teeth! No smart-arsed civilian, who the hell that civilian was, should have been allowed to mouth-off at a copper — *any* copper — the way I had.

I'd bluffed and, dammit, they hadn't had the simple guts to call my bluff. Wrong! *Wrong*! WRONG! And who the hell's fault was it, but men like Badger? Men the grass-roots copper couldn't trust to back them to the hilt.

I shed my saturated clothes and soaked life into my cold body in a hot bath. Then I sat in pyjamas and dressing-gown sipping a hot toddy and relived the day, what was, in effect, the previous day. Somewhat cynically, I found time to wonder where Butterfield was, whether he'd taken my advice and what he was up to.

I thought about the youth; the would-be-stealer-of-car-aerials. Not with guilt, you understand. Nobody had killed him. He'd killed himself. All *I'd* done was shove moderately high voltage through part of my own motor car. Nothing illegal in that. One of his pals had thrown the empty bottle through the window. The youth himself had tried to break the aerial away from the mudguard. So — and whichever way he'd died — *my* consicence was clear.

Nevertheless, what sort of person? A lout, sure; but louts sometimes come from otherwise very respectable families. Sons of doctors, sons of lawyers, sons of hard-working businessmen. They're there among the dross. No more loutish, no less loutish, than the scum who make up the bulk. I'd met them. I'd lived with them. The world at their feet and, for some damn-fool reason, they saw fit to fart deliberately in the face of respectability. Not rebels, hell, they didn't deserve the title of rebel. A rebel has, an aim, a goal, a purpose. These mad bastards had *nothing*. Mutations of the human race. That's all. Mental mutations. Screwed up to hell and no damn good to anybody. Not even themselves.

So, okay, maybe I'd done a nice family a good turn. It was possible. Maybe I'd been instrumental in the removal of an embarrassment.

Meanwhile, what of the Lessford people? The Lessord Citizen Vigilante Committee? They'd really had a gutful. Two shootings, two hangings. They didn't mess around with barbed wire and handcuffs. With them it was the whole hog, every time.

I settled more comfortably in the armchair, sipped hot toddy and tried to work out what sort of people made up this Lessford crowd. Bags of get-up-and-go, that for sure. Not scared of the sight of blood. Medics, maybe. Maybe even butchers. But there had to be a leader; somebody capable of giving orders. And what orders! I figured an ex-Army man. Maybe ex-Navy, maybe ex-RAF. But I plumped for Army. The pattern had a certain "khaki" feel. Ex-officer type. Ex-World War II. Maybe somebody with decorations. Military Cross, something like that.

I decided I'd like to meet him. Meet him, combine our two forces and *really* knock the Kendal outfit over the skyline. With the right leadership, plus my own unique know-how, we'd be unbeatable. Soldiers? Did some fool call Kendal's tearaways "soldiers"? Friend, with an Army man up front, and enough men with guts to obey orders, we'd show them what the word soldier *really* meant. We'd take them apart and put them together again on a re-designed basis. We'd make them crawl on their hands and knees. We'd have them *praying* for prison, if only to get behind walls and bars out of our way. We'd . . . We'd . . .

Funny thing about waking up in an armchair after almost four hours of sleep. When you drop off it's the most comfortable place in the world. When you wake it feels as if you've been sleeping on a bag of hammers. The cushions and springs are like concrete. Your body feels as if it's bruised all over.

It was too early to really start a new day, but too late to go to bed. I compromised. I ran more hot water, enjoyed another long soak, then took my time shaving and dressing. Then I went to the kitchen and tried poached egg on toast. It was a minor disaster. I burned the toast and learned that poaching an egg isn't just a matter of cracking the shell and dropping the contents into a pan of hot water.

I found myself wondering how the hell she'd always done it so neatly. All our married life. Long gone days when I hadn't realised how fortunate I was. Poached eggs on toast? Nothing to it. The toast a light golden colour, swimming with fresh butter. The egg, compact and oval-shaped, no ragged edges and with the yoke sitting there asking to be spilled all over the white at the first touch of a knife. So many things. So many simple, everyday things and, as I was fast discovering, none of them *were* simple. Just that she'd been something of a genius . . . and I hadn't known.

The breakfast that morning of Thursday, March 16th was not a successful meal. Not even a happy meal. The memories were as mixed up and as unpalatable as the food. I was glad when I heard the sound of movement downstairs. I could go into the bank, nod a quiet new day to the cleaners, and at the same time check through various telephone directories for certain addresses.

By mid-morning I was away from Bordfield and in the market

town of Sopwith. It wasn't too big a place, and in no time at all I was knocking on the door of a neat little bungalow — one of an estate of similar bungalows — and waiting for Evans to answer my knock.

He hadn't altered much. Slim, dark, smouldering-eyed. He'd been a fine copper. If, as is claimed, the NCOs create or destroy the pride and morale of an Army regiment, the same can be said of a police force. The so-called "officer class" can do only so much; they can lead, they can set an example, they can provide the backbone. But the sinew and muscle is built up by the sergeants and the senior constables. *They* are with the men on the streets. *They* bind the mass of average coppers into a single unit capable of performing near-miracles of law-enforcement.

Evans had been such a man. I hoped he still had the spit and vinegar of the old days.

There was, perhaps, a slight hesitation before he invited me into the bungalow, then waved me to a chair alongside the glowing gas fire which was part of the central heating system. Having returned to the door of the living room and calling to his wife in the kitchen to brew tea and provide mid-morning biscuits, he settled himself in a well-used rocking-chair, across the hearth from my own chair, picked a gnarled and mended pipe from the mantleshelf, took a slim wooden spill, lighted it from the fire and held the flame to the charred bowl of the pipe.

'It's good to see you, Mr Lennox,' he said warily.

'And you. Forgive me for dropping in out of the blue like this.'

He puffed tobacco smoke, phlegmatically, but didn't answer.

The pleasantries were over. The next move was mine and I had to make it very cautiously.

'Bored with retirement?' I asked gently.

'It's what I worked for.' He waved out the spill, then dropped it into the tiled hearth. 'I try not to get under Sian's feet. I read a bit. Garden a bit. It's a quiet life. I enjoy it.'

'A quiet life?' I echoed.

'I have an ambition.' He removed the pipe from his mouth long enough to allow his lips movement for a quick, wry smile. 'To draw as many years of pension as I did of salary.'

'Just reading and gardening,' I teased softly.

'It suits me fine, Mr Lennox.'

We sat in silence for a while. Sian Evans brought a legged tray, holding beakers of sweetened, milky tea and a plate of chocolate biscuits, and set it mid-way between the two chairs. She seemed nervous.

She murmured, 'Mr Lennox,' then scurried back towards the kitchen.

We tasted the tea and, as I unwrapped the tinfoil from one of the biscuits, I said, 'Things aren't quite what they used to be, are they?'

'In what way?'

'The villains are on top.'

'Are they?' He reached across for a biscuit.

'*Aren't* they?' I countered.

'It's quiet enough here at Sopwith.'

'Ah, yes. But in Lessford. Bordfield.'

'I wouldn't know.'

'You read the newspapers.' I bit into the biscuit.

'The big cities.' He placed his pipe carefully back on the mantleshelf and began to unwrap the biscuit. 'I come from a little place called Pontrobert, Mr Lennox. Sian's from Llanfihangel, that's even smaller than Pontrobert. Sopwith. It's a huge place by comparison, you see. Plenty big enough for us. We don't *like* cities. We don't concern ourselves with them.'

'Quite. But once a policeman, always a . . .'

'No sir.' He shook his head slowly. 'That's what criminals say. But it isn't so, not unless you *want* it that way.'

'And you don't?'

'Mr Lennox.' He chewed the biscuit rhythmically. Deliberately. Rather like a cow chewing the cud. 'I did my job well.'

'None better,' I agreed.

'But, y'know, when a miner comes to the top for the last time, that's it. He may miss the comradeship a bit. Maybe that. But he isn't always longing for the darkness and the dampness and the danger. That's something he's glad to be without.'

146

'We're not talking about mining.'

'There were times I could have done without.'

'All of us,' I agreed. I sipped my tea. 'But good times. When we were on top. When we were where we were *meant* to be.'

He, too, sipped tea, then popped what remained of his biscuit into his mouth before he spoke again.

'You don't mind me being honest, sir?'

'I'd be disappointed if you weren't.'

'What you did. When you killed that man.' He moved a hand in a strange gesture; as if polishing a tiny stain from a smooth surface. 'I couldn't have done that. No matter what. That was something I could never understand.'

'I thought it a kindness,' I said gently.

'Oh no, sir.' He shook his head. 'To take life. You thought you were God.'

'I paid for it.'

'Maybe. I wouldn't know.'

'But I *do* know.' There was harshness in my tone. 'Three years in that sort of place. You pay for *everything* . . . with interest.'

'I can remember,' he mused, 'when you wouldn't have said that.'

'Can you?'

'"Put him inside, then melt the key". That's the sort of thing you once said.'

'Bobby-talk.'

'Aye, happen. But now you *know*.'

He took the pipe from the mantleshelf, the spill from the hearth and lighted the tobacco again.

I sipped tea and watched his face from the above the rim of the beaker.

I said, 'We were once fellow policemen.'

'Aye.' he nodded.

'Friends.'

'Never that, Mr Lennox. You were my gaffer — and a good gaffer — so I never argued. I followed instructions. Happy to. But we weren't friends.'

'For God's sake we were . . .'

'You tried too hard, see? All this pally-pally stuff. It cut no ice with me. You were my gaffer and I might have thought more about you if you'd *acted* like my gaffer. The other stuff wasn't right. It wasn't genuine. It *couldn't* be genuine.' He took the pipe from his mouth and waved it a little. 'All the stupid clothes you wore. Silly clothes. Asking to be noticed. Wanting to be popular all the time. Then killing a man . . . now that wasn't right, Mr Lennox. That was when I was glad I *wasn't* your friend.'

'As others see us,' I murmured sadly.

'What's that?'

'Never mind. It's not too important.'

'And now this stupid 'vigilante'' business. Playing at God again.'

Very slowly, very carefully, I placed my beaker back on the tray. I relaxed in the chair, linked my fingers across my stomach and stared at Evans eye-to-eye.

'Honest,' I said gently.

'You asked me to be.'

'*And* enigmatic.'

'I doubt if I could be that if I wanted to,' he smiled

'The remark about "vigilante business".'

'Six dead, so far. Nothing to be proud of.'

'Six?' I raised an eyebrow.

'Two shot, two hanged, one thrown through a shop window, one drowned.'

'Drowned?'

'They fished his body from the canal early this morning.'

'I didn't know.'

'You didn't know.' The half-smile called me a liar.

'*Pretend* I didn't know,' I suggested.

'About what? About the chains. About the sack filled with boulders? About him going in alive?'

'But you think I *do* know?' I said in as calm a voice as I could muster.

'Mr Lennox . . .' He paused to take a quick draw on the pipe, to keep the tobacco glowing. 'I think you've forgotten the difference between right and wrong. You once knew, that to your credit, but not any more. They tell me . . .' He moved a shoulder. 'They tell me once you've killed a man — killed once — after that it's easy. Like riding a bike.' . . .

'This "vigilante business"?' Firmly but gently I realigned the direction of the conversation.

'You're behind it, sir,' he said calmly.

'Is that what people say?'

He drew firmly and steadily on his pipe, watching my face all the time. If there was a gleam of humour in those dark eyes, it was not very nice humour. The humour of contempt. The humour of a man who knows he's being lied to.

'If I denied it?' I asked softly.

'I wouldn't believe you.'

'All right.' I unclasped, then re-clasped my fingers. 'Let's work on a proposition. Not an admission. Just a theory upon which to base an argument. Assuming I *do* know something about the Citizen Vigilante Committee? Or more accurate *a* Citizen Vigilante Committee?'

He remained silent. Still watching me. Still with the hint of contemptuous humour in his eyes. Still puffing gently on his pipe.

'There could be more than one,' I said. 'Bordfield. Lessford. Each could have its own.'

'It's your theory, Mr Lennox,' he said.

'The shootings, the hangings were done at Lessford.'

'And the shop window? The drowning?'

'The — er — shop window could have been an accident.'

'Another "theory".'

'Evans,' I said and my voice was, perhaps, tinged with impatience, 'we're talking about scum. We're talking about . . .'

He was nodding solemn agreement.

'You see,' I smiled. 'You're with me. You're . . .'

'All killers are scum, Mr Lennox.' He paused, then added, 'That's why Sian won't stay in the same room as you.'

'But you will,' I breathed.

'As a favour. That's all.'

'Evans, I don't need any favours from white-livered . . .'

'A favour to Mr Badger.'

It stopped me. It was a little like missing a step when running up stairs; something coming up at you and hitting you in the face. I found myself breathing heavily as if I'd become slightly exhausted.

Evans removed the pipe from his mouth and used the stem to point and emphasise his words. Quietly spoken words, but words I *had* to believe.

'Mr Lennox, you're a sick man. That's what I'm told. That's what Chief Superintendent Badger tells me and I'm prepared to believe him. For myself I'm not interested. I've already said, I never liked you too much. When you shot a man and made believe you were doing him a favour, that's when I started *dis*liking you. Maybe that's when you first became sick. I don't know. I'm not interested. To me you're a murderer . . . always will be.

'I'm told other people tried to help you. Mr Tallboy. Mr Badger. I'm told they tried very hard to help you, but you wouldn't be helped. You thought the force was no good without you. Couldn't function without you there in front. You even talked other people into believing that. An extra force. An unofficial force with you at the head.' The quirky smile came and went. 'You must have been very plausible, Mr Lennox. This vigilante committee argument. You must have been *very* plausible. Making them believe it was justified. That it wasn't mob-rule. That it wasn't . . .'

'Stop, right there!' I almost shouted the words. 'This man — this pop-star character you're on about — this Badger character. Has he also told you about *encouraging* what you're pleased to call an unofficial force? That he's fed us back-door information? That he doesn't give a damn what tricks he gets up to, just as long as he tames Kendal and his crowd? Has he told you *that*?' . . .'

Nobody will believe me. I've told them, I've insisted, I've even pleaded with them. The experts. The people who should know; the people who make great claim to know. *They still won't believe me*, but it's true. The snap, at the back of my skull just above the nape of the neck. Like a tendon breaking. Like a violin string being subjected to tension well beyond its strength. They don't believe me, but I heard it go! Inside my head; a distinct snap, like the crack of a whip. I *heard* it before I *felt* it; just that split second before I felt it. Then, not pain. Not pain, but a sudden deep-down numbness followed by slight dizziness and, for a moment, slightly out-of-focus vision. Then the vision righted itself, the dizziness became less pronounced, but the numbness remained.

I make no pretence. I was scared. Who isn't scared when a thing like that happens up there in the attic? Something had broken. Something had come adrift. And up there — and despite the smart back-slang talk of the would-be-pundits — very mysterious and inexplicable things can happen. At first I thought of a stroke. A small and not-too-serious stroke. The rupture of a tiny blood vessel, maybe. I unlinked my fingers, clenched and unclenched my fists. Everything was working. Everthing was mobile. So, not a stroke. What little I knew — and the truth is it *was* little — insisted that a stroke equated with restriction of muscle control. Numbness other than that up at the base of my skull, but although that numbness remained the rest of me seemed to be functioning normally. I checked. I moved my legs a little, clenched and unclenched my fists again, and was suddenly aware that sweat was running in rivers down my face and dripping from the end of my chin.

But no pain. Not a hint of pain.

Evans removed the pipe from his mouth, made to push himself from the chair and said, 'I'll send for a doctor.'

'What the hell do I want a doctor for?' The question was a croak.

'From what I can see . . .'

'You're blind, Evans.' God, how I hated the man; hated the fact that he could see something had happened. I rasped, 'Like the rest of 'em. Blind as a bat. You can't see a damn thing. Badger's thrown sand in your eyes. You. Everybody. You see only what *he* wants you to see. Everything else? You might as well be down an unlit mine.' . . .'

'Don't die on me.' He relaxed back in his chair. His tone carried no sympathy; no real expression at all. 'You came here to con me, like you've conned others. It hasn't come off because I've been warned. Now do me a favour. Get out of my house. As soon as you're able, if you don't mind. It would upset Sian if you died on me.' . . .'

As I pushed myself upright, I muttered, 'Screw Sian. And screw you, Evans. I once thought you were a man. You're not. You're a bloody monkey . . . and Badger's the organ-grinder.'

Elephants' Graveyard . . . Elephants' Graveyard . . . Elephants' Graveyard . . .

God only knew what it meant. Just that it was there, in my brain, a burden which kept time with the throb, which in turn kept time with the beat of the VW's engine. The legend of the lost valley where elephants go to die; their last resting place, the location of which only *they* know; a secret place, a hidden place, piled high with the picked bones of great mammals and more ivory than the mind can comprehend.

Elephants' Graveyard . . .

Like a pendulum inside the dome of my skull, but at the same time, and almost as a companion-piece to the steady beat, the numbness. The lack of feeling which nevertheless could be "felt".

Elephants' Graveyard . . .

Figuratively speaking maybe that was where *I* was making for. The legend insists that they know when they are about to die and that the knowledge points them in the right direction and drives them forward. Why not men? Why not *me*?

Not the bank. Not the flat. That wasn't my graveyard. My last resting place — if, indeed, that was where I was making for — was on the outskirts of Beechwood Brook Division. A cottage, built by one policeman and now lived in by another policeman and his wife, who was a policeman's daughter. Dammit, I *was* a policeman. I'd never been anything other than a policeman. In cells, in slop-houses, in exercise yards. Always a policeman. What else and why not? Put an elephant in spangles, make it do stupid humiliating tricks in a circus ring, ring it with a moat and steel bars, encircle its leg with a steel band and link that band to a great hook set firmly in a wall . . . what difference does it make? It remains an elephant. Let it be gawped at, let it be photographed, let its slow cumbersomeness be laughed at. It remains an elephant. It doesn't change, because it *can't* change. Small-minded men cannot change it — cannot rob it of its basic dignity — and were it free (who knows?) perhaps at a moment towards the end of its life it would face a certain direction until an ocean, a mountain range or a desert dropped it in its tracks, and walk. Some instinct. Something *it* knows because, unlike mankind, it has retained its original innocence.

I was in a mood to believe legends. I was in a mood to believe anything. I was in a mood to accept death as a kindness.

I chose lanes to the north of Bordfield. Lanes along which I could keep the VW in third and concentrate as much of my attention as possible on driving. Quiet lanes where, if I lost control, I'd end up in a ditch and not be the cause of a serious road accident. Three times I pulled into the side, braked to a halt and wiped my hands and face with a handkerchief. That handkerchief was sodden with sweat, but still my hands were slippery on the wheel and sweat dripped periodically from my eyebrows and interfered with my vision.

How long did it take me? Who knows? One hour? Four hours? I never asked and nobody told me. Half the time I wasn't one hundred per cent sure which lane I was driving along. What can only be described as a homing instinct guided me.

Again, Elephants' Graveyard . . .

Eventually I reached the gate. I braked, switched off the engine and dropped my suffering head on my arms across the wheel. I think I prayed; some sort of prayer to some mysterious and nameless God. That I might be understood. Not loved — to ask for love was to ask for the impossible — just some degree of understanding.

Then I climbed from the car, opened the gate, walked slowly along the path and knock on the door. The door opened she stood there and words couldn't come. Instead . . . tears.

She performed what can only be described as a miracle. She and her husband, Susan and Chris Tallboy. They did things for me.

Things I didn't deserve. Things I didn't expect. But they did them quite naturally. They took five days from my life, wrapped those days in cotton wool and eased me sweetly and gently back to something approaching normality. They found a medic — their own medic at a guess — and he, too, was in mint condition from the age of *real* General Practitioners. He had wisdom enough to know that pills and potions merely assist nature in righting whatever happens to be wrong; knew that rest and peace of mind could work miracles. 'Relax. Opt out of the rat-race for a while. Forget clocks, forget calendars. Sleep when you're tired, eat when you're hungry.'

I told him of the "snap" I'd heard at the base of my skull, followed by the numbness.

He grinned ruefully, and said, 'I could use long words. I could send you to a nut-cracker and *he'd* use long words. We'd both be guessing. That old grey matter sits up there laughing at us. The experts make what they're pleased to call rules, but if you care to count 'em, the exceptions out-number the rules. So we're back to the guessing game.

'Guess,' I suggested.

'I could be miles out.'

'I'll risk it.'

'Muscles,' he said solemnly. 'We're a mass of muscles. Some we can control. Most of 'em we can't. They can all cramp up. Basically that's all a heart attack is . . . a muscle that's cramped up. Inside the head a muscle does the same thing. A tiny muscle at the back of the head. An arm muscle — a leg muscle — if that gets into a cramp, we can do something about it. Work it around. Massage it. But not up there. Oh, sure, we *can*. Shove a jolt of electricity through it. Jerk it into action with a new-fangled drug. But — a personal opinion — the best way is to give it time to ease its way back to normal at it own good pace.'

It seemed to make sense, so I accepted it.

Meanwhile, I rested and ate good meals. At first I was chary. Evan's outburst — his whole attitude — had shaken me. If he was right — if what he'd said represented the consensus of opinion — that was okay by me. They could all go stuff themselves. I was my own man and always had been. Nevertheless, I was human enought to like being liked. And to be liked by people like Chris and Susan meant a damn sight more than being disliked by people like Evans. But it had to be the real thing. Not sympathy. Not pity. One way and another, I'd screwed things up a little, but I was nobody's lapdog.

I needn't have worried. What Chris and Susan gave me was the genuine article, pure gold and flawless. On the second day I was alone in the garden gazing at (but not particularly seeing) the saffron and white of a clutch of crocus flowers when Chris spoke. I hadn't heard him walk across the grass, but his tone was friendly, although his expression was serious.

'A few words, Lenny?'

'Of course.'

'Off the record.' He was out of uniform, and somehow seemed to give the impression that for the moment he was out of the police force. He emphasised, '*Really* off the record. Just the two of us.'

'Of course,' I repeated, and forced myself to concentrate.

'The vigilante thing?'

'We did the Cross King Street caper,' I sighed. 'We started something.'

'"We"?'

'I was there, Chris. I organised it. The others? No names, let's just say you know them and respect them.'

'The shootings at Lessford?'

'Nothing at Lessford,' I assured him.

'Not the shootings? Not the hangings?'

'You have my word. No shootings. No hangings.'

'No drowning?'

'No drowning.'

'The young tearaway who went through the shop window.'

'We've thrown nobody through a shop window,' I said, and spoke no more than the truth.

'Lenny.' He took a deep breath. 'If I was sure. Straight-down-the-middle sure. I believe you. Hell's teeth, I *want* to believe you. But . . .'

155

'Okay,' I interrupted grimly. 'In addition to the Cross King Street fiasco we shot two bastards at Lessford, hanged two more, pushed a fifth into a canal, threw a sixth through . . .'

'Stop it Lenny!' He caught my arm and squeezed as my voice rose with a hint of hysteria. In a quieter more soothing tone he said, 'I'm a bad host. I shouldn't have asked. Then a quick twisted smile, and, 'Not last night, though. That for sure.

'Last night?'

'Two more.' We'd fallen into slow step around the edge of the damp lawn. 'Lessford again. More shootings.'

'Shotguns?' My one-time occupation triggered off near-professional interest.

'Shotgun. Crossbow. Two separate killings within an hour of each other.'

'Crossbow?'

'Nasty.' He pushed his hands deep into the pocket of his slacks as he strolled in step with me. 'No certificate needed. No licence. Anybody can buy one. A North Yorkshire firm makes some of the best crossbows in the world. A good firm. Beautifully made weapons. And they try to make sure they end up in responsible hands, but what can they do? Having sold them, they can't monitor who then buys them.'

Thus we talked. That day and other days. Out in the garden or inside the cottage. Sometimes just the two of us, sometimes with Susan adding feminine logic and intuition.

Two more "vigilante" killings were committed while I was with the Tallboys. One at Lessford, one at Bordfield. On Sunday, March 14th, decapitation, via shotgun, was carried out as one of Kendal's men made his way to early morning Mass. On Monday, March 15th, the piano-wire garrotted body of a second man was left in a stolen car, parked on a double-yellow line within a hundred yards of Badger's own office.

And on the Tuesday (March 16th) Badger came out to the Tallboys' cottage to visit me. Mohammed had had to swallow his pride and take the trip to the mountain.

It takes a lot to bring a detective chief superintendent out in a muck sweat. I knew. I still know. A batch of bank jobs, a rash of rapes, even a mild multiplicity of murders can be accepted without undue risk of ulcers. But ten killings in little more than as many days!

'They're heading for the timber,' he said drily.

'Some soldiers,' I sneered.

'Old man,' he murmured, 'if I didn't know you better, I'd be tempted to accept that as an admission.'

'Lenny doesn't kill,' said Susan sharply, and I mentally thanked her for voicing what she knew to be a lie, and saving me from indulging in an even bigger lie.

We were in the main room of the cottage. A warm, cosy room; carpeted and rugged with enough, but not too many, chairs. Four of us — five including Cat — relaxed and talking of what had by this time become known nationally as "The Time of the Vigilantes". It was after midnight — probably nearer one o'clock in the wee hours of Wednesday, March 17th — and Badger had been brought home by Chris for an evening meal more than three hours previously. Everybody had recognised the invitation as a ploy; as a means of saving face on the part of Badger and, equally, as a means of demonstrating some degree of magnanimity on my part. In short, of getting Badger off the hook.

I was a guest. I played along. I tried not to be smart, or at least not *too* smart. In fairness, Badger met me half-way. Over the meal there'd been talk of Stowe's son.

Badger had smiled his thanks and said, 'Murphy sang operatic arias.'

'I'm glad.'

'All we needed was to find the right key, then he made all the high notes.'

Chris had asked, 'Inside?'

'Murphy. Warrants out for the others, and enough witnesses to score when we grab 'em.'

'But not Kendal,' I'd said softly, and nobody had denied the remark.

Thus we'd mentioned Kendal — or at least *I'd* mentioned Kendal — but then the subject had been changed. Deliberately?

Diplomatically? I hadn't been sure. I'd merely accepted the changed direction of the conversation, pending another opportunity to talk about *my* choice of subject.

Throughout the meal and later, when we'd relaxed in the warmth and comfort of the main room, I caught an occasional glimpse of those startlingly blue eyes appraising me. The young/old face giving nothing away. And yet the mid-Atlantic drawl was as pleasant as ever and, such was the charm of the man, that I became half-convinced that this visit to Tallboys' home hadn't an ulterior motive after all; that Chris and Badger really *were* buddies and really *did* enjoy a long evening of mutual conviviality now and again.

Badger stuck to his Pall Malls, I kept with my cheroots and Chris and Susan smoked a cigarette from the mother-of-pearl box on the low coffee-table before the hearth whenever they felt like joining the general lung-destruction. The talk was, in the main, on the usual cabbages-and-kings level up to about midnight then gradually — probably because of the slow but steady intake of good booze — more grittier things were touched upon . . . and eventually Kendal.

In a slightly sardonic tone I asked about the reaction of Kendal's tearaways to what amounted to an epidemic of murder. And in a dry voice Badger replied, 'They're heading for the timber.'

Then followed the short exchange I've already mentioned and I said, 'Badger, what makes you so sure I'm behind all this "vigilante" activity?'

'Not you, old man.' The smile came and went in time with the quick journey of a Pall Mall to and from his lips. 'I give you the Star Bingo Hall caper. That I give you, because I fed it to you. Both goons give a fair-to-moderate description because you were nuts enough not to wear a mask. You used handcuffs. Handcuffs are numbered '. . . you should have remembered that, old man. When they're issued there's a record kept. Okay, people "lose" 'em when they retire. They keep 'em as a souvenir. So, the Star Bingo hall, you want me to name names, I'll oblige.

'But no proof,' I said gently.

'Not now.' He shook his head. 'The proof — the handcuffs — I sent them back with a thank you note.'

'Therefore . . .' I waved the cheroot in a small, questioning gesture. 'What's the rest? And why me?'

'We're your friends, Lenny.' It was Susan who leaned forward in her chair as she spoke. I think I have never heard such a depth of pleading. 'We are your friends.'

'Two of you,' I said gently.

'*All* of us. All *three* of us. We want to . . .'

'To help you and use you.' Badger ended the sentence. 'You want the truth? That's it. Help? Okay, but you were unique. Straight from the pen but still a cop. That was the assessment. That's what we hoped.'

'No need for infiltration,' I murmured.

'That's what we hoped,' he repeated. 'We — er — y'know, we screwed things up a little somewhere along the line.'

'Badger,' I said tightly, 'you fed me the Bingo Hall set-up. You handed it to me on a plate. Short of a plan drawing and a time-table . . .'

'The contact, Lenny. That's all. The first contact.' This time it was Chris who made the excuses. A worried Chris. A Chris who knew damn well this whole scheme had been as water-tight as a sieve from the start. 'Kendal's men. Somebody close enough to Kendal to get *you* close. And — y-know — you *had* been inside.'

Badger murmured, 'Not a Hollywood gangster movie with real blood.'

'You!' I stabbed the stiffened forefinger of the hand holding the glass in the direction of Badger. I paused long enough to swallow some of the whisky, then I let him have it. 'You, my high-ranking friend, don't know what the hell you *do* want. Hollywood movies . . . the ones where the copper crawls around inside prison making friends with all the cons in the hope of solving the big one. *That* you don't believe, but *that* you want . . . *your* version. I was inside for a killing. The real thing. Headlines. *Killer Cop*. The whole seven-course meal. I was Lennox. Good old Lenny.' I tried hard to keep bitterness from my voice, but failed. 'The fat man. The jolly man. The man who couldn't *not* make friends.'

I tasted the drink again, then railed on, 'You, Badger. Even you, Chris. You don't know. *I* didn't know until it happened. Inside those places friendship doesn't apply. Nothing! Only hatred. Only scheming. Only mistrust. The only friendships are homosexual friendships. Built on possession. Domination. Jealousy. You have no idea. The books that have been written. The films that have been made. Even the so-called documentaries. Nothing! They don't even touch the fringe. They don't even *start* to . . .'

Quite suddenly I seemed to run out of steam. To have nothing left to say, or at least the inability to say it. Inside I was raging. Inside the stupidity — the crass ignorance — of both Chris and Badger made me boil and simmer, but short of opening my mouth wide and howling obscenities, there was no vocal outlet. The hurtful thing was that it shouldn't have been this way. Dammit, they were coppers. They'd seen it all. They dealt it real-life. They shouldn't have *had* to be told.

Susan leaned forward in her chair, touched my knee with the tips of her fingers and murmured, 'Lenny, we love you,' and I was ill-mannered enough to allow my mouth to twist itself into a sardonic, mocking smile.

The truth is I didn't want "love". Not "love", not "understanding", not 'affection". The last thing I wanted was to be treated like an elderly baby. I wanted — I wanted . . .

What in hell's name *did* I want? In retrospect I have puzzled and wrestled with that very simple question. In the small hours of Wednesday, March 17th, in the comfort of the home of two of the nicest people ever to be part of my life, *what the hell did I want?* Had I been asked that blunt question — had Badger said, 'Just exactly what *do* you want, Lennox?' — how would I have replied?

Kendal was part of it, and perhaps I'd have made Kendal into a bigger part of it than he really was. Collins, too. I like to think Collins was the biggest part of all; the payment in full for his murder; the delivery of justice. Those two, Kendal and Collins, but they weren't *everything*. The rest? The balance? Badger was an element. Badger, and the undoubted fact that I counted him a poor man to be filling my old chair. He'd allowed the inexcusable to happen; he'd allowed crooks — in particular one crook — to rule the streets. *Ergo* he was superfluous; superfluous as Head of CID, superfluous as a police officer, superfluous as a responsible citizen. Badger, then, was there, along with Kendal and Collins. But even that wasn't all. Wasn't everything.

There remained a space, a space left despite all this. Nor was it a small space or even a vacuum. It was a space big enough to notice. To be obvious. Big enough for *me* to notice and it was crammed solid with . . . something.

'We . . .' I stopped, moistened my lips and tried again. I hoped they knew what I was attempting to say. *I* knew, but I also knew I was going to say it very badly. I lacked the words. I think I lacked complete understanding. But, however badly, it had to be said; the effort had to be made. In a carefully controlled, almost gentle, tone I said, 'We have to bottom it. To sort this thing out. To accept certain truths. One of them? I'm the odd man out here.' I raised a hand slightly to silence Susan's protest. 'The odd man out,' I repeated. 'Stretch things. Include Badger and say we're four friends gathered to untangle a particularly nasty knot. I'm still the odd man out. You three . . . all police. Two serving officers and a woman who knows *exactly* what that means. Who's lived her whole life with good coppers. Even great coppers. But me?' I paused, sipped whisky then shook my head sadly. 'No more. Never again. That was smashed. Shattered. More than three years ago. Since then even the broken pieces have been splintered. The old "Lenny"? The man who might once have sat here as an equal? He's gone. Vanished. He doesn't exist any more. For what good he is to you he need never have lived.'

'A little late to break the news.' The observation was caustic, albeit deserved, but Badger's tone matched my own. No animosity. Not even criticism. He continued, 'Lennox, old man, what I expected . . . let's skip that. What I *have* is gang warfare.'

I looked puzzled.

'Get to be the high-rider,' he sighed. 'All the other would-be high-riders are working like hell trying to topple you. Like I say. Kendal's army is beating a not very strategic retreat. Any place, just as long as it's in a hurry. Ten down. None of them want to be number eleven.'

'Not . . .' I swallowed. 'Not Citizen Vigilante . . .'

'Old man,' he interrupted, and his voice was a shade sharper, 'you gave the bastards a cover-story. That crazy card you left. The let-out. The news-rags have made this vigilante thing into a goddam crusade. It is open season on any fink with even nodding acquaintance with Kendal. So those who are no better than he is knock his guys off and are newspaper heroes for the trouble.'

'Not ordinary decent citizens?' I breathed.

Badger and Chris spoke together.

Badger said, 'Ordinary decent rats.'

Chris said, 'Decent people don't kill, Lenny.'

Nobody spoke for all of ten seconds then in a hollow, defeated tone, I asked, 'Therefore, what now?'

'Kendal,' said Badger bluntly, 'has to get his. Eliminate the emperor . . . end of empire.'

'As easy as that?' If I didn't sound convinced, it was because I wasn't convinced.

'Old man, the fink has not created a dynasty. Just him. When *he* goes, the lapdogs suddenly develop teeth. The in-fighting starts. Then *we* can pick them off.'

Dawn was lighting the eastern skyline when we broke up. The room seemed thick and clogged with stale tobacco smoke and equally stale talk. Having said everything, and said some things half-a-dozen times over, we trooped into the garden to send Badger on his way. Then, having watched the tail-lights round the bend, the three of us stood awkward and embarrassed in a group near the gate.

'I'm sorry, Lenny.' Chris's voice was low enough to be rough. Almost rugged. The words seems to have splinters in them, and seemed to tear the lining of his throat as he spoke.

'For what?' I deliberately kept the question as gentle as possible.

'When we met you.' Susan, too, sounded monumentally unhappy. 'A new start,' she muttered. 'That's what we wanted. All we wanted. Not this. I swear, not this.'

'My pet,' I said softly, 'men like Badger have devious minds. The force needs such minds.'

'Bloody computers do all the straightforward police work these days,' croaked Chris.

'True,' I smiled.

'More's the pity.'

'Chris.' I was in an invidious position. A killer, lumbered with the task of quietening the consciences of a good copper and his wife. A ludicrous situation, nevertheless I did my best. 'The only way,' I argued. 'It stops what I inadvertently started. It rids the world of Kendal.' I paused, then added, 'It goes some way towards evening things out as far as Henry Collins is concerned.'

'It makes *you* a murderer,' said Susan gently.

'What I already am.'

'No! What you did . . .'

'Susan, my pet, I don't like Badger. Until this evening I didn't trust him. Now, I have his measure. He's a realist. What he wants, he gets. As for me? All that smooth talk — all that "old man" guff — like everything else it had a purpose. Susan, *I am a murderer*.' I spoke the four words slowly and distinctly. 'To Badger, just that. Nothing more, nothing less. The word "manslaughter" isn't in his dictionary. Only "murder", with or without fancy qualifications. Fine, a murderer. He wants Kendal moving from the face of the earth. He's tried legal means. Normal, police methods. Kendal's too smart. Kendal sits there and laughs at Badger. Laughs at the police and the law. And — to his credit — Badger won't tolerate that. Again, a realist. Kendal's created a monster. Over the last few days some of Kendal's men had been killed. According to Badger by hooligans anxious to smash the Kendal organisation. Maybe take a bite of the cake for themselves. No good. No way.' I shook my head. 'We're talking about a monster. An arm off here. A leg off there. Individual killings. A crime state like nothing on earth. No chief constable — no Home Secretary — would stand for it. And no good coming from it, and Badger knows *that*, too. A monster, my children.' I smiled. I wasn't *quite* old enough in years to be their parent, but I knew I was more than old enough in experience. 'A monster

163

needs decapitating. After that . . . nothing.'

'It's not fair.' Susan wasn't far from tears. 'You've been punished. You're not a bad man. I don't care what they say, you're *not* a bad man. They — they mustn't . . . They shouldn't . . .'

' "They",' I interrupted gently. 'You're talking about an organisation, my pet. A fine organisation. Your husband's part of it. Your father was once part of it. So was I . . . once. Don't condemn it because of one man.'

It was all I could say. That and similar sentiments. Maybe I believed what I said. I couldn't be sure. As sure as hell I *wanted* to believe, but oddly it was a little like fighting to believe something I secretly knew was so much crap. Red white and blue stuff. Britannia Rules the Waves garbage. That brand of belief. "Our policemen are wonderful" — yeah a handful, maybe. The rest? I wouldn't pay them in Smarties.

Eventually we wandered back into the cottage and to our own rooms. I kicked off my shoes, loosened my tie and sat on the edge of the bed and thought a whole lot about a certain senior detective called Badger; a certain senior detective who, although no fool, had missed some very obvious fingerprints; who'd weighed every pro and every con; who'd (obviously) come to the conclusion that Butterfield was as expendable as myself and could therefore be left free to perform in the big trick. The big trick. The "sawing-Kendal-in-half" trick, but don't get mealy-mouthed about things. Call it by its right name.

Murder!

No sweat about trials. No pacing around wondering what the verdict might be. No interviews, no paperwork, no enquiries. Kendal stood in the way of all things, therefore Kendal had to go. A copper couldn't do it. It might screw up his Constabulary Oath. But that was okay. Me? I wasn't a copper. I'd *been* a copper. People — people who mattered — still *remembered* me as a copper. But I *wasn't* a copper. Nor ever again would be.

The same thing applied to Butterfield.

We made a moderately good team.

The gun was waiting for me at the flat.

I'd left the cottage without saying goodbye to either Chris or Susan. Without even thanking them. It seemed best; no involvement; a few less answers they'd have to provide if things went wrong. We'd all been conned. Some more than others. Maybe Susan more than Chris; maybe Chris had at least guessed at Badger's motive in organising the big "Welcome Home" gag for the prodigal son . . . maybe guessed but hoped he'd been guessing wrong. It wasn't important. Nothing was too important any more.

And the gun was waiting for me. There on the tiny Formica-topped working surface of the kitchen; in a neatly sealed shoe-box, in its nest of wood-wool, with a spare magazine sitting alongside it. Just over thirty-two ounces of superb killing machinery.

The Browning GP35 semi-automatic pistol. Capable of pumping 9mm Parabellum bullets out of its ugly little snout at a very satisfactory rate of knots. And, unless you're up on ballistics, don't waste time counting the number of bangs; that feed system holds a 13-round box magazine, *ergo* a mere six-shot revolver is very small fry. A good enough weapon to be the standard NATO military pistol. A handgun much favoured by British airborne troops in World War II. Some shooter!

I weighed it experimentally in my hand. Just to hold it — just to allow my fingers to curl comfortably around its grip — gave an almost God-like sense of power.

Almost reluctantly I returned it to its box and replaced the lid. Then I brewed instant coffee, lighted a cheroot and, quite cold-bloodedly, contemplated various possibilities. With or without Butterfield? I decided I needed him. Even with the Browning, I needed an extra pair of eyes to watch my back. To tell him or not to tell him? And, if to tell him, how *much* to tell him? That was a slightly more difficult question, and yet the answer was fairly obvious. If he came he had to *know*. Everything. He must be given the choice, but if he chose to come he had to know exactly what he was letting himself in for. Everything. Hopefully, we'd get out. Get away with it. Unofficially the police — in effect

Badger — was on our side. He'd as good as promised to give space in which to make a getaway; to mark time on the enquiries for twenty-four hours. Away. Aboard a ship. Maybe across the Channel. A day-trip job, where full-blown passport regulations weren't necessary. To Northern Ireland maybe. Somewhere — anywhere — beyond the shore-line. Then get lost for perhaps a year while the police performed the required pantomime. And at the end of it an "undetected murder", and we could settle down to respectability again. That was part of the bargain. The unspoken part. The part hinted at. The part Badger had talked around in vague unfinished sentences . . . like a good sketch artist placing quick, disconnected lines on a sheet of drawing paper, and the end product being plain to recognise. Ah, yes, but Badger! And the lines *hadn't* been connected. Therefore, in fairness, Butterfield had to be told everything.

Which led to the question of a plan of action.

These involved, minute-by-minute, yard-by-yard plans. Remember the Great Train Robbery? On a grander scale, remember Operation Market Garden? Plans are made to screw things up. That ancient snippet of wisdom: plan carefully, then assume that if things *can* go wrong, they *will* go wrong. From which it follows that the ideal is a firm and unqualified agreement upon the target and the outcome . . . and after that take it from the top of the head.

That was the conclusion I reached. No involved plan. Heads down, go in, take things as they come, then butcher Kendal . . . *after* he'd named the killer of Henry Collins.

Odd. Nobody came up from the bank. Not Stowe. Not Curtiss. Nobody. It was as if I hadn't been away; hadn't taken unexplained leave of absence. Badger again. That I didn't doubt. This man, Badger, was a match for Old Nick himself. He could bring high street banks to heel. *And* the gun had been delivered, via at least one door with a damn good lock as part of its furniture.

All this strangeness, all these "impossibilities", and yet I felt a strange calm. A coldness. A numbness; as if the numbness which had been inside my head some days before had spread, to give a

166

peculiar, unnatural tranquility. I (hopefully with Butterfield as my assistant) had accepted the role of professional killer. Unpaid of course; no so-called "contract". Nevertheless, that's what it boiled down to.

To kill Kendal . . . just that and nothing more. The means had been handed to me on a platter. The opportunity? That was mine to make, but with the Browning pistol cocked and ready the making of the opportunity shouldn't be difficult. As for motive . . .

Collins, of course. Always Collins. But (and I was being honest with myself) that was only the trigger motive. Motive enough in the circumstances, but in effect the detonator via which to fire the real explosive. In the parlance of the underworld, I owed.

Three years of it. Three years of contempt and humiliation. Three years of filth and degradation. What had gone before hadn't counted for a damn thing. Clearing the streets of scum, keeping Bordfield a decent, respectable place in which to live, going without sleep, going without meals, working until I was ready to drop — and that for years on end — and not complaining, not even considering it as anything special. All that, sum total — *nothing!*

Oh, I'd killed. A mercy killing, if ever there was one. And I'd been ready to pay. Any reasonable price. Necessary . . . of course. And (as I've already mentioned) the judge had tempered justice with mercy, and four years hadn't been too impossible a stretch. A mere three years with remission. But time has breadth as well as length, and the place — even places — in which I'd spent those three years had been the important factor. With animals and surrounded by foulness. Not an open prison. Not even one of the so-called "progressive" prisons. Oh, no! Each one hand-picked . . . or so it had seemed. A deliberate and continuing abasement. A constant and ever-increasing mortification.

I owed.

And, by God, I was going to repay.

Butterfield hesitated for, perhaps, thirty seconds and thereafter was positively eager.

'You mean kill him?' he verified.

'Ten have died already,' I reminded him.

'And Badger'll let us get away with it?'

'That's what Badger says.'

I'd telephoned and he'd come running. I'd reflected that his employers must have held him in high esteem to allow him to come and go as he pleased. He'd come to the flat, but because bugging devices still held high priority — and I'd been away from the flat far too long for me to ever be sure again — I'd greeted him, touched a finger to my lips then guided him back into the street and into one of those Olde Worlde bun shops where fur coats, floral hats and hearing-aids are almost a requisite for admission. At a window table, overlooking the street and within sight of the bank entrance, I told him. I used as unemotional a voice as possible, held nothing back and watched his face as I spoke. Then I quietly propositioned him, and that was his reaction.

He spread Cornish clotted cream and strawberry jam on a home-made scone, as he said, 'You know where he lives, of course?'

'A hotel in Lessford.'

'The George and Dragon. The whole top floor.'

'Not quite The Savoy, though,' I murmured.

'Not big,' he agreed. He bit into the scone then with a forefinger guided the overspill of cream and jam into his mouth. 'Not even star-rated. But I don't think they want to be star-rated. Very private. Small and select is what they aim for, I think.'

'You know the place?' I asked.

'I've been there a couple of times.' He chewed and swallowed. 'Drinks with passing acquaintances. Men-about-town.'

'He owns the place,' I murmured.

Butterfield raised surprised eyebrows.

'Why not?' I smiled. 'A sort of modern feudal castle staffed by his serfs. What safer headquarters?'

Butterfield mumbled something as he popped what remained of the scone into his mouth.

'Do you know him?' I asked.

'Kendal?' He seemed surprised at the question.

'Know him?' I nodded. 'Have you seen him? What's he like to look at? Big? Small? Fat? Thin . . .

'I don't know anybody who has,' he interrupted.

' "King" Kendal?' I mocked. 'The original blushing violet?'

'He doesn't leave the hotel. That's what I'm told.'

'Not exactly the high life,' I observed.

As he reached for another scone, he asked, 'Do we leave a visiting card?'

'No.'

I sipped my tea and watched him spread more cream and jam. Me? I wasn't hungry. Drinking the tea was merely something to do with my hands, and an indirect way of paying for the privacy provided by the cafe.

Almost off-handedly, he said, 'You have this gun.'

'The Browning pistol.'

'What do *I* have?' he asked.

I stared at him.

He said, 'You've already described it. A modern feudal castle. We have to reach the fifth floor.'

'I'm not contemplating having to fight our way there,' I said slowly.

'Still . . . a possibility.'

'Suggestions?' I invited.

He took his time. I had the distinct impression that he was suddenly treating me as an equal. Not the follower, of course, he had yet to mentally elevate himself into the role of leader, but nor was *he* the follower. It tended to irritate a little, and yet in retrospect why not? We *were* equals. In the event of a snarl-up — in the event of an arrest and trial — we'd stand alongside each other in the dock. I therefore frowned a little, waited and held my peace while he carefully split and creamed the newly-chosen scone.

'I think we'll have to fight.' He concentrated his attention upon the knife, cream and scone as he spoke. 'I think we might have to kill more than Kendal.'

'It doesn't seem to bother you.' My tone was a little hard and

169

accusing.

'No.' He looked up and asked, 'Does it bother *you*?'

'I don't enjoy killing people,' I snapped.

'No?'

He smiled as he asked the question, and the smile called me a liar. And dammit he was half-right . . . and knew it.

'Not just *anybody*.' It was a qualification to my previous remark. A meaningless and silly qualification. 'Scum,' I said. 'They're different. In those circumstances . . .'

'Vigilante stuff,' he mocked gently.

'Butterfield.' I put authority into my voice. 'This thing I'm doing — this thing *we're* doing — a crusade, of a sort. Illegal, perhaps . . .'

'*Perhaps?*'

'. . . . but necessary.'

'We aren't coppers any more.' He took jam and spread it carefully on top of the cream. 'You're not a chief superintendent. I'm not a common or garden flatfoot.' He tasted the prepared scone, chewed, then drank tea. 'We killed a man. Remember? The powers-that-be might think he fell through a shop window and cut his own throat. But we know better. Now you, Mr Lennox, might kid yourself into believing that by electrocuting him we were "crusaders". Speaking personally, I'd say "outlaws" might be a better word.'

'You're — er — getting at something, Butterfield', I said suspiciously.

'Of course.' He took another bite of the scone, then cleared his mouth before he continued. 'We're after Kendal. I liked Chief Superintendent Collins, therefore, if Kendal's responsible . . .'

'Kendal's responsible.'

'I won't sleep less at night if we eliminate Kendal. But common gumption insists that by this time Kendal will be alert. He'll be expecting something. If he's any sense, he'll have surrounded himself with a wall of real tearaways. To get at him, we'll have to go through that wall. You have a gun. You might be able to shoot your way through.'

'Some of them might have guns,' I grunted.

'True.' He nodded. 'Therefore, we need something special. More than just one gun. *I* need something too. I can come up with a pick handle. I can lay my hands on a very nasty spring-loaded knife — blade almost nine inches long. That's our armoury. Not much cop. Given an educated guess, we haven't a hope in hell.'

'Meaning you're not prepared to try?' I said contemptuously.

'No, not that.' He shook his had. He finished the scone, dabbed his lips with his napkin and leaned slightly across the table. 'The first man you killed,' he said softly. 'The surrounding circumstances. That's what we need. Similar circumstances. It gives us something of a chance.'

'You — er —' I watched his eyes carefully. 'You have a plan?'

'Oh yes.' He nodded.

'I'd be interested to hear it.'

'Mr Lennox,' he smiled, 'you're *going* to hear it. You're going to *agree* to it. Otherwise, it's a solo run. I've no doubt Kendal's wreath will be even more expensive than Badger's.'

It was a good plan. For almost spur-of-the-moment thinking it was a *very* good plan. I'd have been a fool not to agree.

Nevertheless . . .

When we'd parted — when Butterfield had left to gather the bits and pieces needed — I'd been forced to acknowledge one more slice of a very nasty truth. A truth about myself, and a truth about Butterfield.

Butterfield had resigned the force, and officers resign every day for a thousand and one different reasons. But with Butterfield it had been for a very special reason . . . or, at least such was the firm conclusion I reached. Butterfield had sought what he might have called "adventure", but for him that word had a peculiar meaning. In effect, he was a thug who'd refused to recognise himself as such. He'd wanted action. Fights. Blood by the gallon. He'd seen the force as a means to an end; the end being a very belligerent way of life, justified by the wearing of a uniform. In a phrase, he'd been a bad copper. The worst sort of copper. He could have been a crook, a professional hoodlum. Equally, he could have joined the shadowy world of the mercenary soldier. What he could *never* be was part of a highly disciplined, civil controlled law-enforcement body.

And yet . . .

Had I the right to sit in judgement? Had I even the right to mentally criticise? I'd killed a fellow creature. Twice! I'd blown a man's head off. I'd thrown a switch and sent an already-dead youth through a plate-glass window. There was no way of forgetting all this. No way around it. No way of kidding myself that, whatever Butterfield was or was not, I wasn't already two up on him.

Back at the flat I gave the matter careful thought.

There was, of course, no suggestion of pulling out. I was committed. I've already explained, I owed. The debt had to be paid, and I needed Butterfield's assistance in the paying. Nevertheless, I remembered both things and people and was sad. Maybe I *had* ended up as Badger's catspaw. Even that wasn't important any more. The strange numbness returned to the nape of my neck and seemed to draw a curtain across clear thought, but I *could* think (in an odd, illogical manner) and I decided I should write a letter.

Why? God knows.

Addressed to whom? I wasn't sure, and it wasn't too important.

In the event, and even after four attempts, it was a stange letter. It explained things badly, if at all. A rambling, meaningless splurge of words and random thoughts. "The vigilante idea was mine, therefore I must accept responsibility." "I recruited Butterfield. It follows, therefore, that whatever happens is my fault." "I hold the belief that the police must stay on top. Lawfully if possible, but if that isn't possible by any other necessary means." "I intend to kill the man responsible for the death of Henry Collins. I also intend to rid the world of Kendal." That sort of stuff, which explained nothing and excused less. And yet it had to be written, but I don't know why. I addressed an envelope to Chris, sealed away the letter, then went down into the bank and gave the sealed envelope to Stowe.

'Keep it,' I requested. 'A year from today, if I haven't collected it personally, post it.'

'Lenny.' We were in the privacy of his office and for the first time he used the word Lenny rather than the more formal Mr Lennox. The hint of a worried frown touched his expression, and his eyes held a look of sad concern. 'You're not your old self, yet. The — er — re-adjustment isn't complete.'

I found myself saying, 'I don't think complete re-adjustment figures in Badger's plans.'

There was a moment's silence, then rather slowly and very gently, he said, 'I owe you a lot, Lenny. I owe Chief Superintendent Badger very little.'

'We all owe,' I muttered.

'Of course. Perhaps life consists of giving and receiving. If the balance is right, the equation equals happiness. If wrong, misery.' A quick smile brushed his lips. 'A banker speaking, perhaps.'

'It makes sense.'

'Forgive me. Your balance is — er — not quite right.'

'I'm not miserable,' I argued, without real conviction.

'But unhappy.'

'As you say, the re-adjustment isn't yet complete.' I hesitated a moment, then added, 'I think it soon will be.'

'Just don't let Chief Superintendent Badger upset the balance,' he warned, gently. 'The line between dedication and ruthlessness is very fine.'

It was as far as he was prepared to go. Indeed, the impression was that he thought he might have stepped a little farther than he'd at first intended. He was a fine man. He didn't flaunt his qualities of absolute honesty — good men rarely do, indeed they are often unaware of them — and, although we'd met so few times, I knew we could have been friends and that I'd have been proud to have him as a friend.

We shook hands and I left the office.

Back in the flat I threw myself onto the bed and slept. I felt exhausted, but didn't know why. The numbness in my skull was still there; a minor irritation but not much more. I slept the sleep of a sick child; a restless sleep but without nightmares. Nevertheless, a sleep over-spilling with dreams. My wife was there; young as she was when I married her and not wracked with the disease which eventually took her from me. Chris and Susan, too. And Collins. There, opening and closing their mouths; shouting at me, but unable to make themselves heard above the mob-roar of scores of men I'd met and lived with during the last three years; men who hated me and whom I in turn hated. And yet, strangely, not a noisy dream. Not a frightening dream. Vivid and perhaps full of meaning. But *what* meaning? That was the question which eluded me. No words came. There seemed to be an invisible barrier — a sound-proof barrier — and I heard nothing. Nothing, that is, beyond the wordless roar of the mob, and that only as a rise and fall of a muffled crowd. A strange dream. A dream which robbed the sleep of recuperative quality.

It was dusk when I awoke, and I washed and made myself ready for my rendezvous with Butterfield.

Strangely, it was a very unostentatious hotel. About twenty yards along a side road leading from a main thoroughfare, it stood between an office-equipment firm and the offices of one of the better-known house agents. It seemed almost huddled; as if having its shoulders squeezed in an attempt to deny it what limited space it claimed. And yet it gave off a sense of class, as if it had no need of neon lights and the like to emphasise the fact that it was a no darts-and-dominoes establishment.

I pushed my way through the swing-doors and entered a world of thick-piled carpet, subdued but adequate lighting, and gentility which managed to steer clear of any hint of primness. At a guess, a watering-place catering for the nouveau riche and in the main used by that section of the populace.

Certainly the prices were high enough to keep the plebs at bay. My double whisky and water could have been bought at almost half the price in some pubs and, as I carried it across the bar lounge to where I'd spotted Butterfield relaxed in a corner armchair, the thought struck me (and not for the first time) that the lunatic who first coined the phrase "crime doesn't pay" was very light on practical experience.

Butterfield nodded silent greeting as I lowered myself into the neighbouring armchair.

He raised his glass to his mouth and murmured, 'Four of them.'

'What?' For the moment I didn't catch on.

'Heavies,' he explained softly. 'The guy behind the reception desk. Chances are he has something very nasty hidden under the shelf.'

'Oh!'

'The bar-keep.' He glanced at the counter. 'He watched me very closely. He watched *you* all the way across the room.'

'And the other two?' I asked.

'There's an armchair.' He sipped his booze. 'Don't look now, I can see him beyond your right shoulder. He's supposed to be reading a newspaper. He turns the pages now and again. But his eyes don't move. If he is reading, he picks one word, then stares at it till he figures it's time to move on a page.'

'And the fourth?'

'Out in the corridor.' He gave a quick grin. '*What's On in Lessford*. Seen it? It's on the wall. Framed. Usual gummidge. The cinemas. Local theatricals. Even lectures and church services. There's a female. She's been studying it so long she should be able to quote the name and address of the printer.'

'A woman!' I stared.

'They even have prisons for 'em these days,' he said sardonically.

I tasted my drink and thought things over for a moment. I was glad to have Butterfield available. Whatever his shortcomings as a copper, he seemed to have the instincts of a born fighter. A born killer.

'I have the Browning,' I murmured. 'What about you?'

For a fraction of a second he moved the edge of his unbuttoned, loose-fitting mac. What looked to be the handle of a samurai sword nestled comfortably in one of the poacher's pockets.

'Hong Kong,' he confided softly. 'I've a brother in the Royal Navy. It's spring-loaded. Blade a little more than nine inches long. You could shave with it.'

'What the hell . . .'

175

'We finish our drinks. We smile sweetly at the bar-keep. Then we leave.' He seemed to have worked out a plan of campaign. Indeed, he seemed to have taken over, but because it seemed a simple, uncomplicated scheme and therefore as likely to work as any other, I didn't interrupt. 'In the foyer I handle the goon behind the reception desk. *You* position yourself alongside the woman — block her view of the counter for a few moments — then be ready to make for the lift.'

I raised my glass and stared him full in the face. If there was friendship in my gaze it was there unintentionally. The man disgusted me. He was what I'd sworn I'd never be or even become, a killer who got his kicks from killing. It was there in the cold amusement at the back of his eyes. The anticipation. The thought of what was in store. And (dammit!) I'd opened the door for him. Without me — without what I'd started and the culmination of what was about to happen — he might have lived his life without once committing murder.

Therefore, my fault, but I loathed him none the less for that.

Nor was I mistaken or even likely to be mistaken. I'd lived in close proximity with his kind for too long. They *can* be recognised. They have an air. A "feel". They have something missing; a vacuum in their overall character which with practice can be spotted. Their laughter is without humour. Their sorrow is without compassion. Their every emotion is shallow and without depth.

And Butterfield was of that breed.

I finished my drink, replaced the glass on the table. Butterfield nodded, tipped what was left of his drink down his throat and stood up.

'No unnecessary blood-letting,' I murmured weakly.

He gave a quick, derisive grin, walked towards the door of the bar lounge and I followed, knowing that I was trapped and with no way out.

The foyer was long and narrow. Beautifully furnished and decorated, but badly proportioned. A little like a broad passage. The woman was still studying *What's On in Lessford*. I positioned

176

myself alongside her; pretending to read the list and shielding her view of the reception desk. She couldn't see, but I could, and as I watched I was at once horrified and open-mouthed in wonderment. Evil? Oh yes, my friend, there is a beauty in evil. It remains evil but the simple, uncomplicated quality, plus the manner of execution, removes it from the gutter and places it up there with every other work of genius.

Butterfield strolled to the desk. He even smiled at the receptionist. He stopped, flipped a page of the opened ledger and pointed. The receptionist looked puzzled and twisted his head, the better to read what was for him upsidedown. He made as if to lift the ledger and turn it, but without haste and quite naturally, Butterfield beat him to it and, carrying the opened ledger, walked to the receptionist's side of the counter. The finger — the left forefinger — remained on the page as Butterfield returned the ledger to the counter top. The receptionist leaned forward slightly, and as he did so Butterfield's right hand slid behind the folds of his mac.

I heard the snap of the blade leaving its housing and saw the weapon for the first time. Christ! Butterfield hadn't exaggerated. That blade was almost a foot long, and the handle was hefty enough to be held double-fisted. And it moved with all the silent speed of wet rubber against wet rubber. Up, in a terrible slicing movement, and the single blow almost decapitated the receptionist and sent him staggering back from the counter. There was a pause — the fraction of a heart-beat — before the blood gushed from the wide-opened throat, but Butterfield used that tiny pause to spin and push the man, and thus prevent the scarlet bore from staining either the counter or the ledger. Then Butterfield's hand disappeared beneath the counter and reappeared holding a pump-action twelve-bore shotgun.

Murder had been committed in far less time than it takes to tell . . . and without sound or sign.

Butterfield glanced at the closed doors of the lift, and I stepped across the foyer and thumbed a button, the button glowed red, as did a tiny, downward-pointing arrow above the button.

The woman turned, began to smile, then stopped smiling when

she saw the blood-dripping blade and the shotgun.

In a cold, soft voice, Butterfield said, 'You know the rules, madam. I take it you want to live.'

She gave a tiny, frightened nod. She was scared, but not screaming-scared and, as Butterfield had suggested, she knew "the rules". She froze the tiny movement she'd made towards her handbag and stood motionless as the lift arrived with a soft hiss and the doors parted. The lift was empty.

Butterfield turned his attention on me and snarled, 'All right, where's the damn gun you're supposed to be holding? Start pointing it at things. Get her in the lift and keep the bloody doors open.'

The killer, you see. The "natural". He'd taken over and I'd neither the time nor the desire to argue his authority. The foresight snagged slightly as I yanked the Browning from my waist-band. I threaded my finger through the trigger guard, made a tiny gesture with the gun and she obediently stepped into the lift. I leaned against the door to keep it open.

Meanwhile Butterfield had tucked the shotgun under one arm and was holding the blood-soaked blade of the knife between his teeth. From the pockets of his mac he took two flat, half-pint-sized whisky bottles. From their necks sprouted linen fuses. He held the bottles between the fingers of one hand and dipped into his hip pocket with his free hand and produced a cigarette lighter. I think the linen must have been soaked in saltpetre. Something. Whatever, it hissed and sparked at the touch of the flame and, as he returned the lighter to his pocket, he stepped across the foyer, plucked one bottle from his fingers and hurled it into the bar lounge. I was unable to see clearly, but I guessed he'd thrown it at the bar counter, where it would splash flame among the bottles of spirit. The second bottle he threw at the stairs at the end of the foyer and, as the glass broke, a wall of fire rose and curled up the walls to form a barrier to anybody wishing to reach the upper rooms.

Then he was in the lift, shotgun in one hand, and in the other the knife with which he threatened the woman.

'Drop the handbag, lady. Then raise your hands and face the

far wall. And don't even *look* as if you might start something.'

She obeyed, the lift doors whispered shut and he pressed the top, red button. The one which didn't give a floor number. The one marked Private.

As the lift made its smooth ascent, Butterfield leaned the shotgun against the side of the lift and took two more bottles and the cigarette lighter from his pockets.

'Get her facing the doors,' he ordered. 'And when we arrive . . . *move!*'

The Boss Man, you see. The situation and the individual. And I accepted it because in it lay my only hope of survival. I'd dreamed up a nightmare, and was now part of that nightmare, and I had sense enough to realise I had no choice other than to ride it.

I prodded the woman in the ribs with the snout of the Browning, and said, 'You heard the man. Face the doors and keep your hands high.'

The lift stopped. The doors parted. Butterfield pushed the woman in the small of the back and she stumbled into the corridor . . . and died. The shots ripped into her from the right. Four — probably five — snapped off in quick succession. Had it been Butterfield or myself we, too, would have died. Instead they killed *her*, and she fell face-downwards half-in and half-out of the lift.

'Leave her,' snapped Butterfield. 'She'll jam the doors. Keep the lift out of action.'

Already he'd lighted the fuses and, without moving from the temporary shelter of the lift, he swung an arm first to the right, then to the left, and sent fire-bottles crashing along the unseen corridor.

He grabbed the shotgun and said, 'Right, behind me and at a rush. You take the left, I'll take the right . . . and for Christ's sake use that trigger.'

Whatever else we'd done, we hadn't silenced the internal telephone link-up, and God only knew what was waiting for us beyond those lift doors. A shoot-first-and-apologise-later reception, that for sure. The dead woman was hard proof of that.

And oddly the sight of the rag-doll body of this unknown woman flipped the coin and brought my roaring fury back with a rush.

Butterfield threw the knife into the corridor, then followed it in a near-horizontal dive. He rolled on the carpet in order to be a moving target and as I followed I heard the short bark of a handgun, followed by the roar of the twelve-bore as it answered. I followed at a crouching run, hit the far wall of the corridor, then dropped to one knee and aimed the Browning in a two-handed grip, pointing up the left half of the corridor. There was flame and smoke, and in it I saw a figure holding one arm to shade his eyes while in the other hand he held a revolver. I squeezed the trigger twice and he dropped.

Then there was silence except for the steady roar of the spreading flames. We stayed there waiting, watching for some sign of movement, but there was none, then, still cat-timid, we rose to our feet.

'Not too difficult,' grunted Butterfield. 'My man's dead. What about yours?'

'I'm not sure.'

'Keep your eyes skinned.' He picked up the knife in his right hand. 'I'll *make* sure.'

'Kendal,' I rasped.

'I'll ask.'

Carefully we made our way along the wall of the corridor. Nervously. The Browning weaving and ready, as we approached the man I'd shot. He wasn't dead. He had a stomach wound; not bad, but painful enough to keep him groaning and pleading for relief with his eyes.

Butterfield hauled him clear of the encroaching flames and at the same time, kicked the fallen revolver well away from desperate fingers.

'Kendal.' Butterfield dropped the snout of the shotgun onto the root of the man's neck and curled a finger around the trigger. 'I'm not counting. I ask once. No reply . . . no head. Which is Kendal's room?'

The man tried to raise his pain-contorted face, but the shotgun pinned him as firmly as a moth on a card. He moved a hand and groaned the words.

'The door. It's — it's marked No Entry.'

'Who's in with him?'

'Nobody.' Then, as he saw disbelief in Butterfield's expression, his voice rose. 'I swear . . . *nobody*! He — he likes to be alone.'

'A Garbo complex,' mocked Butterfield.

'Honest,' whimpered the man. 'If he needs somebody he rings.'

'I think you're lying.' Butterfield's tone was almost conversational. 'I think I'll kill you . . . to be on the safe side.'

'No!' The Browning dug hard into Butterfield's ribs. The smoke was catching my throat, and it made my voice harsh and dry. 'We believe him.'

'*I* don't believe him.'

'You've out-lived your usefulness, Butterfield.' I increased the pressure on the trigger. Fractionally. But he felt it, and knew I wasn't bluffing. 'There's a fire escape. Find it. That's your only other choice.'

Butterfield moved his shoulders in a couldn't-care-less gesture, and meant it. The killing of the wounded man was obviously as unimportant to him as the swatting of a fly. He unhooked his finger from the trigger-guard of the twelve-bore and handed the weapon to me with a smile of utter contempt. I was weak, and I'd pay for my weakness . . . the unspoken accusation was plain to read in his eyes.

'From here on, you fly solo,' he murmured.

'I prefer it that way.'

'You won't make it.'

Leave the knife, too,' I said coldly.

'Look, that's *my* . . .'

'Leave it!' I snapped. 'I know who I'm looking for. I know where to look. Solo, as you say. Just find the fire escape and run.'

Again the movement of the shoulders, then he dropped the knife onto the carpet before sprinting down the corridor and through the curtain of fire; following the direction pointed by white arrows painted on scarlet boards.

'You.' I kicked the knife well out of his reach as I spoke to the wounded man. 'If they ask — if anybody asks — my name's Lennox. All this was my idea. Mine. Understand? All this, to reach Kendal. And when I reach him, I intend killing him. That's the "why". In the event of anybody asking.'

The man had told the truth. The door had No Entry stencilled on its surface. Nor was it locked, and when I entered there was no reception committee waiting, and the held-ready shotgun was not needed.

A huge room (at a guess two large rooms converted into one massive living-place) immaculately furnished and decorated and the centre-piece was a king-sized bed. A king-sized bed with a gold, king-sized silk coverlet and a mass of king-sized pillows propping up . . . who else but a king? "King" Kendal.

That was the first real shock. That it had all been for nothing. I didn't have to kill him. The ancient with the scythe was already taking practice swings. The eyes were alive though. Red-rimmed and gleaming like burning coals. And the voice; a little weak, perhaps, but still carrying the authority which had carried him to the top.

But the rest?

A stick-insect. Skinny to the point of fleshlessness and covered with parchment-like skin which gave the appearance of being at least four sizes too large for the withered body.

'You reached me.' The twig-like fingers drummed silently on the silk of the coverlet. 'I heard the commotion. I thought it might be you. You're a man, Lennox. A real man.'

I held the shotgun steady on his skull-thin face and said, 'It wasn't easy, Kendal.' I moved closer. 'Keep those fingers in sight, friend. I don't think you've long to live, but . . .'

'Not long.'

'You can count it in seconds if you misbehave or if anybody walks through that door.'

'Nobody comes unless I call.'

'Good.' I took a deeper breath than usual to steady myself. 'Be advised. Don't call.'

I was near enough to read the eyes. No fear. A touch of admiration, perhaps, but little else. This one might even have deserved the title "king".

'Collins.' The name almost stuck in my throat. 'Maybe you didn't know him.'

'Henry Collins. Chief superintendent. I know everybody, Lennox.'

'Somebody killed him.'

'He died. Don't exaggerate.'

'You're a damn liar. He was murdered.'

The eyes blazed and for a moment I thought (weak as he obviously was) he might try a spring from the bed at my throat. Then the rage quietened and a smile touched the bloodless lips.

'You have balls, Lennox. They told me. They daren't lie. You have balls.'

'Whilever I hold the thick end of this thing.' I moved the shotgun slightly. 'Anatomical strengths and weaknesses don't apply. He was murdered. Who murdered him?'

He gave me a name and it didn't mean a thing.

In the distance, and growing louder, I heard sirens. Fire and police. I'd heard them too often in the past not to recognise them. One part of my mind did mental calculations. At a guess, Butterfield had had time to get clear of the immediate neighbourhood.

'Where do I find him?' I asked.

'He's safe.'

'That's not what I asked.'

'Lennox.' He spoke as if to a respected acquaintance. 'No man's *worth* that much. Nobody! Collins. Okay, Collins was your friend. Fellow-fuzz. The hell, he was a nothing. Fancy uniform. Flash manners. What the hell else? He's dead. Like you, like me, like everybody. It comes. He's not around any more. You can't do a resurrection job.'

'Where's the bastard who killed him?' I repeated coldly.

'Inside.' He sighed. 'I'm explaining, Lennox. I'm putting you right. You're my kind, otherwise I'd tell you to take a jump.'

'Where? Why?'

'Purse-snatching. Christ Almighty! That's his *size*. He's not worth all this aggro. A mugger . . . what he did to Collins. No bigger. He'll never *be* bigger. Some cheap gimmick from a Woolworth's counter. That's his limit. He couldn't . . .'

'Where?' I interrupted.

'Armley. Leeds.' The skinny hands moved slightly. 'Six months in a granite tomb. Lackey to some heavy who rules a handful of cells. Jesus, he's not *worth* it.'

'Your man,' I reminded him.

'Don't make me laugh!' Again the sudden rush of fury to the eyes. Then the blaze died as he continued, 'I employ *men*, not punks. The punks I control. Not the same thing.' There came a soft chuckle. Dry. A typical "stick-insect" sound. 'You've been suckered, Lennox. A man like you. Suckered by a smart-arse like Badger.

'Badger?' We suddenly had an enemy in comon.

'He wants to know things. Anything. Everything. A grass at every corner, but he's still blind and deaf. That annoys friend Badger. That stops him from sleeping nights. He has to *know*. Sometimes I feed him crap — pure crap — but I spice it up a little for the streets and he takes it, and chews it, and believes it. For a time. Just for a time. Then I let him know it's crap, and that almost drives him up the wall.'

'A little more dangerous than Ludo,' I opined.

'With a self-opinionated fink like Badger?' The dried lips curled. 'Feed him dog-dirt. Make him believe he can recognise caviare when he sees it. He'll eat it and enjoy it. They don't come more foolish . . . or easier.'

'He hates you,' I murmured.

'So? He's so far down the queue, he's out of sight.'

I could hear the fire appliances outside, and the racket some floors below us as men began to control the fire. A wisp of smoke crept under the closed door but, no matter, this man Kendal fascinated me and I wanted to know as much as possible before I killed him.

He seemed to sense it. Agree with it. He settled himself a little deeper in the pillows and talked, as if totting up figures and reaching an acceptable total.

'The secret, Lennox. To *keep* it secret, see? Everything. To make them guess, but make damn sure nobody *knows*. What they don't know, they'll invent. They'll imagine. A great thing, the imagination. It makes everybody a fool. Loch Ness Monsters. Flying Saucers. The Abominable Snowman. God knows what else. Imagination. The first step towards believing what isn't.

'I run a tight outfit here, Lennox. And I mean *tight*. Nobody sees me, unless I send. Nobody! No photographs. There's a cool thousand, ready cash, for anybody who can show me one photograph. Just one. Anywhere. Any time. Even a verbal description. Has Badger ever told you what I *look* like? Age? Height? Build? That sort of thing?'

'No.' I shook my head. Outside and downstairs the hubbub was growing. I hadn't much time left, but I still wanted to know things. Nevertheless, I *had* time; time enough to squeeze the triggers of the shotgun.

The quick, dry chuckle preluded the continuation of his talk.

'Nobody, see? Not even Badger. "King" Kendal. Holy Christ, do I *look* like a king? But nobody *knows*. Imagination. The dumb creeps *made* me a king. To them I'm ten foot tall. I run an "army". Some army! Hand-picked, Lennox. That's all. Hand-picked and well paid. Twenty. No more than thirty, and always on call. They obey orders. No questions. That's my "army". A good "army". More than the Kray twins ever had. More loyal. More obedient. It's all I need. All I've ever needed. I send word out. "Do this". "Do that". It gets done . . . or else. *That's* my "army", Lennox. All the shit-scared creeps who daren't say no. Not *my* men. Creeps my men control.' He paused, then, said, 'Badger's sure to ask.'

'What?'

'What I look like. How I live. As much as you can tell him.'

'It's possible,' I agreed.

'As a favour, Lennox. Don't tell him. Not everything. Let him go to his grave not knowing.'

'I'll think about it.'

'The condemned man's last request, eh?'

'I'll think about it,' I repeated.

Quite calmly, he said, 'You're here to kill me.'

'It would be a wasted journey otherwise.'

'Fine,' he murmured softly. Then, 'Fine. A good ending. Very appropriate.'

'You've given me a name,' I reminded him.

If he heard me he made no comment. He turned his head slightly on the pillow, and said, 'You see me, Lennox. You know what's wrong with me?'

'Cancer?' I suggested.

'Cancer is clean by comparison, my friend.'

There was no self-pity, nevertheless the tone held a quality which discouraged interruption.

'Pox,' he continued, and that one word was a spat obscenity. 'The old syphilis, Lennox.' The stick-fingers made a tiny brushing movement as if to push aside any argument or disbelief. 'Not the sore-on-the-lip gag. Not *that*. I used to horse around. Y'know, women are there to be screwed. I believed it. Still believe it. I thought I picked carefully. But not carefully enough. Sure, I had some sort of cold spot. That's what *I* thought. The aftermath of a bad chill, and it cleared away in no time at all. Then later, another chill. 'Flu, maybe. Sore throat. Something of a headache.' The parched lips moved in the ghost of a contemptuous smile. 'Pox, Lennox. It comes camouflaged. 'Flu. A cold in the head. *Anything* but pox, and then it's too late. The so-called tertiary stage. That's when it hits you. That's when you *know*. And it's too damn late! Chronic, see? It has you by the balls, and no way is it going to let go until you're in a box. The skin, the liver, the heart. It makes its own lousy choice. The bones, maybe. The brain. Maybe more than one place. Like I say, cancer is a gentleman by comparison.' The pause was long enough to make me think he'd finished, but he hadn't. 'With me it's the heart and the liver. "Poxed up to the eyeballs". It *means* something, when you're like this. You're here to kill me. Great! But you're too late, Lennox. Years too late. A diseased dame killed me before you went inside. Slow-motion with side-effects you wouldn't believe. I only hope she's still alive . . . with the same sort of problems.'

One of the skinny hands moved. The fingers curled around the barrel of the twelve-bore and raised the barrel until the snout was in line with the middle of his face, and little more than six inches from the smiling lips.

'Make it good, Lennox. Don't louse it up. One shot and the "king" abdicates.'

He was still smiling as I squeezed the trigger.

'Lock a civilised man behind bars — especially an educated man, especially a man who held the responsibility of a detective chief superintendent — and the spiral staircase analogy becomes even more emphasised. He's disorientated almost beyond belief. He doesn't know up from down. He doesn't know right from wrong. He needs easing gently, very gently, back to normality.'

'There was a good job waiting for him,' Tallboy said. 'Somewhere to live. Comfort a lot of people would give their eye-teeth for.'

'The operative word is *gently*.' The guy in the white coat scowled his annoyance at Tallboy's inability to understand. 'Three years inside, then *that*? It was like a pauper being handed a million pounds and being expected to adjust, without help. It was crazy.'

'The intentions were good.' Tallboy sounded miserable.

'They always are. My God! The number of people who need treatment because of "good intentions". He didn't expect it. He wasn't prepared for it. So, it knocked him sideways, what else?'

'Are you saying he's mad?' muttered Tallboy.

'We're all mad, don't you know that?' He looked almost as sad as Tallboy. 'My profession seeks normality, knowing it can never be found. Sub-normal. Abnormal. The two divisions of mankind. But no middle ground. Superior. Inferior. The "average" man doesn't exist, and yet we're expected to use him as a yardstick. The man without hang-ups. Without guilt complexes. Without over-enthusiasms. Without illogical likes or dislikes. I tell you . . .' He paused and sighed. 'Lennox is no more mad than you or I. A different madness, perhaps. A madness we can't understand. The yearning to get back to prison, for example. Why?'

'Is that what he wants?'

'He's admitted everything. Not just to me. To Badger. To at least four senior detective officers. Everything! He's refused Legal Aid. He's already pleaded guilty on all counts at the committal court. He seems almost *eager* to get back inside. To Armley Prison, Leeds.'

'Armley?'

It's the only prison he ever mentions. Perhaps he has friends there.'

'That's only a short-stay prison,' said Tallboy. 'Committals. A Reception Prison. He'll stay there maybe six months, till they decide where to send him for the rest of his sentence. He can't have friends there. Great Heavens, man! Lennox can't have *friends* in any prison.'

'All right.' He waved his hands in an empty, helpless gesture. 'I'm only telling you what I know. What I've gleaned from his talk. Armley. Maybe he looks upon it as a womb-substitute. I've come across stranger things.'

'The hell with that for an explanation.'

'All right, I'm wrong. It won't be the first time. The only thing I do know. He's like the rest of us. On his own spiral staircase. And rightly or wrongly — up or down — he's determined to move.'

And that was it. They talked a little longer, but got no farther. Other than confirming Tallboy's original opinion, that he didn't like the guy in the white coat.